# WHEN
# WE WERE
# SISTERS

CYNTHIA ELLINGSEN

# WHEN WE WERE SISTERS

FOREVER

NEW YORK  BOSTON

Forever
Hachette Book Group
1290 Avenue of the Americas, New York, NY 10104
read-forever.com
twitter.com/readforeverpub

Originally published in 2021 by Bookouture, an imprint of Storyfire Ltd., Carmelite House, 50 Victoria Embankment, London EC4Y 0DZ

First Forever US edition: June 2023

Forever is an imprint of Grand Central Publishing. The Forever name and logo are trademarks of Hachette Book Group, Inc.

The publisher is not responsible for websites (or their content) that are not owned by the publisher.

The Hachette Speakers Bureau provides a wide range of authors for speaking events. To find out more, go to hachettespeakersbureau.com or email HachetteSpeakers@hbgusa.com.

Forever books may be purchased in bulk for business, educational, or promotional use. For information, please contact your local bookseller or the Hachette Book Group Special Markets Department at special.markets@hbgusa.com.

Library of Congress Cataloging-in-Publication Data
Names: Ellingsen, Cynthia, author.
Title: When we were sisters / Cynthia Ellingsen.
Description: First Forever US edition. | New York ; Boston : Forever, 2023.
Identifiers: LCCN 2022057904 | ISBN 9781538740873 (trade paperback)
Subjects: LCGFT: Novels.
Classification: LCC PS3605.L43785 W47 2023 |
DDC 813/.6—dc23/eng/20221208
LC record available at https://lccn.loc.gov/2022057904

ISBN: 9781538740873 (trade paperback)

Printed in the United States of America

LSC-C

Printing 1, 2023

*To Jennifer Mattox, Stephanie Parkin,
and Frankie Wolf, sisters in writing*

# WHEN
# WE WERE
# SISTERS

# PROLOGUE

Mist swirled around the house on the hill, the view like a memory I had revisited too often in my mind. I dug my toes into the sand, the rough grains giving way to the wet cold underneath. The waves churned steadily against the shore as a sharp breeze blew in from the ocean, and I shivered.

In some ways, it felt like minutes since I'd been back to the North Carolina coast. I could practically see me at twelve years old, racing down the wooden steps that led from the edge of the bluff to the beach grass and then the sand. My grandmother always stood at the top, watching me and my sister, her smile as bright as the sun.

Each time, I'd held tight to Charlotte's hand as we'd raced into the ocean. Fresh air would fill my lungs and the cool crash of the waves slapped against the mosquito bites that covered my legs. We would dive under, then swim towards the horizon with steady kicks.

That one day, I had swum with her until we were past the waves, then I flipped onto my back to float, enjoying the way the salt water seemed to lift me up. I felt alive and invincible, grateful for each moment with the sister I'd been separated from my entire life. Turning my head, I'd watched as she pushed her body towards the sandbar, something I hadn't yet been brave enough to do.

Charlotte had been raised in the suburbs with a pool in her backyard, but I'd grown up in Ireland. The only swimming lessons I'd had were indoors and there hadn't been many of them. Besides, there was a big difference between the controlled, still water in a chlorinated pool and the relentless, stinging tear of the ocean.

Charlotte beckoned me to follow her out. Even though I was afraid, something pushed me to flip onto my stomach and try. I drove my body with surprisingly strong strokes, my breath quick as the water splashed against my face. The ocean became deeper, colder, and my limbs began to feel heavy, but I pressed on.

Charlotte looked back at me and waved her hand. I waved back, trying to indicate I planned to join her at the sandbar. She gestured and called out, but her words were lost in the wind. I watched as her face changed to panic. Her hand stretched up, clawing the air, right before she went under.

My heart nearly stopped. It was early in the morning, so we were the only two people in the water. My grandmother was too far away to do anything. I refused to lose my sister, even if it might mean losing myself in the process. Gritting my teeth until my jaw ached, I swam through the ocean as fast as I could.

I dove down like Charlotte had taught me during our seaweed hunts, keeping my eyes open in spite of the pain. My third try, I spotted dark hair drifting through the water like the tentacles of a jellyfish. I reached down and grabbed it, yanking her up with every ounce of strength I had. She broke the surface, gasping and choking.

"Hang on." The weight of her body half pulled me under, but I fought for the both of us. "I've got you."

It would have been impossible to make it to shore, but the sandbar was in sight. My lungs burned and my limbs were heavier with each inch gained. Just as I lost the ability to go farther, the strong arms of my grandmother wrapped around the both of us, dragging us to safety.

That day, I realized I would do anything to save my sister. It was hard to believe that, in the end, she would still make the choice to leave me behind.

# CHAPTER ONE

Sliding on my sunglasses, I walked back through the sand to the beach lot where I'd parked.

The morning chilled me as I cracked my car window to let in the saltwater air. I had forty minutes until the meeting with the lawyer, so there was time to grab a quick coffee and take a look around. It had been years since I'd last been to Woodsong Harbor, my grandmother's coastal North Carolina town, and it looked like something you'd see on a postcard.

Pastel buildings lined the streets, most of them shops or restaurants with lush flower boxes and windowpanes that shone like the sun. Trees bloomed overhead, their blossoms draping over the roads in a resplendent display of pink and white. The aroma of fresh flowers mixed with the scent of the roasted coffee and pastries that wafted from the open storefront doors.

It was early, but Main Street was awake. Based on the families strolling along the sidewalks and the bicycles zipping by, this was a walking town. There were several people seated at outdoor tables in front of a brunch spot, complete with heating lamps and a decorative overhang of white lights and climbing flowers. The guests were a mix of old and young, and most of them looked at the paper instead of their phones, which was nice to see. The food on the tables was a decadent mix of French toast and fancy omelets.

I kept driving until I found a cute little coffee shop. There was a parking spot right out front, and I did my best to park between a beat-up pickup truck and a silver Mercedes. It had been a while since I'd parallel parked, but I cranked my way into a spot without bumping anything, and pulled up as close to the truck as I could to avoid hitting the Mercedes on my way out.

The bells on the door of the coffee shop jangled as I walked in. The floor was a polished concrete and the walls a smooth gray brick. Metal tabletops stuck out from the walls, each decorated with a square vase of bright flowers that seemed to stretch up to the series of small lights that hung down from the ceiling like stars. It was a place to think and dream, and if I'd had the time, I could have spent hours sketching the ocean while seated at one of the window tables.

Others must have felt the same, because the shop was crowded. Shelves on the walls were stacked with cellophane-wrapped bags of chocolate nonpareils, homemade caramels, and saltwater taffy. The price plaque attached to the shelf listed them at eleven dollars. I drew back, self-conscious to think that, even at thirty-eight years old, they were something I couldn't afford.

"What can I get for you?" The teenage girl taking the coffee orders gave me a friendly smile. She had blonde hair and a bright smile.

The metal board behind the counter listed the drinks but not their prices. There was a sugar-free section with all sorts of delicious-sounding choices. Still, it seemed like a safer bet to keep it simple.

"Just a double latte," I said.

"Eight dollars, please."

"Actually, can I change that to a single latte?" I asked quickly.

"Sure. Six forty, please."

Hiding a wince, I held out my credit card. It was about ten lattes from being declined. Thank goodness I didn't plan to be in this town long, because it would be impossible to survive.

Sipping at the warm froth of the milk topped with a blend of cinnamon and nutmeg, I breathed in the peace of the morning from a table that afforded a view of the ocean. Classical piano music tinkled over the speaker and I wondered what would happen if I faked car trouble and tried to video chat into the reading of the will instead of showing up in person.

The lawyer had already vetoed that idea. I'd contacted him after receiving the letter and requested to call in, but he was adamant that I come in person. There had been other beneficiaries, such as my father, some friends, and local charities, but my grandmother had stipulated that Charlotte and I were to be together for the reading. I probably wouldn't get more than a necklace, but the fact that my grandmother had included me was enough for me to make the trip.

I took another sip of the latte, and its warmth comforted the chill in my heart. There was a family with young children that had caught my eye a few tables over. Two girls, and the smallest was dipping a straw into the froth of steamed milk with a big smile on her face. The two of them made me think of me and my sister, and what it would have been like if we'd been raised together. It also made me question where the time had gone.

I'd expected to be married with a family by this stage in my life. When I was in my early twenties, I'd been engaged. He was a great guy, but I'd been scared that it wouldn't work and our family would end up broken. It was funny to think how different things could have been if I had been brave enough to take the risk.

One of the little girls caught me staring, and quickly I returned my attention to the view outside. The waves rolled in and out. My problems seemed small compared to the size of the ocean, and I tried to focus on that.

The caffeine had just started to make me feel brave enough to head to the lawyer's office when the door to the coffee shop burst open. An attractive man in a black T-shirt and jeans stormed in. He went up to the counter and said something to the barista, his dark eyes flashing. She put a reassuring hand on his arm.

"Does anyone own a white Ford SUV?" she called.

Quickly, I raised my hand. "Yes. I do."

Did my car get hit? That wouldn't work, time-wise. I'd have to find a ride to the lawyer's office, because I couldn't be late.

The man stormed over to my table. "Hi. I get it that you, like everyone else in this town, are here to kick back and enjoy your vacation." His dark gaze swept over me. "You might also want to respect the idea that other people are trying to work."

"You lost me," I said.

"You're blocking the hatch on my truck and I need to unload it."

"Let me get this straight," I said. "You're frustrated that you had to take five seconds out of your day to ask me to move my car back? When, really, you could probably move yours forward?"

The guy seemed so surprised that I'd stood up to him that he was at a loss for words. Most people probably catered to him because he was so attractive, but I didn't find rudeness enticing. Quite the opposite.

"Sure." I grabbed my keys. "I'd be happy to move out of your way."

My latte was half-full. To ensure no one would swipe my table, I draped my sweater over the back of my chair and headed towards the door. The sun was too bright but I could see what the man was talking about, as I'd done a terrible job parking and was practically on top of his truck. Nevertheless, I felt a greater sense of dread about the Mercedes that was parked behind me, because I definitely didn't want to hit it.

Somehow, I backed up without incident. The man came out and yanked open the hatch on his truck to unload piles of metal, the muscles in his arms straining with the effort. He moved it to a cart and wheeled it into the shop next door without so much as a thank-you.

The window was etched with the word *Blacksmith*. Even though it was dim inside, I could make out several intricate metal sculptures that were impressive. Still, it wasn't the type of shop where the work was so urgent that it required being rude.

When I went back into the coffee shop, the dark-haired woman who had been hard at work making espressos greeted me with a fresh latte in a to-go cup and a wax paper bag with a pastry inside.

"On behalf of our town," she said, "I apologize for my brother. Logan's been grumpy ever since his wife left him."

"He probably just skipped his morning coffee," I said, and she laughed.

"I'm Lauren."

"Jayne."

My sister had been given the pretty name. Charlotte. I'd never liked reading *Charlotte's Web* when I was growing up.

"This coffee shop is lovely," I said. "Thank you for making me feel welcome."

Lauren had to own it. As a former business owner, I recognized her dedication. It said a lot that she'd given me a coffee and a pastry because someone in the shop had been rude.

"Thank you." She shared a smile. "I've worked hard on it. I hope you'll come back."

The line had started to form again, so she gave a little wave and stepped back behind the counter. It wasn't like I'd be back in this town again, so I decided to make an impression on Logan that maybe would stay with him. Gripping the cup of coffee and pastry bag, I stalked into the blacksmith shop.

The smell of the shop made me flinch. It reminded me of old pennies or nickels, a smell that seemed more intense coupled with the fire roaring in the grate at the back of the room. The metal pieces placed around the space were beautifully crafted; the larger sculptures could have made it into any gallery showing in the city.

Logan stepped out from the back room, wiping his hand across his sweating forehead. He was headed to the front door, maybe to grab another load. When he spotted me, he stopped.

"The shop's not open yet." His tone was still gruff, but less confrontational. "What do you need?"

Sleep, for one. I'd left my friend's apartment at four o'clock in the morning to make the drive and I was tired. I also needed a plan, because there was a mess waiting for me back home. Most of all, I needed courage, because I did not want to walk into the lawyer's office and face the feelings and memories I hadn't dealt with in years.

What would this guy say if I told him all that?

Instead, I cleared my throat. "I need to remind you that everyone's going through something. Kindness matters." I set the coffee and pastry bag on a table. "Here. I hope your day gets better."

He looked stunned as the door banged shut behind me. Somehow, I managed to pull out without hitting the Mercedes or the truck, even though my hands were shaking with nerves. I arrived at the lawyer's office with minutes to spare.

Through the entry window, I saw the receptionist chatting with someone. It had been over twenty-five years, but I would have known her anywhere.

It was my sister.

# CHAPTER TWO

My first impression was that Charlotte was shorter than she appeared on social media, but just as put together. Her dark hair was up in a sleek ponytail and she wore a crisp white linen sheath accessorized with a coral-and-turquoise necklace. I watched, gripping the steering wheel, as the receptionist nodded and led her down a hall.

The waiting room was quiet when I walked in. I pretended to look at the scenic portraits of old boats hanging up on the wall, but couldn't focus on a thing. The receptionist returned and gave me a polite smile.

"How can I help you?" she asked.

"I'm here for an appointment with Martin Sommers," I said, fidgeting with my bracelets.

The delicate silver bands had been gifted to me by my mother. She'd passed away five years ago of cancer, and I wore the bracelets on days I needed her by my side. I could only imagine what she would say about this situation. Most likely, that no heirloom was worth the price of heartache.

Ironic, considering the half-written letter I'd found in my mother's favorite book. It had been pressed against the pages like a dried flower. *Dear Jayne, There is a truth to be told but I am not brave enough to say it…*

I'd wondered what it had meant, what she'd wanted to say. It was most likely something she'd written when she'd first found out she had cancer and wasn't feeling brave enough to tell me.

Still, the idea that there was an unfinished conversation between me and my mother had left me feeling unsettled.

"Follow me, please."

The flare of the receptionist's rose-colored jacket swished back and forth as I followed her down a long hallway decorated with beach scenes. My shoulders tensed each time we approached a door. The receptionist paused at the fourth one, which was open.

"You can go in," she said, and Charlotte glanced my way.

The summer we spent together flashed through my mind like a movie reel. Making jewelry from seashells, sharing ice cream, crying at goodbye… We'd exchanged heartfelt letters for a month after I'd left. Then she'd cut me off.

My heart wanted to demand, *Why?* Instead, I managed a polite, "Hi."

"Hello." Charlotte gave a pert nod. "Good morning."

Her voice. It was delicate, like a song, but so full of confidence.

I remembered being in awe of her the day we sat cross-legged in the sand and she explained her life plans. If being the president of the United States proved boring, she'd said, she wanted to be an astronaut. I'd decided then and there to do better in math, so that we could orbit the Earth together.

"I'm Martin Sommers," the lawyer said, stepping forward. He was tall, and his thin lips gave him a stern appearance. "It's nice to meet you. Shall we begin?"

The polished mahogany conference table was set with a tiny notepad, a pen, a bottle of water, and a small tin of peppermints at each seat.

I settled in, wiping my sweating palms on my pale blue dress. It felt strange to think my sister was close enough to smell her perfume. It was sweet like lilac and lemon.

Even though I didn't know Charlotte at all, social media had kept me informed about her life. She was a successful salesperson at a large finance firm and had married a ruddy-looking real estate investor who golfed at resorts across the country. She didn't post pictures of her two teenaged sons, but often shared images of her palatial home in Cary, North Carolina, with its marble entryway, elaborate mantel arrangements, and iron gates. The doors were locked to me, and I'd often felt like an intruder looking at her page. Still, I wanted to know who she'd become. Social media might not be an honest interpretation, but it was better than nothing.

Leaning back into the soft leather of the chair, I started to doodle on the notepad. It took a few minutes for me to notice I was drawing the two girls at the coffee shop. I stopped, worried Charlotte might think I was drawing a memory of her.

The lawyer opened a leather folder. "I would like to begin by saying that I have worked with your grandmother for the last forty years. Your grandparents were my clients from the start of my career and the finest people I've had the pleasure of knowing. Your grandmother has made some unconventional requests; however, she was in excellent mental health when we drafted her will." Peering through reading glasses, he said, "She begins with a letter."

*Dear Charlotte and Jayne,*

*One of the greatest moments of my life was the summer that the two of you came to spend with me. Jayne, I adored getting to know your kind heart and beautiful spirit. It meant everything to me to see you and Charlotte bloom together like two beautiful flowers alongside the shore.*

*I am aware that there has been heartache and confusion over the past several years and that a relationship between the two of you may feel beyond repair. I do believe, Charlotte and Jayne, that if you spend some time fighting to get to know one another rather than fighting each other, you will have the ability to reclaim what was lost. I do think it would be possible to rebuild your relationship.*

*Life is complex, as are our beliefs, perceptions, and emotions. I understand that this might be too much, and if so, I understand. However, thank you for being here today. I will rest in peace knowing that I did everything in my power to bring the two of you back together.*

*With all of the love in my heart,*
*Your grandmother*

It felt hard to breathe. It had been a nice idea to put me and Charlotte in the same room, but there was too much that had happened, too much left unsaid. That type of hurt couldn't be erased in fifteen minutes, and Charlotte had made it pretty clear over the years that she didn't want to try. I hoped my grandmother's expectations hadn't been high that this meeting would solve everything, because I could already tell we weren't going to walk out of this office exchanging contact information.

The lawyer cleared his throat. "Shall I continue?"

Charlotte raised her eyebrows and gave a quick nod, as if the letter had been a strange interruption at a very public dinner.

"The bequeathment was drafted in her words," he said, and began to read: "Charlotte and Jayne, our time together was the most magical summer of my life. Therefore, I would like to leave you the beach house in hopes that you can re-experience that magic once again."

The words hung in the air like the crest of a wave. The idea stood, poised and picture-perfect, before it crashed into me in a burst of noise and confusion.

*The beach house?*

"I'm sorry." Certain I had misunderstood, I said, "Could you repeat that?"

The lawyer cleared his throat. "Of course." He read the two lines verbatim, without an ounce of irony. My heart started pounding.

I'd assumed my grandmother had brought me here because she'd left me a piece of jewelry. Maybe a thousand dollars. But an entire house? The house at the *beach*?

Involuntarily, my gaze shifted to Charlotte. Her expression summed up my feelings.

The idea that I was about to be handed a property, *that* property, was a shock. I had loved my grandmother, but I hadn't known her that well. I'd been afraid that it might hurt my mother if I developed too close a relationship with her. Either way, I didn't deserve an inheritance like this.

The lawyer continued to read: "Charlotte and Jayne, there are a few conditions. You might recall that your grandfather and I purchased this home in the seventies as a remodeling project. Changes in his job gave us less of an opportunity to devote ourselves to that pursuit. Even so, we couldn't bear to let it go."

Charlotte clicked her pen in a steady rhythm. One glance from me and she stopped.

"Therefore, I've decided that the two of you will have to live there together and finish the remodel for me."

Charlotte set down her pen with a clatter. "Sorry?"

The lawyer gave us a rueful smile. "Yes. She was quite excited about this idea. The terms are clearly outlined in the following portion of the will, but do you have questions about what I've read so far?"

There was a fully bloomed tree out the window where bees hummed around the fragrant blossoms. Part of me wished to be out there with it, smelling the flowers. Even the threat of the bees seemed safer than confronting my feelings about this.

Charlotte opened her tin of mints. "I'd like to hear the terms."

The lawyer slid his glasses back on and read: "My dear girls, you must work together to remodel the beach house. There is a bank account in place for this. I do request that you complete the rooms in the order that they are assigned in this document and finish in six months, beginning no later than one year from today.

"I will provide a stipend of two thousand dollars a month for personal expenses, and I ask that you remain in town for the duration. Ken and the boys are welcome to stay, Charlotte. However, you and Jayne are required to work on the house together. In addition, I ask that the two of you share one dinner per week in an effort to get to know one another.

"Once the house is remodeled, you can sell it or keep it, but you must agree on the outcome. If you do not follow the terms of the will, the house will be sold as is, with the proceeds donated to charity. The purpose is to ensure I've done everything in my power to bring the two of you back together as sisters once again."

The lawyer folded his hands. "What questions do you have for me?"

I took a long drink of water, trying to catch up with my feelings. Six months with my sister... once, I would have given anything to have that time. Now, there were so many factors to consider.

Charlotte and I hadn't spoken in years. I barely knew her, and she didn't know me. It felt like she'd spent her life avoiding me, so I couldn't imagine that she'd say yes to six months under the same roof together and, if she did, I doubted I'd be able to bring the best version of myself to the situation.

This past year had been one of the worst of my life. I'd failed at my lifelong dream of opening a children's art studio, shuttering its doors only two years in. I'd spent the last three months working around the clock to repay my massive debt. The stress had ruined yet another relationship, and I still needed time to process all that had happened. This inheritance could save me financially, but emotionally, I wasn't quite sure I was ready for it.

Charlotte looked as baffled as I felt. Her full lips were pursed and her eyes troubled. I had forgotten how striking her eyes were; blue flecked with glints of amber that made them bright.

"How soon are we expected to start?" she asked.

"Theoretically, you could start tomorrow. However, I imagine you'll have loose ends to wrap up at home." He got to his feet, sliding the folder under his arm. "I'll step out so the two of you can talk this over and decide when and if to set a date."

The door clicked shut and the silence stretched between us like years. Finally, Charlotte spoke.

"I would like to see the house, first and foremost. Evaluate the condition. We can come back here in the morning and go from there."

I hadn't planned on staying in town. The amount that remained in my bank account would barely cover a bed-and-breakfast. Still, I gave a weak nod.

"When would you be available to get started?" Charlotte asked.

Really, I could get started right away. I worked as a floater at a preschool during the day and waited tables at a high-end restaurant at night, but both places would be fine without me. I also didn't have to worry about a lease, as I'd spent the last few months living on my friend's couch.

"I'm flexible," I said. "Is there a time that works for you?"

It felt strange to talk like we were making plans to hang out.

"Soon," she said, riffling through her phone. "The boys finish school at the end of May."

"The boys" were my nephews. Ones I had never even met. The lump in my throat made it hard to swallow, and I took a quick drink of water.

The support I'd given my friends' kids was endless. I'd attended each birthday party, spent hours on their art projects, and cheered for them at plays, dance recitals, and sporting events. I'd have done all that and more for my nephews, if Charlotte would have let me.

Now I was about to live with her family? The thought made the room feel upside down.

"Does that work?" Charlotte pressed.

I didn't know how to answer. Would it work? My sister had never responded to the Christmas cards I'd sent, or the attempts I'd made over the years to connect online. Were we really supposed to live together for six months and pretend like all of that had not happened? I rested the cold water bottle against my hot cheek, trying to find the right words.

"It's not the start date," I said. "Six months is a big commitment. I need to know what happens when the time's up. Will you sell?"

If Charlotte wanted to keep the house as a vacation home, I couldn't afford it. I had no idea what the property was worth, but since it was on the beach, the taxes alone would bury me.

Charlotte raised her perfect eyebrows. "Is this all about money to you?"

"No," I said quickly. "I'm trying to figure out what's realistic, that's all."

"Well…" She lifted her chin. "I'm trying to figure out why you're in the will at all. You didn't even go to her funeral."

The words felt like a slap in the face.

"You're one to talk about skipping funerals," I told her.

Her eyes flashed. "Listen. You have no—"

"Sorry. Let's not do this," I cut in. "I'm just as shocked as you are. Right now all I want is to get the information I need to decide how best to move forward."

Charlotte let out some sort of a grunt, picked up her phone, and began texting.

I looked out the window at the leaves dancing on the trees. This wouldn't be easy. The comment she'd made about the will had hit its mark. She didn't feel that I deserved to be a part of this, and maybe she was right.

The lawyer strode back into the room. "Have the two of you decided on a plan?"

Charlotte set down her phone. "Not yet."

"I'm struggling," I admitted. "I'd have to sell the house when we're done because I wouldn't be able to afford the taxes. I don't know that Charlotte wants to do that, but I don't want her to miss out on the inheritance, so I'm stuck."

Charlotte furrowed her brow.

The lawyer nodded. "Charlotte, what are your intentions?"

She hesitated, then glanced at her phone. "We can sell."

My heart beat a little faster. For a split second, I felt hopeful that we might find a way to work through the heartache that hovered between us, but I knew better than to get my hopes up.

"Perfect," the lawyer said. "Shall we go see the property? The houses on the Row are so beautiful, especially at this time of year."

"What's the Row?" I asked, getting to my feet.

"The ten Victorians that overlook the beach," he explained. "Locals refer to that street as the Row."

The day had warmed up outside and the Carolina breeze blew hot against my arms. Butterflies danced around the flowering bushes, birds sang in the trees, and the sun sparkled against the view of the ocean off in the distance. It was such a beautiful day, but it was hard to take it all in, considering the emotion rushing through me.

It had been years since I'd been inside the house, and I couldn't believe my grandmother had given me this opportunity. Still, I was scared.

It wasn't realistic to think that Charlotte and I would spend a few months together and suddenly become best friends. There were years of hurt and heartache between us. Fixing that would not be as simple as slapping a coat of paint on something that had seen better days.

# CHAPTER THREE

There's not much that I remember about my home life in California other than the few images imprinted in my brain: a small lemon tree that sat in a brown bucket in the corner of a sunbathed porch. A cloth doll with a frilly dress that Charlotte liked to play with that I would hold when our parents fought. The smell of Chef Boyardee beef ravioli and applesauce—foods I'd avoided since that time.

The thing I did remember in vivid detail was the moment I realized my mother and I had left. We were on a plane to Dublin, looking at the buildings and houses below glowing bright in the night. My mother had to take care of her father, who was in the early stages of dementia, and had made the trip sound so exciting that it took me a while to understand the fact that my father and sister had not boarded the plane.

"Will Dad and Charlotte come in the morning?" I'd asked, curling up against the window with my fluffy princess blanket and an apple juice from the gift shop.

"No, sweetie." My mother, always so pretty with her high cheekbones and strawberry-blonde hair, ran an affectionate hand over my blonde curls. "Lottie's too young, and I have to put my focus on my father. But it will be a grand adventure for the both of us, just you wait and see."

I sat up. The whir of the plane was suddenly too loud and the windowpane cold.

"They'll come, though," I said. "This week."

My mother fiddled with the clasp on her purse. "No, sweetheart."

"What?" I said, confused.

It was late, and I was getting tired.

"They will come visit later in the year," my mother said, taking my hand. "I need time with my father at the moment, because he's sick."

It was hard to picture my mom's father because I'd met him when I was too young to remember. I imagined him in bed with a red nose and a box of Kleenex, eating soup, like in the cartoons.

"We'll come home when he's better?" I said.

My mother ruffled my hair. "This is going to be an adventure. It's a new country for you and it's home for me. Life is something to be seen, explored, devoured..." She pretended to eat my nose and I giggled. "So, that's what we'll do."

I twisted the blanket around my hand, picturing my sister. We'd been in the middle of a game we'd made up with our horse and princess collection all week long. I didn't want her to play it without me, but more than that, I didn't want to be without her. I started blinking fast, trying to fight back the sudden sting in my nose.

"I want Lottie to come," I said.

My mother looped her arm around my thin shoulders, pulling me in tight.

"Me, too," she said softly. "She can't, though. It will be for the best in the end."

I started crying big gulping sobs and the man in the seat in front of us shot my mother an irritated look. He had orange earplugs in and a black sleeping mask perched on top of his head.

"Hush, sweetheart." Gently, she squeezed my cheeks. "This isn't the place. I'm going to tell you something I've figured out, so listen close. It's okay to take a wrong turn in life, but once you realize you're lost, it's not okay to keep speeding past the exits. Do you understand?"

I didn't, but it made me proud that she was sharing something so grown-up with me. I stared out the window at the lights. Maybe it would be okay if Lottie played princesses while I was away, because she could tell me all about it when I got back. Leaning against the window, I imagined my sister snuggled up in the blankets in her bed, and I drifted into a fitful sleep.

Hours later, the wheels jerked to a stop on the runway, and my mother slid up the window shade. She was the first to clap and whistle when the captain announced we'd landed in Dublin. I started cheering and clapping, too, mainly because I didn't want to get left behind.

*

The drive from the lawyer's office to my grandmother's house was only five minutes. Dogwood trees lined the street, raining down their perfumed blossoms like a welcoming committee. The ten houses that made up the Row were tucked back behind long driveways and most of them were gated in, but there was no escaping the abundance of corner towers and sunburst panels that shaped this street. My grandmother's house was #7 and I let out a slow breath as I pulled in.

Martin had already parked, and he stood in the driveway, looking up at it. "Isn't it something?"

Charlotte sat in her white Range Rover, the muted sounds of the car phone breaking the silence of the morning.

"It is," I said. "It's beautiful."

So many shadows had clouded it in my memory. Now, it practically gleamed, the sun shining down like a spotlight. I'd explored several different corners of the world, but the #7 house on the Row was one of the most stunning homes I had ever seen.

It towered above us in a dramatic display of deep-gray clapboards accented with burgundy slate and forest-green trim. Two large chimneys flanked each side and a belvedere sat on top like a crown. Ornate wooden garlands added to its allure, as did the inviting porch that wrapped around the front of the house. Every intricate detail, from the portico balustrades to the bay windows, was perfect.

The muted sound of Charlotte's phone call ended and was replaced with electronic dance music, which surprised me. It came to an abrupt stop as she opened the car door. She stepped down, her posture perfect and ponytail bouncing, a pair of designer sunglasses hiding half of her face.

"Sorry for the wait," she called, picking her way across the broken pavement of the driveway. "I was stuck on a call."

"No problem at all," Martin said. "Shall we go in? It's outdated, but I'm impressed every time I walk through."

Our group climbed the steps. I admired the old stained glass with the decorative rose in the window above the door, the ornate handle, and the spacious entryway that greeted us the moment we walked in.

Charlotte left her sunglasses on as she peered at the space. "I didn't know it had fallen into such disrepair. I'm not sure we can get this done in six months."

The observation brought me back to earth with a bump.

My eyes swept over the foyer, where the wallpaper was peeling, a section of the floor was crumbled, and a hole gaped in the ceiling from water damage. The carpeting and tiles needed to be replaced, and a million cosmetic details like the wallpaper, fixtures, and paint would also need to be redone. Plus, the house smelled musty, as if age had blown through to rob it of its sweet splendor.

"It looks daunting, but it's possible to get it done," Martin said. He peeled off a piece of wallpaper and crumpled it. "I know your grandparents had hoped to put more work into it. Your grandfather enjoyed discussing his plans for the house with me."

I hadn't known my grandmother well, but I barely knew my grandfather at all. He had been overseas the majority of the summer Charlotte and I had stayed, which was part of the reason my grandmother had invited us. She'd said she needed the company. It had been the best summer of my life and somehow she'd made it sound like I'd been doing her a favor.

"Yeah." Charlotte paused, looking out over the living room. "It was hard on Grandma when Grandpa died. I imagine this house had too many memories. We should have…" She shook her head as her voice broke. "Sorry." She waited for a moment, then said, "My family visited her in Florida several times before she died. If we had known the house here had fallen into such a state, we would have helped out."

Charlotte turned away as if studying a piece of wallpaper, but I saw her take her sunglasses off for a second to swipe at her eyes. My grandmother had died back in January, but it had to be painful to be back at a place where they had spent time together. I wanted to offer words of comfort but didn't know what to say.

Martin did it for me. "Your grandmother knew how much you cared for her," he said kindly. "She knew she was loved."

I swallowed the lump in my throat and shifted my gaze to the pictures of my grandparents that hung in the hallway. My grandfather looked a lot like my father. Full lips, a strong jawline, and sharp eyes. My grandmother was softer, with her heart-shaped face and wistful expression.

Charlotte cleared her throat. "Do you know if there are any major problems?" Her voice was brisk, and I could tell that she was determined to appear unaffected. "I see several cosmetic issues, but what about structure?"

"The roof has a number of areas that need mending," the lawyer said. "There are some plumbing problems and the electricity is not up to code."

For a split second, Charlotte glanced at me. Her sunglasses remained on but it had seemed like she'd planned to commiserate, then, just as quickly, changed her mind. The idea that she'd even considered it made me feel another rush of hope.

"That shouldn't be too difficult," I said quickly. "The budget's there and it's not like we'd be roofing or rewiring ourselves, right? I hope not, because I don't want to join my grandmother in heaven quite yet."

The lawyer laughed, but Charlotte did not. Her demeanor became frosty and I wondered if the comment had been insensitive, which was not how I'd meant it to sound. We stopped at the bottom of the grand staircase and I hesitated, wondering if I should apologize.

"This leads to the living areas upstairs," Martin said. "There's another staircase at the end of that hallway that leads back down to the kitchen. Shall we go up?"

Charlotte led the way, noting that several of the banisters needed repair. "There are three bathrooms up here," she said, once we'd reached the top. "One in the first bedroom, one's in the hallway, and the other is off the master. I would like to check them to see if there are any big issues."

The first two bathrooms needed some work, but the master bathroom was a mess. Water damage had taken hold in the ceiling and the plaster was bowing. It was also speckled with mold.

"Yikes," I said.

"We'll have to rip it all out." Charlotte slid her sunglasses back on her head and shined her cell phone's flashlight at the spots. "Plus, see how deep the mold has gotten. It could be a big problem if it got into the wood." She turned off the flashlight, looking troubled. "I hope she didn't live here when it was like this."

"No," Martin said. "The fire would have made that difficult."

Charlotte and I responded at the same time. "*Fire?*"

Martin cleared his throat. "It was downstairs. Let me show you."

This time, Charlotte did make eye contact with me. It was brief, but we shared a worried look.

Martin led us to a door off of the back of the kitchen. Charlotte's shoulders went rigid. The sunroom behind it had been completely charred and the dusty scent of old ash lingered in the air. Instead of being rebuilt, the space had been left to wither away.

"What on earth happened?" she demanded.

Martin cleared his throat. "The fireplace was not fully out and an ember popped onto the rug. Your grandmother was not home, but by some miracle the neighbors were grilling outside at the time. They noticed the smoke and called the fire department. This was right before she'd moved to Florida. I think coordinating a repair was too much for her straight away and she planned to get to it one day but ran out of time."

I walked over to the back wall. There was a black tarp covering a large portion of the lower wall. I lifted up a corner to find charred section of boards that, when I leaned down, gave a clear view of outside. "Is it safe to stay here?" I asked, indicating the gap. "People could probably get inside if they tried, and nothing's stopping the mice."

"I don't think it's been an issue," Martin said. "However, I'd suggest installing some sort of a padlock on the door that leads into the house until you can repair the wall. I doubt there are mice as the door leading to the main house has been shut."

I nodded, hoping this was one of the first rooms on my grandmother's list, since the rooms had to be remodeled in the order that she'd prescribed.

"That said," Martin continued, "Woodsong Harbor is quite safe, and I don't anticipate a problem."

We walked in silence through the rest of the main area. It was easy to see how grand the house had once been. In spite of the challenges, there was so much potential.

"Well, what do you think?" Martin asked, once we had completed the walk-through and stood on the front porch.

The amount of work to be done was daunting but I was excited. If anything, it helped to justify my role in this. It wasn't like I had stolen someone's silver spoon—I'd have to work hard to make it shine.

"It's a lot," Charlotte said, sliding on her sunglasses.

I noticed that she had a small smattering of freckles across her nose, just like my mother. I'd loved my mother's freckles so much when I was little that I'd drawn them on my nose with her eyebrow pencil.

"I also need to discuss it with my family," Charlotte added. "I'd like to sleep on it."

Martin checked his watch. "I'll be in my office first thing in the morning. Shall we set an appointment around nine?"

Once we'd settled on nine thirty, the three of us headed to our separate cars. The lawyer sat in his, making phone calls and returning texts, but Charlotte sped off immediately. I started my car but hesitated, unsure where to go or what to do next.

I wondered if it would be possible to camp out for the night. Or if I could sneak through that opening in the back of the house since it would be mine, anyway. Tempting but not safe, and getting caught would be incredibly embarrassing.

The house stood tall and strong in my rearview mirror, memories swirling around it like ghosts. The entire situation still felt surreal but, for the first time, it seemed possible that my grandmother's plan might work. If Charlotte agreed to go through with this, I might finally have the chance to reconnect with my sister.

# CHAPTER FOUR

"Jayne, hurry."

My mother nudged me through a wrought-iron gate and up a brick path, dragging our two enormous suitcases behind her. I trudged up to the front stoop of a small cottage attached to a row of other cottages, tired from the trip on the airplane and slightly motion sick from the cab. My mother rapped on the door, which was yellow with a black knocker.

The door scraped open, and my mother dove into the arms of a wiry man with sharp brown eyes. He was only a fraction taller than my mom, and he had tight curly gray hair.

"I missed you," she said, holding him tight.

"Who's this?" he said, in the same singsong lilt I'd heard people speaking since we'd left the plane.

I stepped forward. "I'm Jayne."

"Plain Jayne." The words were said with a twinkle in his eye, so instead of feeling angry like I usually did when most people said it, I was fascinated. "Do you like sweeties?" He produced a brown bag and handed it to me. "Apple drops. Bet you've never tasted anything that good."

I reached into the bag and pulled out one of the circular blobs of candy. He was right. They were sweet but spicy and weren't like anything I'd had before.

"What do you say to your daideo?" My mother beamed.

"Thank you," I said, then crunched down.

Daideo, my mother's father, helped move our suitcases into his home. It was spacious, with a big back window that looked out over a large garden. It smelled stale, like old man, but the rounded doorways, unfamiliar pictures, and stacks of books were intriguing.

I spent the day teaching Daideo how to play Go Fish, going on walks with him and my mom, and doing my best to laugh a lot at his jokes, because she kept bursting into tears.

Finally, when we were feeding birds by a pond and my mother started crying again, Daideo snapped, "If you don't want to be here, get back on the plane."

I grabbed my mother's hand. "Can we?" I whispered.

It had been fun, but I didn't like it that she was crying or that her dad had yelled at her. It made her seem young, like me. My stomach started to tremble, and I wondered whether or not my mother could protect me in this strange place.

"We're staying." My mother squeezed my hand and wiped away my tears with her red leather gloves. "I need to help Daideo."

Time marched on. It turned out, Daideo didn't yell very often because he preferred to have as much fun as possible. He was good at knock-knock jokes, he liked to bake cookies, and he took me and my mother to St. Stephen's Green at the same time every day to feed the ducks, rain or shine. He was silly, too. He liked to pretend he couldn't remember my name, he'd put on his socks but forget his shoes, and once, he made us a second batch of eggs right after I'd finished the first breakfast he made me.

I also liked the kids that lived in the cottages near us. We played in the gardens in the back and it felt like everybody knew everybody. Even though school in Ireland was different, there were times I forgot I was somewhere new, as I didn't allow myself to think too often about Charlotte and my dad.

The holidays arrived in a flurry of snow and anticipation. Daideo loved Christmas and had decorations everywhere. There was a little glass tree with lots of lights on the kitchen counter, a big tree in the living room, and stockings hung over the mantel of the fireplace. On Christmas Eve, he sipped on eggnog and read a Christmas story to me and my mother, his face lit in a prism of colors from the lights on the tree.

My mother reached over and squeezed my hand, and I leaned against her, staring at the stack of presents. There were already so many, wrapped in foil paper with fancy bows. I remembered the way Charlotte had put as many bows as possible on her head the Christmas before.

"I want to talk to Lottie," I said suddenly, interrupting the story.

Daideo tugged at my toe. "Let me finish, acushla. We have to find out if St. Nicholas is going to do the deliveries in time."

He started to read again but I jumped to my feet. "No. It's Christmas and I want to talk to my sister!"

Charlotte and I had spoken a few times since I'd first arrived in Dublin. Quick phone calls that ended in tears, but at least I'd heard her voice.

My mother gave an eager nod. "I was going to call tomorrow, but we can do it tonight."

Daideo held the book tight. "It's hard on the children, Aubrey."

"It will be fine," she said. "Let's finish the story later, okay?"

Daideo went to the kitchen and started arranging a plate of cookies.

My mother took a drink of eggnog, then picked up the phone. My dad answered and I spoke to him first, surprised at how deep his voice sounded compared to the light brogue I heard each day.

"I miss you, Daddy," I said.

"I miss you, too." His voice seemed to catch for a minute, but I knew my dad was too big to cry. "This Christmas hasn't been the same without you."

"Can I come home?" I said, picking at the rubbery phone cord.

"Jayne." My mother put a hand on my shoulder. "Ask to speak to Charlotte. We need to find out if she got her presents."

My mother and I had spent days visiting all the toy shops downtown to find the perfect gifts for Charlotte. We'd found her a wooden puzzle, a beautiful doll with hair as dark as hers, and the coziest pair of red mittens.

There were some muffled sounds in the background. Then my dad came back on the line. "I'm sorry, Jayne. She's not up for talking today."

"Did she get her presents?" I said, confused. "I want to talk to her."

"I'm sorry, honey," he said. "She won't come to the phone."

"What do you mean?" Then, because everything felt so wrong, I shouted, "Charlotte! Lottie, get on the phone. I need to talk to you!"

My heart broke as I heard her say, "Tell them to go away."

"We love you, Jayne," my dad said. "I hope to see you soon."

My mother called right back, and even though Daideo tried to distract me with macaroons, I got the gist: Charlotte didn't want to talk to me, but she definitely didn't want to talk to my mother.

Moments later, my mother hung up the phone, her face stricken. Without a word, she went into her room and shut the door.

Daideo ruffled my hair. "Santa will see both you and your sister tonight. Take comfort in that."

I waited until Daideo went to join my mother in her room before creeping over to listen at the door.

"I miss her," my mom sobbed. "Every second of every day."

"Then go back." His voice was firm. "Trust the nurses to care for me."

"I can't leave you here," she said.

"My life is here," he said. "Your mother's grave is here. I'm not leaving her."

There was a moment of silence. "It will be okay. Charlotte won't remember much of this."

"But Jayne will," he said.

"I need these last years with you."

These last *years*?

I shoved open the door and stumbled into the room. My mother and Daideo had been sitting on the bed. They both got to their feet, my mother clutching a shredded tissue.

"What do you mean, these last years?" I demanded. "You said we wouldn't be here long. You said we were going home soon!"

My mother took a few steps towards me. "Honey, calm down."

I grabbed the first thing I could get my hands on. Her slippers. I threw them at her with all my might. No one scolded me; they just watched as if stunned.

"Dad's going to flip out when I tell him that you planned to keep me here that long," I told her. Wildly, I looked around for something to break. Striding towards the mirror, I reached for a perfume bottle. "He'll come get me and—"

"He knows."

The words were quiet, but they sliced right through me. Slowly, I lowered my arm.

"What?" I whispered.

Granted, I hadn't missed my dad the way I'd missed Lottie. He worked all the time and I barely saw him anyway. But he was still my dad, so why would he let me leave?

"Jayne, come sit." Even though I was filled with fury, I sat on the bed next to my mother. She put her arm around me and said, "Daideo has something called Alzheimer's disease. It's a sickness that's taking away his ability to manage on his own."

I frowned. "What do you mean?"

He grabbed my ear and gave it a gentle tug. "It means that in a year or two, I won't recognize you. I won't be able to live in this house anymore, because I'll need someone to take care of me. I also…" He looked at my mom, as though for permission, and she nodded. "I also have cancer in my stomach. The good news is that sometimes I can't remember I have it."

"Spending time with Daideo right now is something I have to do." My mother's voice was brisk. "Charlotte can't be here right now because she's little and needs a lot of care and attention, and I won't be able to give that to her when Daideo starts to get really sick."

"He's not sick," I said, confused.

They exchanged a look.

"You can't see it yet, but the time will come. It would be too hard on Charlotte to have to go back when that happens," my mother said. "But she's coming to visit in February with your father. They'll stay for three weeks."

"Three weeks," I whispered.

Outside the bedroom window, snow began to fall.

"It's a white Christmas," Daideo said quietly.

My mother dabbed at her cheeks with a scrap of tissue. "Let's get you in bed so Santa Claus can come, okay?"

"Three weeks," I repeated, trying to picture it. I'd take her to see the ducks, right away. "I need to know that she's coming for sure."

"Nothing's for sure, acushla," Daideo said, ruffling my hair. "But hope is the brightest star in the sky."

"She's coming," my mother insisted. "I promise."

As I lay in my bed that night, I hated the idea that, instead of being next to Charlotte's, my stocking was on the hook of a strange mantel in a home on the other side of the world. I fell asleep wishing I knew how to get on the roof. I'd wait there for Santa and beg him to take me back to my sister, so that I could spend Christmas with her by my side.

*

There were only a few bed-and-breakfasts in Woodsong Harbor, and they were all out of my price range. I decided to type a bid into a hotel search engine, fully expecting to have to drive forty-five minutes to an affordable motel off the highway. To my surprise, my bid was accepted at one of the bed-and-breakfasts here in town.

Emerald Pines was a charming house painted green. It was off the main road, in a quiet neighborhood with large porches and even bigger front lawns. There was a patch of trees in the back that gave it a wooded feel.

"You must be Jayne." A woman with ash-blonde hair met me at the front door with a friendly smile. "I'm not clairvoyant or anything; it's simply that everyone else has checked in. Let me show you your room. I'm Betsy, by the way."

Betsy led me up a sweeping staircase to the very end of a tastefully wallpapered hall. "Now, it's quite small, which is why it's on the discount site," she warned, her hand resting on the knob. "If you don't like it, let me know, and I'm sure we can find you something somewhere in town."

"No, I'm sure it'll be fine," I said, imagining the drive back to the highway motels. This would be a thousand times better, even if it was the size of a closet.

Sure enough, the room was adorable. The ceiling slanted down, cutting the space in half, but it was lovely. Cream-and-royal-blue wallpaper, thick cozy carpet, and a single bed that looked like an antique. It had the slightest scent of oranges and roses, probably a potpourri of some sort, and a tiny sitting area with a full bookshelf. I'd been so busy the past few months that I hadn't had a chance to read, which had once been one of my favorite pastimes.

"This looks great," I said.

Betsy bustled over and fluffed the pillows on the bed. "I'm so glad. I'm a widow and don't need much space, so it seems like a palace to me. Silver lining, right?"

"I'm sorry." I set my purse on the dresser. "When did your husband die?"

"Oh, ages ago." She gave me another warm smile. "Now, I always set out cookies at four. Dinner is at six o'clock, or I can bring up a cold plate for your room, and breakfast is from seven to nine. Do you need anything special to help out with your stay?"

"No, thank you," I said. "This is perfect."

"Ring if you need anything at all." Betsy exited as efficiently as she'd arrived, calling over her shoulder, "Have a lovely day."

The door clicked shut. The old-fashioned bell clock by the bed read eleven thirty, which meant I needed to find something to eat for lunch. I searched my phone to find a restaurant nearby that was affordable, and settled on a burger place by the beach.

The burger was a perfect combination of chargrilled meat and crisp lettuce, so I sat on a nearby bench beneath a tree and devoured it. The shade and breeze from the ocean kept me cool as I researched things to do in town on my phone. The most appealing options were the forest trails that stretched up into the hills. I tossed the empty to-go container and walked back to Emerald Pines to make the drive out there.

I had no sooner pulled out the keys to my car than I spotted a rack of bikes with a plaque that read *Guests Only*. It had been ages since I'd been on a bike, but it sounded fun. Selecting a mint cruiser with silver trim, I pedaled down the sidewalk tentatively at first and then like a pro.

The wind swept through my hair as the ocean glimmered in the distance, the view of the town as perfect as a painting. It was hard to believe that Charlotte had spent so much of her life here, when my role here had been so minor. My thoughts went back to the house. Even though I questioned whether or not I deserved it, I hoped Charlotte would agree to move forward.

I didn't have any experience with remodeling, but it definitely appealed to my artistic side. The house was already special and, with hard work, it had the potential to be extraordinary.

The sidewalk narrowed into the parking lot for the forest trails. The signs noted that some were for walking and others were for biking. I decided to walk, since the cruiser might not make it if there were too many ruts.

The cool oasis of the forest was inviting and I headed in. The deep green of the trees lulled me into a sense of peace. When the path turned into a wooden footbridge over a creek, I stopped at the edge of the wooden railing with my eyes closed, listening to it pass by.

Once I'd enjoyed the fresh air, I headed back to Emerald Pines. There, I curled up with a stack of books in the cozy chair, the sun warming my legs. My eyes grew heavy and I fell asleep for a minute or an hour, I really didn't know. Soon, the light was long in the room and I opted to ask Betsy to send up a cold plate so I wouldn't have to dress for dinner.

The smoked salmon and summer salad were refreshing. Finally, I settled in for a long soak in the claw-foot bathtub in the small bathroom, which felt like the height of luxury. The warm water, coupled with eucalyptus salts and scented candles that reflected in the water, helped soothe away the tension in my shoulders.

My cell rang from the bedroom, cutting through the stillness of the summer night. Worried that it was the lawyer calling to tell me that Charlotte had decided to opt out, I scrambled out of the tub to answer, dripping water all over the floor.

For once, it was a relief to hear a computerized voice inform me that I was past due on my credit card payments and needed to make a payment immediately. The creditors had hounded me for months and I'd learned to accept it, even though I'd always been a person who paid my bills on time. This was the first month I'd had to put off my phone payment, and I wondered how long it would be until that was shut off, too.

At least I wouldn't be able to receive any more messages like this. Since I no longer had an apartment, I would also stop getting those menacing letters. Not that any of that would make my debt go away or help pay for the skyrocketing cost of my diabetes medication.

Selling the beach house would, though. I had dared to research the amount houses like the ones up on the Row would sell for, and the numbers nearly knocked me down. Even once the proceeds were split with Charlotte, I would be left with a stunning amount of money, right when I needed it most.

Snuggling into the blankets, I tried to picture the two paths my life could take: If Charlotte said no, I'd be back to working two jobs for at least the next two years, until I was finally out of the woods. If she said yes... I could barely wrap my mind around the thought. Starting to doze, I pulled the comforter close around me. I fell asleep imagining Charlotte standing at the iron gates of her house, deciding whether or not to let me in.

I had been asleep for two hours when shouting jolted me awake, followed by the thick smell of smoke. I sat up straight, confused about where I was and what was happening. I'd left the window open to let in the night breeze, and outside, the trees glowed orange through a thick haze in the air.

The forest behind the house was on fire.

Coughing, I stumbled to my feet. I had slept in a T-shirt and a pair of underpants, but the only thing I could think of was to get out. I grabbed the quickest thing I could find, the bathrobe and sandals I'd left by the door. Then I rushed into the hallway.

The lights were on and Betsy was racing up the steps. "I have to get everyone out." Her eyes were bright with panic. "It's too close."

The house was big, with at least ten rooms. I jumped in to help, taking the opposite side of the hallway and banging on the doors. The guests began to emerge, sleepy and disheveled. Once every door had opened, I ran down the stairs and out of the house.

There were fire trucks everywhere, their lights illuminating the area in a strange red glow. The firemen stretched the hoses along the side of the house, rushing back and forth, shouting instructions as they ran. The neighbors from the houses on each side stood on their front porches, hands pressed to their mouths.

I moved to the side of the house, watching the smooth arc of water hiss from the hose towards the smoldering flames. It felt like a dream or a nightmare, and I hung back as the firefighters battled the blaze. The moment they put out one section, the flames flickered to life on the opposite side of the forest like those fake birthday candles that would never quite blow out.

The breeze shifted and the flames leapt to the lawn. One of the guests shouted, pointing. The firefighters turned the water on the grass and then back to the forest. Finally, the water began to have an effect. The forest hissed and steamed as the flames died out. Smoke rose from the wet trees and drifted towards the full moon. The stale scent lent a familiarity to the air, like the smell of a chimney during winter, or a campfire down by the beach.

Everyone started talking, their voices full of relief. One of the couples staying at the bed-and-breakfast headed back towards the front door. Betsy gently took the man's elbow and said something to him. He nodded and the couple rejoined the crowd on the front lawn.

"I'm so sorry," Betsy called, her kind voice soothing in the chaos of the night. "The firemen have told me that we'll have to stay out for a while. They need to make sure that the smoke levels in the house aren't unsafe."

The group settled in to wait, some taking a seat on the gliders on the porch and others on the front stoop. I stood to the side of the porch, noting that I was the only guest without a partner and certainly the only one dressed in a bathrobe. While I had spent my time banging on the doors to get people out, everyone else had spent their time getting dressed.

Turning my attention to the fire trucks, I drew back at the sight of Logan, the grumpy guy from the coffee shop. He stood at the back of a truck, removing his fire coat. He had soot smeared across his sweating face and, as I watched, he unloaded a case of small bottles of water. He brought them over to the group, handing them out as if we were guests at a barbecue.

I was tempted to make my escape, but there wasn't anywhere to go without being in the way of the other firemen. Logan handed out water bottles to the couples on the bottom steps and then spotted me. He turned and stalked off to the truck without offering me a thing.

I was about to call out in protest when he turned away from the fire truck carrying a bottle of water and a big blanket, his helmet swinging from his arm. His eyes seemed to graze over me as he slid the rough gray wool into my hands.

"Here." His hair was wet with sweat. "You win the fire safety award. If there's a fire, you don't get dressed, you get out. Nice work."

One of the other firemen called for him, and he shot me a wink before heading off.

Pulling the blanket tight around me, I watched as he shook the sweat out of his hair, then pulled his helmet back on and broke into a jog. It was hard to believe he was the same guy who had confronted me in the coffee shop. It was also a bit embarrassing that I'd lectured him about kindness when he saved people's lives in his spare time.

I wished I'd kept my mouth shut. Now that I had a chance of staying here all summer, I was sure to run into him again.

The house settled quickly once everyone was safely inside. I even heard muffled snores through the wall next to me, but as hard as I tried, I couldn't get back to sleep. Even when I pulled the pillow over my head, the smoke smell in my hair was too strong.

Finally, I got up and took a shower, hoping it would calm me enough to go back to bed. Once I crawled back between the sheets, though, I couldn't stop picturing Logan in his fire gear, battling the flames as they moved towards the house. Letting out a sigh, I gave up on sleep and headed downstairs.

Betsy had mentioned that the kitchen closed at 10 p.m., but she'd also said to let her know if I needed anything. There was a nice collection of tea on the counter next to the coffee supplies. Chamomile usually worked wonders helping me to sleep.

I had just opened the cupboard to search for a microwavable cup when a cheerful voice said, "Is there something I can help you with?"

"Oh my goodness, you startled me." I put my hand to my heart. "I came down for a cup of tea. I hope that's okay."

"I was doing the same thing." Betsy bustled into the kitchen and put on a kettle. "Seems to be the theme of the night. That fire sure startled *me*. Thank you so much for your help getting everyone out. I appreciated that." She paused, then shook her head. "It was impossible for me to sleep, picturing this place going up in flames." She indicated I should take a seat at the table by the window. It was much smaller than the one in the formal dining room, where breakfast would be served. "I would offer you something stronger to drink," she said, pulling a box of cookies out of the cupboard, "but I don't have a license to serve alcohol this late."

I smiled. "I already had that delicious glass of wine you sent up. Too much alcohol would get my sugar out of whack."

Betsy had been arranging the cookies but stopped. "You're diabetic?" When I nodded, she reached up into the cupboard and pulled out a sugar-free box.

"Thank you, but I'm good." The kitchen chair had a burgundy cushion and I settled in. "I'd just like a cup of tea to help me get back to bed."

Betsy put back the box of cookies and joined me at the table. "I've never seen a fire in real life. I mean, one that was actually burning things down."

"Me neither," I said, thinking of the wreckage in the sunroom at my grandmother's house.

It was a relief to think that she had not been home when the sunroom caught fire and that the neighbors had been so quick to act. I wouldn't be sitting here if they hadn't, because the beach house would have been destroyed.

"It was scary," I admitted.

"It was." Betsy pushed a strand of curly hair out of her eyes and considered the kitchen. "It's been a little dry here, but I didn't expect this. I've worked for years to make this place into what it is. The moment when the wind shifted and the flames came so close…" She pressed her hands into her cheeks. "I can't tell you how that made me feel."

I could relate. The sense of ownership, hard work, and incredible risk it took to try to make your passion a livelihood was something I remembered well. More than that, I knew the devastation that came with watching it all fall apart.

"What made you want to start a bed-and-breakfast?" I asked.

The tea kettle whistled and she filled our cups. "Well, I grew up in New York City. I loved to go to the museum and sit in front of the same painting for hours because I would see so many different people pass through. I kept trying to strike up conversations with strangers. Hearing about the lives of others has always been infinitely fascinating to me, so I figured I had two choices: work as a stewardess or open a hotel. I was a stewardess for twenty years and finally saved up enough to open this place."

I smiled at the story. It was clear she'd told it a hundred times, but she still managed to make it charming.

"I'm glad you did," I told her as she handed me the steeping cup of tea. "I was having such a peaceful night until the fire. My tiny room is perfect."

"Good," Betsy said, laughing. "Now, what do you do?"

The mug warmed my hands as I debated how much to share. There was a risk in talking too much, especially since I was going to be here for the summer.

"It's embarrassing," I said.

I led with that to see how Betsy would respond. She didn't widen her eyes and lean forward like someone seeking out gossip. Instead, she gave a sage nod. "Things feel that way, sometimes."

"I started a children's art studio," I admitted.

Betsy's eyes lit up. "That's darling. Pottery? Painting?"

"There was something for everyone," I said, remembering the joy I'd felt that first day, watching the kids explore the paints and sensory items and build giant cardboard boats. "I didn't have much of a head for the business side of things, so it ended up being a disaster."

"In what way?" she asked, removing her tea ball.

I set mine on my napkin, watching as the color chased itself to the edges.

"I made too many mistakes. Admission was too low. The rent was too high. I didn't set boundaries on the supplies. I gave too many free kids' parties to silent auctions and didn't set blackout dates… The list goes on for days. Ultimately, I didn't know how to run a business and, on top of that, I felt guilty for making it about money, because I loved what I did."

Betsy nodded. "It can be hard to accept the idea that work doesn't always have to be work."

"Yeah." I sipped at the tea. "I was so happy to have my studio that I felt like I should have been paying someone for the opportunity. In the end, that's exactly what happened."

My shoulders tensed as I remembered the embarrassment of being forced to dilute the paint because I couldn't afford it. One of the parents had brought a jar to me and said, "I think one of the kids got to your paints. They're full of water."

"I put everything I'd had into the business and then some," I said. "It didn't want to fail on its own—it dragged me right down with it." The smell of smoke lingered in the air, along with the spicy scent of the chamomile. Shaking my head, I said, "Sorry to sound so full of self-pity. I closed the doors three months ago, so I'm doing my best to accept it."

"I'm so sorry," Betsy said. "Had you been to business school?"

"No," I said, laughing. "I majored in elementary ed, so I only got as far as two plus two—which might have been the problem."

Betsy chuckled with me but then got serious. "Well, you learned some valuable lessons. Maybe one day you'll try again."

That wasn't going to happen. Even if I had all the money in the world, it wouldn't change the fact that I had no idea how to run a business. The experience had been a lesson in humility and heartbreak, and I'd had enough of that to last a lifetime.

"Doubtful," I said. "I appreciate the kind words."

"What brought you to town?" Betsy asked after we'd sipped our tea in silence.

"My grandmother passed away earlier this year. She left me and my sister her beach house." The words sounded surreal, like I was talking about something that had happened to someone else. "My sister is deciding whether or not to agree to the terms of the will. I should know tomorrow."

Betsy clasped her hands. "No wonder you can't sleep! Where's the house?"

"Up on the Row?" I said, trying out the term the lawyer had used.

Betsy's eyes widened. "I adore those homes. Which one is it?"

"The one that's a bit run-down," I said. "My grandmother planned to remodel it herself but never got to it."

Betsy wrinkled her brow. "May I ask, who was your grand-mother?"

"Iris Wilmington. Did you know her?"

"Yes. I am so sad to hear she passed away." Betsy shook her head. "I knew her through the local social events. I often wondered what happened to her after she moved to Florida. Your grandmother was a lovely person. You must miss her terribly."

I took a sip of tea to hide my emotions. Fear had kept me from getting too close and, looking back, I regretted that decision.

"I should let you get to bed." I took my cup to the sink. "Can I wash this or…?"

Betsy bustled over. "I'll take care of it. You get some rest."

My body was so tired that it felt like a journey just walking up the stairs. I was grateful for the chamomile but, in spite of my exhaustion, my mind was racing so fast I didn't know if I would get to sleep at all.

# CHAPTER FIVE

I'd finally drifted off after tossing and turning most of the night. My cell rang at eight, and I blinked in the bright sun filtering through the white lace curtains of the bed-and-breakfast. I fumbled to answer the call before it went to voicemail.

"Hello?" I asked, sitting up straight.

"Good morning, it's Martin Sommers."

"Good morning."

I'd never been a morning person. It usually took me about an hour to wake up, with the assistance of a good breakfast and a strong cup of black coffee. Thanks to the adrenaline that had rushed through my body at the sound of his voice, it felt like I'd already done all that and more.

"I'm calling with good news." He sounded cheerful. "Your sister has decided to move forward with the terms of the will."

I tossed the covers back and slid out of bed. On some level, I'd convinced myself that Charlotte would back out. My body was suddenly tense and I had no idea what to do, where to go, or what to think. This was life-changing in so many ways.

The fact that I was going to inherit something of such significant financial value made me feel uncomfortable. So did the fact that I was also going to spend the next six months under the same roof as my sister. It was something I'd longed for since I was six years old, but now that it was going to happen, I didn't know what to think.

"Jayne, are you there?" the lawyer asked.

"Yes." My voice sounded weaker than I would have liked. "That's great news."

"I need to confirm that you are also planning on moving forward?" he asked.

"Yes," I said. "Absolutely."

The moment the words left my mouth, my heart started to race. I opened the window. I couldn't see the section of the forest that had caught fire the night before, but I could smell the faded scent of ash in the air.

"Excellent." I could practically imagine him crossing something off a to-do list. "Now, I'll need you to sign the paperwork and receive the keys. Does nine thirty still work for you?"

"Yes." The adrenaline was starting to make me feel off. "I'll see you then."

I hung up and fumbled through my purse for a meal bar. Ripping open the wrapper, I took some quick bites and drank water until I started to feel a bit more level. My diabetes was under control and it was rare to have any type of issue, but I was exhausted and off schedule, and food was the first thing I needed if I started to feel strange.

The biggest thing that would help would be a real breakfast. I could smell eggs and sausage cooking downstairs. I imagined Betsy had made a delicious spread.

Quickly, I put on a pale blue sundress and brushed my hair. I'd always been blessed with thick blonde hair that looked good whether it was up in a half ponytail, wet from the shower, or windblown after a day at the beach, so it never took me long to get ready in the morning.

Then I headed down to breakfast, surprised at the speed at which life could change.

\*

I pulled up to the lawyer's office in my clunker of a car, parking it next to Charlotte's sleek ride. It made me feel embarrassed, but I reminded myself we'd lived different lives. I didn't know the details of hers, but I was hoping that with time, I would.

The receptionist greeted me with a friendly smile. Today, she wore a navy-colored suit. She led me to the same room and shut the door.

Charlotte sat at the long table, this time dressed in a pink-and-white-striped seersucker dress with a strand of pearls. She and the lawyer were discussing a yacht club they were both familiar with, and I hung back for a moment, not wanting to interrupt. Spotting me, Martin got to his feet.

"Good morning," I said, hoping that I didn't look as lost as I felt.

Charlotte nodded. "Good morning." She had on a bright pink lip gloss that matched the pink pinstripes in her dress. Subtle, but stylish.

"To you, as well." Martin pointed at a fruit tray and a selection of coffee. "I brought this in to celebrate the big occasion."

"Thank you," I said. "That's so nice."

Charlotte had a small plate of strawberries and kiwi in front of her place at the table. My favorites, as well. I took the same, half hoping that she'd notice and smile, but she barely looked up.

My seat at the table was ready to go, with a fresh bottle of water, new pen, notebook, and tin of mints. I put the plate of fruit next to it all. The entire situation felt surreal, like maybe I was still asleep.

Martin slid on his glasses and sat back down. "Well, this is what your grandmother hoped for. Rest assured that I will be in the office throughout the process, ready and willing to answer any questions or concerns the two of you have.

"The main thing is that you are both responsible for staying within budget. However, Fran, the accountant you'll work with, is an excellent resource. She will handle payments to the contractors and will supply you with a biweekly status report on the budget. You will receive your first stipend once you move into the house, and they will come monthly after that."

My pulse quickened. It was hard to believe I could start to pay off my creditors and not stress about how I was going to afford my medication. Two thousand a month wasn't going to change my life, but it would make it possible to see the light at the end of all of this.

"Now, Charlotte will be working remote, but the nature of her job allows for flexible hours. She has requested for the work on the house to be scheduled around her hours on those days. Is that agreeable?"

I nodded. "Sounds good."

"We also need to determine a start date," he said. "What is good for the two of you?"

"The first week of June," Charlotte said.

The lawyer nodded. "Jayne, how is that for you?"

My preference was to start tomorrow. Returning to the pace of working in the preschool during the day and going straight to waiting tables at night sounded exhausting. There had been a time when I'd gone to lunches with friends, lived for outdoor concerts in the summer and cozy game nights in the winter. That had all fallen by the wayside when my life became about survival.

The idea of going back to all of that was not appealing, but at least it would give me the opportunity to be there for the preschoolers' last day of school. Still, I felt scared to leave town, or more precisely, Charlotte. The idea of driving away with the knowledge that she was leaving, too, filled me with anxiety.

"You won't change your mind, will you?" I asked.

"No." She frowned. "Will you?"

I wanted to tell her that there was nothing I would rather do than spend the next six months with her, but of course, it wasn't as simple as that.

"I won't back out," I said, lightly pressing my hands on the table. "The first week of June would be perfect."

Martin opened his briefcase. "Then allow me to pass out the paperwork, so that you can get started signing." He handed out two black folders with several pages that went over terms and conditions. "I'd like to draw your attention to the order of repairs. This is a particularly important point to address, as your grandmother wanted you to follow this list. In the interest of time, some tasks can overlap, but she wanted you to stick close to the schedule."

I looked down at the list.

1. Structure
   - Roof
   - Damaged wall in sunroom
   - Structural changes or updates
2. Water damage
   - Master bath upstairs
   - Entryway
   - Additional?
3. Remove wallpaper
   - Living room
   - Dining room
4. Remove tiles
   - Main room
   - Bathrooms
5. Replace bathroom fixtures
   - Master bath
   - Guest baths

I began to skim after number four, but the list had twelve steps with varying degrees of detail.

"It has to be done in this order?" Charlotte said, clucking her tongue. "There are areas where it might make sense to switch it up."

Martin shook his head. "She was firm on this point."

"Then we'll have to book some of these repairs now," Charlotte said. "The roofers, at least. It's impossible to get someone in without a few weeks' notice. We should be able to get quotes remotely. Martin, would you be able to let them into the house if they require access?"

"Yes, that shouldn't be a problem," he said.

It surprised me that my sister had even thought of that. I was still trying to take in the reality of what was happening.

"I'm happy to help with whatever I can," I said.

Charlotte sifted through the papers. "I'll look through and see what can be taken care of prior to the official start date. Either way, I'm impressed. This is much more efficient than the company I work for. My grandmother should have run a business."

My cheeks colored. The remark couldn't have been a dig at my failed venture, because I doubted my sister had cared enough to research me online. Nevertheless, I couldn't help but feel exposed as I studied the accounting page, with this list of numbers and figures that I'd never imagined within my reach.

Once we'd finished signing, while Martin flipped through our folders to make sure we hadn't missed anything, I found myself staring down at my hands. They had been shaking at breakfast but were steady now. Charlotte meanwhile was occupied with her phone, occasionally sipping her water but never looking up.

Review completed, Martin tapped the packet. "Now, before I hand you the keys, your grandmother would like me to read this letter." He cleared his throat, then began:

*Dear Charlotte and Jayne,*

*Once this letter has reached you, I will be watching over you in all things. Well, if that's allowed up there. I don't know the rules, yet, but I guess I'll learn!*

*The reason I asked the two of you to remodel my beloved beach house together is because, as I mentioned in my previous letter, that summer we were all together has forever remained in my mind as one of the happiest summers of my entire life. I have never laughed so hard, or been so enamored with two such beautiful souls.*

*The two of you were cheated in so many ways by your separation. I pray that during these six months, you will open your hearts to one another and seize the opportunity to heal the pain of the past. It might not be easy, but nothing worth doing ever is.*

*Please stay with it, my darlings. Don't give up. If I have learned anything during my life, it's this: the only thing worth fighting for is love.*

*I will go to my eternal rest with the hope that the two of you will reconcile and finally have the opportunity to become true sisters to one another. If that's not the outcome, that's all right. At least you will have tried, and I did, too.*

*Kisses and hugs,*
*Your grandmother*

The lawyer waited a brief moment and then got to his feet.

"Here are the keys." He handed us each a set. "Of course, I do ask that you do not move into the house until the start date that we've agreed upon, but you're welcome to revisit it today if you'd like. I wish you nothing but joy as you work to bring your grandmother's house to the splendor that she'd always envisioned."

Letting out a breath, I said, "Thank you," and headed for the door.

\*

My mother met me at the door of Daideo's house, her face lit with excitement. The school day had worn me out and I was ready for a snack, but it had been a while since my mother had looked so happy.

She'd been crying a lot because Daideo couldn't remember certain words and sometimes lashed out in frustration. The night before, he'd thrown the dinner she'd cooked on the floor because it had onions.

My mother helped me take my coat and mittens off and we sat on the couch. The heat from the vent in the floor warmed my cold feet.

"I didn't want to say anything because I wanted to make sure everything would be okay." She clasped her hands so tight her knuckles turned white. "Daddy and Charlotte are headed to the airport right now, getting ready to board a plane. They'll be here in the morning!"

The breath left my lungs. "I'll be at school. I'll miss them."

My mother laughed. "They'll be here for three weeks, silly. You won't go to school tomorrow, or even next week. I can keep you out for a week to see your sister."

From her upbeat tone, I knew I was supposed to be happy, but Mrs. O'Connell was right in the middle of reading *The Secret Garden* and I didn't want to miss that. Plus, we were supposed to do sand art later next week and Sally Donaldson had asked me to sit with her at lunch.

It wasn't fair to ask me to forget about all of that because my dad and Charlotte had finally decided to show up. Besides, I felt nervous about seeing them again. I'd gotten taller since we'd been here. What if Charlotte didn't recognize me?

"I'll see them after school," I said, getting to my feet. "Is there any bread left for toast?"

My mother followed me into the kitchen. "It's okay to feel scared. It's been months since we've seen them, but they're coming. They're coming!" She picked me up and kissed my cheeks with glee, and I wriggled away.

The smile fell from her face. "What is wrong with you?"

"Nothing." I opened the refrigerator. "If we don't have toast, we'd better have muffins."

That night, the phone rang in the middle of dinner. My mother answered while Daideo stared out the window. I didn't try to talk to him when it got late because he seemed too tired, and he couldn't keep up with the things I was trying to explain.

I had been busy putting butter on my potatoes when my mother answered the phone, so I'd missed who called. When she came back to the table, she stumbled into her seat, like she was sick. She sat there and stared straight ahead like Daideo, running her fingers over her necklace.

The next morning, she came into my room with the sun. "Rise and shine." Her voice was thick and raspy. "Time for school."

My eyes blurred open. "I'm not going to go. I'm ready to see her."

My mother pulled the shades on the window, straightened the bedspread, and gave me a firm kiss on the forehead. "They've had to reschedule. Charlotte has the flu. They'll come next month."

I let my mother dress me while I tried to take in what she'd said. The starched uniform was stiff on my skin and my teeth started to chatter.

"You're cold." She grabbed a thick, hand-knitted wool sweater from the closet and tried to put it on me.

I shrugged her off. "It's not uniform. I can't wear that."

My mother pulled me into a tight hug, resting her chin firmly on top of my head. This time, I didn't push her away.

"Daideo is not well," she whispered. "We'll be back home soon."

I held my body rigid until she let go. Then I stared down at my shoes. They were getting too tight, but I didn't want to tell her, for fear she'd start to cry.

*

I drove up the crumbling paved driveway to the beautiful house on the Row. It was enormous, falling apart, and with the light of the sun falling on it just so, an absolute work of art.

One thought kept repeating in my mind: *This is mine. This house is mine.*

Even though I had to get on the road, I'd wanted to take a moment alone with it. I planned to have a quick lunch, walk on the beach, and then head home.

The sun was bright and the birds were singing. The property had a lovely expanse of trees across the way, a blend of pine and dogwood. The nettles were dry on the ground, and it felt remote, in spite of the fact that the ocean was just on the other side of the dunes.

What a special place. Wrapping my arms around myself, I turned to drink it all in. The sun glinted off the top windows and I could practically picture my grandmother standing in the front door, welcoming me as she'd done so many years ago.

The temptation to explore each and every crevice of the house was strong, but there was a chance Charlotte would also stop by before her trip home. I didn't want her to catch me snooping through stuff, even if it did belong to me now. Instead, I took my lunch out to the back porch.

Our group had only come outside for a minute during the walk-through and I hadn't had much of a chance to look around. The view of the ocean was spectacular. The multilayered hues of white sand down past the bluff made my heart sing, and the tangy air felt like saltwater taffy on my tongue.

Once I'd eaten lunch, I headed for the gate that led to the steep steps descending to the beach. The staircase had been built into the side of the bluff, and it was falling apart. The railing, which had once been ensconced in rubber, was bare, save a few sections, and it was covered in rust that was sharp on my hand. Nevertheless the posts had held strong and the wooden steps didn't wobble as I made my way between the dry, thick grass, which probably housed an impressive array of snakes. I made a mental note that the steps needed to be on the list of home improvements, sooner rather than later, since they allowed access to the beach.

Once I had made it to the bottom, I took off my sandals and let my toes sink into the powdered sand. The sun was warm on my cheeks and the feelings coursing through me were too big to catch up with. I took in slow, deep breaths, trying to calm down.

I walked for about thirty minutes, until the midday sun felt hot on my shoulders. Then I waded into the water. I'd forgotten how the ocean seemed to tug my feet out further with every step, the current trying to pull me into its steady rhythm. Reaching down, I splashed the salty water onto my shoulders and then my face, letting the waves crash over the hem of my dress.

The soggy fabric brushed against my shins as I finally made my way back towards the stairs to my grandmother's house.

I had just about made it to the rickety steps when a now-familiar face waved from down the beach. Logan. He was at least twenty feet away, walking alongside a golden retriever who clearly adored him. I was tempted to make a run for the steps because I was still embarrassed about telling him to choose kindness when he was a public servant, of all things, but I pasted a cheerful smile on my face.

"Hello again," I called.

He slid his aviators up onto his head. "That was some fire last night, wasn't it?"

Today, he wore a green T-shirt that showcased his strong upper arms.

"It was." The strap on my dress had slipped, and I straightened it. "The owner of the bed-and-breakfast said it's been dry."

"Yeah, I think I've been called in more in the past month than all last year."

His golden retriever strained against the leash, nuzzling her nose against my palm.

"Sorry," he said, giving a small laugh. "She's curious."

"I love dogs." The collar read Shamrock, and I scratched the soft fur on her neck.

Shamrock tried to move closer but Logan gently pulled her back. "It makes me feel so guilty to have her on this leash," he said. "She's a good girl but she's a rescue and gets on the defensive pretty quickly with dogs she doesn't know. I let her run free when there's nobody around."

I appreciated the fact that he was realistic about how his dog might affect other people. It made him seem infinitely more considerate than he'd appeared in the coffee shop yesterday.

*Yesterday.*

It felt like ten years had passed since then.

"Well, I hope she gets a chance to run free," I said.

We smiled at each other. Then he put on his sunglasses and nodded. "Have a good day."

Resting my hand on railing of the steps, I wondered if Charlotte was up there. Most likely not—she'd probably headed home—but the idea that she would soon be there with me every day made my eyes fill with tears.

There were hurts and history that couldn't be changed, I knew that. Yet I hoped it was possible for all of that to be washed away. I'd always wanted to spend time with my sister and, finally, I was going to get the chance.

*

Charlotte and my father made it to Ireland in March, six months after my mother and I had moved there. We decorated Daideo's cottage with balloons and streamers, and I'd made a huge sign that said *Welcome Daddy and Charlotte!* Daideo kept asking whose birthday it was and my mother had stopped trying to explain it.

I sat on the couch with my legs crossed tightly, clutching the string of a red balloon in my hand. My mother had told me again and again that Charlotte was on her way, but I was scared that something would happen and she wouldn't make it. When a strong knock sounded at the door, I leapt to my feet.

"Is it them?" I whispered.

"Go ahead, answer it," my mother said with a big smile.

I pulled open the door and stopped short at the sight of my sister. She looked different. Her face was bigger, she was taller, and her dark hair had grown long, sticking out from under a pink hat with a fluffy pom-pom. It had snowed earlier in the day, but the sun was out, glittering on the frost. My father stood behind her with his hand on her shoulder, but I could only see her.

"Hi, Lottie," I said.

"Hi," she said, so quietly that I could barely hear.

We stared at each other, frozen in place, until my mother said, "Hug! Give her a hug."

The sound of my mother's voice made Lottie jerk back in surprise. She looked past me at my mother and her face went blank. Then she turned back to my father and buried her face in his leg.

Daidco said, "She's a shy one, then? Good to see you, Todd." He stepped forward to shake my father's hand.

"Graham," my mother reminded him.

If my father was surprised that Daideo had confused his name, he didn't show it. Instead, he walked inside with Charlotte attached to his leg and bent down to look at me. Then he pulled me into his arms.

He smelled cold from the outdoors, but beneath that he smelled like my old house and storybooks before bed. I clung tightly to his neck, listening to him whisper, "I've missed you, sweet Jayne. My beautiful Jayne." Then he rested his cheek against mine, holding me tight.

Charlotte hadn't let go of him, so I brought her into the hug and the three of us clung together, until my mother cleared her throat.

"Graham, I'd like to have a moment with the children," she said.

My father squeezed me tight, then stood up. My mother kneeled down next to Charlotte with a balloon in her hand.

"Lottie." Her voice was quiet. "Please look at me."

Lottie shook her head. Finally, my mother let go of the balloon and hugged her right there on my father's leg. My mother held her, kissing her head, even when she refused to budge. I started to feel jealous and grabbed Lottie's hand.

"Want to come to my room?" I asked.

Lottie nodded and followed me back to my bedroom. She wandered around, touching my toys and looking anywhere but at me. Not sure what to do, I pulled out my small doll collection and two wooden horses. Her face brightened and I started our princess and horses game from so long ago.

I heard a sound at the door and looked over. My mother stood there, watching. "Can I come in?"

Charlotte's face turned to stone.

"No," I said, shaking my head.

There was no other choice—I stood up and shut the door.

Charlotte spent the remainder of the day avoiding my mother. The shadows grew long and the smells from the kitchen more intense. I recognized it as chicken pot pie, one of my mother's specialties and one of Daideo's favorites.

"Dinner," my mother called.

My stomach was rumbling and I headed for the kitchen, but Charlotte stayed right where she was.

The small table in the dining room was crowded with two extra chairs that Daideo had borrowed from neighbors. The chicken pie sat steaming in the center of the table, next to a bowl of carrots and another piled with dinner rolls. Every plate was neatly set with a cup of water, and there was a pink sippy cup of milk for Charlotte.

My father was seated, but he got to his feet when he saw Charlotte wasn't with me.

"Where's your sister?"

"In the room." I slid up into my chair at the table. "Daddy, the butter is so good. Try it."

"Delicious," my father said, taking a bite of bread.

He squeezed my shoulder before heading back down the hallway, followed closely by my mother.

Daideo spooned up chicken pie to our plates. We sat and waited. Then we heard Charlotte shout, "No. You go away!"

I got up and ran down the hallway to see what was happening. Charlotte was in the corner of my room, holding a wooden horse and refusing to budge. My mother was trying to talk to her, and she had her face buried in my father's leg again.

"Lottie." I got down on my knees and pulled her into a hug. "Come sit by me."

Charlotte hesitated. Then she followed me down the hall without looking at my parents.

The five of us gathered around the table, and Daideo said a blessing over the food. My mother tried to talk to Charlotte, but she and I were busy giggling and making faces at each other. My mother finally sat in silence, picking at her food, while Daideo and my father talked.

"We'll take a walk at the park after this," Daideo said. "Show Charlotte the ducks." He took a hearty bite of pie. Once he'd swallowed, he said, "Graham, if that bed in Aubrey's room is too small for you, the two of you can trade with me. Mine's so big I could use a boat to make it across."

My parents exchanged glances.

"No, that's okay," my father said. "I've booked Charlotte and myself a room at the inn down the road. I think she'll sleep better there."

"Nonsense." Daideo looked puzzled. "You need to stay with your wife."

"No, Dad," my mother said. "He doesn't have to stay here. It's fine."

Daideo looked back and forth between them. "Did you think my memory was so bad I'd forget you were married? Or is there something you need to tell me about that?"

The tension in the room made Charlotte and me stop giggling. I picked up my fork and dipped it into the gravy in the pie, tracing it across the crust. My father gave my mother a pointed look, and she gave a slight shake of her head.

"I'm not going to lie about it, Aubrey," he said.

My mother's mouth dropped open. "Graham—"

Daideo glared at the two of them. "Shame on you."

"Not in front of the girls," my mother said, wiping her mouth with one of the cloth napkins she so carefully ironed.

"What?" I said. "What are you talking about?"

My father sat in silence for a minute. Then he said, "Your mother and I are no longer married. We got a divorce."

"Graham!" My mother's face turned red. "We'd agreed—"

"*You* agreed." My father's eyes were cold. "I am not about to sit here and let your father think that I am the type of man who would let my daughter stay in another country without me, or my other daughter be without a mother. I have not had a choice in the matter—you have made that perfectly clear—and it isn't right." He turned to Daideo. "Yes, sir. We are no longer married and I am sorry for that, but I am not going to lie about it."

A lump of chicken stuck in my throat and I started coughing, until my mother handed me my water. "It's all right," she said, rubbing my back. "Everything's all right."

Daideo took furious bites. My mother fiddled with her necklace. Then she looked at me and Charlotte.

"Girls, if you didn't understand all of that, your mommy and daddy are not married anymore," she said. "It was a hard decision but one that we made before Jayne and I came here to take care of Daideo. Your father and I still love you both with all of our hearts."

There were so many questions whirling in my head, but I didn't quite know how to ask them. It didn't seem to matter whether my parents were married or not, considering we hadn't been in the same house anyway. My father and Lottie were here, which was all I'd wanted.

The rest of the dinner was silent. My mother whisked away the plates and brought out an apple cake and coffee. Her apple cakes were never good and Charlotte didn't want any, so we headed back to the room to play. We'd started our game when we heard raised voices from the dining room.

"Divorce is not right," Daideo shouted. "You've shamed this family!"

Daideo had given me a small record player for my birthday. I picked out one of the red plastic records and put it on the player, turning the volume up as high as I could. Charlotte started dancing along to the music and I took her hands. We spun around the room, laughing and singing.

There was a sound at the door, and once again I looked up to find my parents watching. My father stood with his arms crossed, looking defeated. My mother looked ready to cry.

This time, it was Lottie who walked over to the door and shut it.

# CHAPTER SIX

The dry spell had ended by the time I returned to Woodsong Harbor four weeks later. The trees were lush and green, while frogs sang from somewhere deep in the woods. The rubber of my sandals echoed against the wooden steps of my grandmother's house, and the stained-glass flower above the door welcomed my return.

Charlotte had texted me the day before that she planned to arrive midmorning. I'd hoped for the same but had gotten a slow start, thanks to a late-night going-away party hosted by my girlfriends at the hibachi grill down the street. We'd performed a few hilariously awful karaoke songs that descended into dance numbers and stayed up much too late on my friends' roof, laughing and sharing stories. It was exactly the send-off that I'd needed.

Even though I would only be in Woodsong Harbor for six months, I didn't have plans to return to Raleigh. The sale of my grandmother's house would give me the freedom of a fresh start. I wasn't quite sure where that would be yet, but I was grateful for the change of scenery while I figured it out. Most of all, I was grateful for this time with my sister, even though I had no idea how it would all turn out.

The house smelled like Charlotte's perfume when I walked in. She was out on the back deck, sitting at a table that hadn't been there before, and wore a bright pink workout shirt. Her hair was up in a ponytail again and she was doing something on her computer.

I set down my suitcase and walked to the back door, my heart pounding with nerves. The house was quiet, which meant her family must be sleeping or down at the beach. I'd worried half the way down here about bumping into them right as I walked in, because I had no idea what to say.

*Hi, congratulations on marrying my sister? Sorry I wasn't at the wedding?*

*Hey, there, boys. I'm the aunt that you've never met?*

Swallowing hard, I walked out to the back deck. "Hi," I said.

Charlotte jumped and looked up. "Oh, hello." She set down her phone and pulled her sunglasses over her eyes. "How was the drive?"

Charlotte looked like she'd just taken a shower or had been in the ocean, because her dark hair was wet. She'd wound half of it into a bun on top of her head, and then put three colorful rubber bands in different sections of her ponytail. It made her look incredibly young, especially since she wasn't wearing any makeup, and I could imagine what she must have looked like as a teen.

She seemed like the kind of girl who would have led the cheerleading squad and had a gaggle of friends, but still sat quietly in class taking notes. It was a mixture of intensity and aloofness that made her seem almost unapproachable.

"The drive was good." I sat in one of the chairs around the table, grateful for the shade of the red sun umbrella. "I've been looking forward to meeting your sons. Are they at the beach?"

"No." Charlotte took a sip from something that looked like a strawberry smoothie. "Ken's bringing them tomorrow. Evan had a bunch of eighth-grade graduation parties today and Ken wanted to have his car here, so it worked out. I figured it would also give us time to settle in."

I breathed a sigh of relief. Even though I wanted to meet them, I'd also wanted the time to ease into this. Plus, I was worried that once her family was here, they would spend all of their time together and I'd remain on the outside.

Not quite sure what to say, I shifted my attention to the furniture. "This wasn't out here before," I said. "Did Martin set it up for us?"

In addition to the patio table, there were two chaise longues with red-and-white-striped cushions. I could imagine settling in on one with a good book, listening to the ocean crashing down below. Was it really possible that I'd have the time to do that now?

"I pulled it all out of storage." Charlotte regarded her work. "The cushions need cleaning, but the rest is in good shape."

"You did this? I'm super impressed."

Charlotte was small but obviously strong. She looked like one of those women who ran a mile first thing in the morning and did kickboxing at night.

"Where's the storage?" I said.

"The mudroom next to the sunroom." She grabbed a notepad off the table and stood up. "I'm thinking the first thing we'll have to do is another walk-through. I know we need to work in the order that Grandma suggested, but I want to make sure that nothing got missed, or if there are areas we could consolidate. Six months isn't that long and there is a lot to do here."

"Hold on." I held up my hand, and she raised her eyebrows. "Sorry," I said, my cheeks getting hot. "It's just… we haven't seen each other in years. I'm all for jumping right in and getting the work done, but I'd also like to chat a bit first. Get to know you."

Charlotte looked cool and removed behind her sunglasses. With a hearty sigh, she sat back down. "Sounds good."

"Great." I cleared my throat, embarrassed that the conversation now felt forced. "Tell me about your job."

"I'm in sales for a finance firm." The smell of salt air tinged with fish blew through and Charlotte wrinkled her nose. "That's left over from the tide, I think."

"So, sales for a finance firm?" I echoed. "Tell me about that. I don't know much about the finance world."

"I bring in new clients for an investment firm. The firm manages mutual funds and the like. In the beginning of my career, it meant a lot of networking and meetings, but I've now been there long enough that people come to me. It will make it possible for me to work here without too much of a problem. What about you?"

"I have a degree in elementary education with a focus on art," I said, hoping to avoid the topic of my failed art studio.

Charlotte studied me. "You're a teacher?"

"No, but I was helping at a preschool before this," I said. "The kids all hugged me one by one of the last day of school last week. It was sweet. I love kids."

"You don't have any, though?"

"No." I laughed. "They're not handing them out at the fruit stand, last I checked."

She gave me a wry look. "Sometimes I'm tempted to hand my boys out at the fruit stand. They're pretty good most of the time, though."

"It will be nice to meet them," I said, careful to keep my tone neutral.

My mother had wanted to meet them, too. So badly. She'd been devastated to lose Charlotte, but once she heard that she had grandchildren that she would never see, she was inconsolable. I don't think she ever got over it.

There were so many times I'd wondered what had kept my mother and Charlotte apart for all those years. Surely, later in life, Charlotte could have better understood the choice my mother had to make? Daideo had started to lose his faculties in a big way about two months after that visit from Charlotte and my dad. There had been days when I didn't get to see my mother at all, because she was so busy trying to take care of her father and hold down a part-time job. That time had been hard on me, but it would have been unbearable for Charlotte.

Looking back, I had to admit that it was selfish that my mother hadn't sent me to live with my father and Charlotte during this time, but I knew the reason—she didn't want to be alone. It was hard enough for her to leave Charlotte behind, she'd told me, but it would have killed her to be without both of us. All the same, I wished that she and my father had figured out a better way to manage the situation.

I'd wondered if that letter I'd found in my mother's book was the start to some sort of apology.

*Dear Jayne, There is a truth to be told but I am not brave enough to say it…*

"Would it be all right if we got started?" Charlotte got to her feet. "There is quite a bit to do. I think we should start by picking out our rooms."

"Sounds good," I said.

The reminder of the history between us had made it hard for me to want to continue with the small talk. Nodding, I followed her inside.

Upstairs, Charlotte pushed open the door to the first room. "I would like this bedroom." She glanced over her shoulder at me. "If that works for you."

The room was small but tastefully decorated, with cream-colored wallpaper with navy accents, a few pieces of antique furniture, and two windows that overlooked the ocean.

It looked vaguely familiar, but I couldn't remember which room we'd stayed in when we were kids, only that we'd been in the same room together. There had been two twin beds and mine was right under the window. I'd fallen asleep each night listening to the waves and the soft sounds of Charlotte's snores. There had been so many nights when I'd stayed awake on purpose that summer, so that I could tuck her in once she fell asleep.

"Is this where you stayed when you visited Grandma on your own?" I asked. "You were here a lot, right?"

"Every summer." Charlotte strode down the hall. "There are two other rooms here. It's completely up to you, but I was thinking the boys could stay in this middle one and you could stay down here." She pushed open the door at the end of the hall and my heart skipped a beat. "You might remember this one."

"I do," I said quietly.

The room was wallpapered yellow with two corner-facing windows that looked out over the ocean. The two windows gave the room a lot more light and the yellow color scheme made it seem even brighter. Even though they weren't there anymore, I could imagine the twin beds where we had slept.

"Yes, this one's perfect," I said.

Charlotte took a seat on a blue wingback chair at the foot of the bed. "I thought it would be a good fit." She flipped her ponytail before opening her notepad. "So, we need to call in a few places to help us get started before we can even get going on this list. I've already ordered a construction dumpster that will arrive tomorrow. We also need to begin researching contractors, starting with structural issues like the wall in the sunroom. Step one—before we begin any of this—we'll need to empty the house. Move everything out but the main things, like our beds and a table in the kitchen."

"Where will we put the furniture?" I settled in on the bed, the yellow quilt shifting beneath me. "Is the storage room that big?"

"No." Charlotte jotted something onto her list. "It's not big enough for all of it, and when we work on the flooring, it would be such a hassle to push everything to the side and work around it. The best bet is to hire a moving company to transfer it all to a storage unit."

"That's a good idea."

Storage units were not that expensive, and we would need the furniture out of the way.

Charlotte checked a line on her notepad. "Next up: cleaners. Everything is a little grubby."

"Or a lot grubby," I said.

The bathroom with the mold growing on the ceiling was a mess. The toilet had hard-water stains and the sinks had definitely seen better days.

Charlotte brushed a piece of lint off the arm of the chair. "I think it's best if we start with a clean slate. This place hasn't seen a broom in at least five years."

"We could clean it ourselves," I suggested, as a gentle breeze shifted the curtains by the window. "I'm not sure we have the budget for cleaners *and* movers. Cleaners can be expensive."

Charlotte raised her eyebrows. "Jayne, I'm going to tell you something right now: I'm happy to work hard on the remodel. I'm happy to get my hands dirty and peel off wallpaper and rip up tiles. However, I refuse to waste time cleaning if I can pay someone else to do it."

"What if the accountant says no?" I asked. "That it's not in the budget?"

"Then I'll pay for it myself," she said. "Life is too short to waste time cleaning."

I ran my hands along the starburst design in the quilt, wondering if Charlotte would have felt differently if she'd grown up with me. Our mother had been a passionate cleaner. She'd often spent her time blasting classical music through the house while dusting, sweeping, and mopping. Eventually, I'd made it a habit to join in.

"We can ask the accountant when she brings our stipend checks," I said.

Martin had sent an email prior to our arrival with detailed information. It had touched on certain points in the will, such as the requirement of following the specific order of the list, and had also mentioned that Fran would drop off our stipend checks late afternoon. It was such a relief knowing I had that money coming to me, because the creditors had not stopped calling.

"I'd forgotten she was stopping by," Charlotte mused.

Yeah, because she didn't need the money.

"I'll text her now and ask her to knock so we can say hi," Charlotte said, before sending the message. "Now, we will also need a ton of cleaning supplies. I'm not quite sure how or where to get those. There has to be a hardware store in town that could deliver them."

The sticker shock of the eight-dollar latte jumped to mind. I could only imagine paying the same for a container of Windex, plus a delivery fee.

"I'm going grocery shopping later tonight," I said. "I'll pick them up, assuming Fran will reimburse me."

"Thank you." Charlotte crossed something off her list. "Now, I do think—aack! What is that?"

"What?" I said, looking around.

Charlotte gestured wildly at an enormous spider perched in the corner by my bed. It was dark brown with long legs, and I jumped to the floor.

"That was not there when we walked in. I bet it was in the bed." I shuddered, imagining it crawling across my pillow. "I'll use my shoe."

"No!" Charlotte gave me a horrified look. "Let me put it outside. Hold on." She ran out of the room and returned with a small drinking glass.

"The spider will jump," I said, moving over to the opposite side of the room. "Don't do that. It'll—"

Charlotte brought the cup down over the spider, then slid a piece of paper between the glass and the wall to contain it. "There." She tapped on the glass. "I'll be right back."

The fact that Charlotte had bothered to save a spider from being squashed was impressive, but she'd always cared about things like that. It was something I'd forgotten about, but during that summer we'd spent together, she'd had such a heart for the starfish that washed up on the sand that she liked to walk the beach, trying to throw back as many as possible. One day, my grandmother had somewhere for us to be and Charlotte burst into tears to see how many starfish would be left behind.

I'd held her hand in the car, trying to explain that maybe the starfish looked forward to the part of their life where they could rest instead of swim. I don't know if she bought it, but she'd stopped crying by the time we'd arrived.

Now, I smiled at her when she walked back into the room. "That was nice of you," I said. "Saving that spider."

She shrugged. "It was a living creature." Taking her seat in the chair, she said, "Now, I think we should call in a home-inspection company to see where we're at. They can tell us all of the things we'll need to focus on that might not be on the list, because those same issues will crop up when it's time to sell."

"That's a great idea," I said, settling back in on the bed. "How do you know to do all this?"

Charlotte picked up her notepad. "Ken and I used to flip houses when he was starting out in real estate." Her eyes met mine for a brief moment before she looked away. It struck me that, in spite of appearing so confident, Charlotte sometimes seemed shy. "One of our good friends was an inspector, so we'd buy him dinner once in a while, and he'd do reports on the foreclosures that we'd buy. I can't tell you how many times he saved us, spotting things that needed to get done during the remodel."

"So, you already know how to do all of the remodel stuff?" I asked hopefully.

"No." She smoothed her hair. "It shouldn't be too hard to figure out, though. Ken has experience with most of the things on our list and he can walk us through. There's also YouTube."

The idea that Ken would be stepping in made me nervous because I didn't want him to take over.

Charlotte must have noticed my hesitation, because she added, "You and I are supposed to do this together, but there's nothing to say we can't draw on his expertise." She looked down at her list. "It will take about a week to get the inspector here, do the inspection, and get the report back. In the meantime, we need to determine the basics. Let's start with this floor and move downstairs," she said, getting to her feet. "We'll cite the things that we notice so that we'll have a better idea of how it looks to us before the professional report comes in."

"Sounds like a plan," I said. "Where should we start?"

"I'd like to start with the master," she said, heading towards my grandmother's old room.

It meant a lot to me that she'd acknowledged that we were supposed to do this together. Feeling encouraged, I said, "So, what do you like to do for fun when you're not with your sons or working?"

Charlotte turned to me, her pretty face set in a polite smile. "Jayne, I appreciate that you'd like to chat, but if you don't mind, I'd prefer to focus on the house. That's why we're here."

The words felt like a slap in the face, especially considering the fact that she'd gone out of her way to be kind to a spider. We were here to rebuild a connection, but the comment made her stance on the situation very clear. I smiled and nodded, hoping she couldn't tell how much she'd hurt me.

"Sure," I said. "Lead the way."

I'd never felt more alone than I did during the two hours I spent walking around the house with Charlotte. She kept us moving at a clipped pace, as if stopping to chat would be a waste. It was so uncomfortable.

Finally, once we'd gone through each room, Charlotte looked at her notepad and then at her watch. "I think we've done enough for today. I'm going for a run," she announced, and started to head back up the stairs.

"Wait," I called.

She stopped, her hand resting on the railing. "Yes?"

I wanted to tell her that I'd been thinking about this day since the moment I'd gotten in my car to drive back to Raleigh. I'd imagined the conversations we would have, regrets that we would share, and, ultimately, the start of a relationship between two sisters. One look at Charlotte's cool, distant expression, and the words got stuck in the back of my throat.

"Nothing," I said.

Charlotte bounded up the stairs. Moments later, she stomped back down modeling a new round of designer workout wear. This time, it was blue running pants and a white tank top. She wore earbuds and by the subtle way she stepped to the beat, I knew she was already listening to music.

"I never stopped missing you," I told her, knowing that she couldn't hear a word.

She pulled out an earbud. "What?"

"I said I hope you have a nice run."

She half waved and headed out the front door, probably to run through the hills and trails near the house.

Collapsing onto the sofa in the living room, I fiddled with my bracelets. There hadn't been a single moment when Charlotte had intentionally shown me something of herself. I'd caught glimpses, but not as much as I would have liked.

I curled up into a ball on the couch and pulled the pillow close to me. It smelled like age and dust, but I held it close, trying to remember if I'd ever been here, in this exact spot. The ridiculous part of me half wished that I could fall back through time, to that brief and bright moment when we'd felt like sisters.

# CHAPTER SEVEN

I spent the evening working my way through a biography about a runner and fell asleep a little past ten. The house was so old and drafty that it creaked and groaned all night. Tossing and turning, I imagined the roof caving in after each groan. Finally, I fell asleep, snuggled into the deep bed buried under three blankets while the ocean breeze cooled my nose.

I shot awake at 6 a.m., thanks to a series of pings. They were all text messages from Charlotte:

*Movers scheduled for 10:30 a.m. Monday.*

*Set a reminder to park on the street before they come. They most likely drive a large moving van.*

*Ken and the boys arrive late morning.*

I stared at the messages in confusion. Flipping my phone to silent, I pulled a pillow over my head and managed to fall asleep until the sun streamed into the window at eight. It shone directly in my face, as if Charlotte stood over me with a flashlight.

Hauling myself out of bed, I pulled my hair up into a ponytail and threw on a pair of shorts and a T-shirt. Then I checked my phone. Charlotte had texted me three more times. I realized she was one of those people who liked to get up at the crack of dawn to fire off texts and emails, without considering the fact that most people were asleep. I wanted to be armed with a strong cup of coffee before facing her, so I hoped she wasn't hard at work in the kitchen.

It was a relief to spot her out on the back deck with her computer, tapping away at the keys. Once I'd lingered over a cup of coffee and oatmeal, I headed out to see her. The minute I pulled open the door, she pointed at her computer.

"Good morning," I said, and she gestured again. "Did you get some sleep?"

Charlotte gave the computer a bright smile. "Excuse me, gentlemen. I'll be right with you." Hitting a button, she pulled out her earbuds and whispered, "I'm in the middle of a meeting."

I'd assumed she was working on her computer. It hadn't occurred to me that she was on camera. The laptop was angled away from me, thank goodness, so I didn't get any surprise camera time, but I was embarrassed all the same.

"Sorry," I whispered back. "Good thing I didn't come down here in my bikini."

The corner of her mouth twitched. Putting her earbuds back in, she said, "Shall we continue?"

Since Ken and the boys were arriving late morning, I decided my best bet would be to get out of the house for a while, so that I wouldn't be in the way when they arrived. I was nervous to meet them and wanted to give them time to settle in and catch up before jumping into introductions. I would have preferred for it to be me and Charlotte in the house, but on the other hand, the opportunity to spend time with my nephews was a big deal.

On the short drive into town, I decided it would be a good use of time to get my hands on a bicycle. The sun was bright, it was another beautiful day, and it would be a lot more fun to zip down the hill that led up to the Row than to drive my tanker around town. I went out in search of a thrift shop, but it turned out that the retail shops didn't open until ten.

Instead, I pulled into a parking spot in front of the coffee shop to say hi to Lauren. It had been a few weeks and she might not remember me, but I'd liked her and wanted to make some friends in town, since I'd be here for some time.

When I parked, I gave a glance around for Logan's truck. That exchange we'd had on the beach the morning I'd headed back home had been friendly, so I didn't want to rile him up with another parking mishap. It would be just my luck to park in front of a fire hydrant by mistake. I couldn't even begin to imagine the fallout from that one.

The scent of roasted coffee beans hit me the moment I walked in. The fans clicked overhead and even though several of the tables were taken by people reading books or working on their computers, the Monday morning vibe was as prevalent as it would have been back in the city. Spotting me, Lauren waved.

"Hey!" She had two people working, and stepped out from behind the counter to greet me. "Long time no see. And you were *not* supposed to give your latte to my brother."

I laughed. "I figured he needed it more than me."

"Or a kick in the you-know-what." Lauren's smile had a deep dimple, and her dark hair was up in two French braids on each side of her head. She wore beaded earrings that were the perfect complement to the green in her summer dress, and I pegged her to be around my age.

"What can I get you?" she asked.

It hadn't been my plan to buy anything, but since she'd asked, I felt obligated.

"How about the sugar-free grasshopper?" I asked, hoping it wasn't the price of a small house. "The kids' size. I already had coffee this morning."

It was described as a chocolate-chip mint ice-cream mocha with whipped cream, chocolate drizzle, and chopped chocolate-covered mints. Mint was one of my absolute favorite flavors, whether we were talking gum, candy, or coffee. I was excited to try it.

Lauren brewed some espresso, gracefully working around the girls behind the counter. The blender whirred and once it stopped, she dumped the light green concoction into a plastic cup over the shot of espresso. Then she doused it in whipped cream labeled sugar-free, before drizzling chocolate over the top.

"Voilà!" She passed it across the counter, the icy container cooling my hand.

"That looks amazing." I took a quick sip through the paper straw. "It *is* amazing."

"Thank you." She smiled. "I try."

I pulled out my wallet and she waved it away.

"I still owe you a coffee," she insisted. "Enjoy."

"You don't owe me anything," I said, grateful for the kindness. "Thank you, though. I really appreciate it. Actually, I do need your advice. I'm here for the summer and need tips on where to go for fun."

"Come sit for a minute." Lauren stepped out from behind the counter and sat at a table by the front window. It held a small iPad and a notebook. "This is how I spend most mornings," she said. "Catching up on the clerical. If they need a hand behind the counter or someone calls out sick, that's where you'll find me instead. Now, why are you here for the summer?"

Sipping at the grasshopper, I said, "I'm remodeling my grandmother's beach house."

"How fun!" She ran her thumb over the beads on her earrings. "Are you doing the work yourself or contracting it out?"

"No, I'm doing with my…" I hesitated, but had to get used to saying the word. "My sister and I are working on it together. We'll contract some of it out but do our best to do the rest."

"It will be a great experience." Lauren rested her cheek on her hand. "I can't begin to imagine remodeling with Logan." She grinned. "We'd probably like, stick each other to the wall with wallpaper glue on purpose."

Their relationship charmed me. For all of Lauren's little digs at him, it was clear she adored her brother. If things had been different, I might have had that type of friendship with Charlotte.

"Speaking of Logan, I'm obligated to tell you that he's an expert at carpentry," she said. "If you need a floor redone, banisters, building, he's your guy. He'll pop up on your search either way. He's one of the best around here."

The idea of seeing Logan again made my cheeks hot. "I'll keep that in mind."

"Where is the house you're remodeling?" she asked.

I explained and she smacked the table. "*Jayne*, I've been there! One summer Logan and I hung out on the beach a bunch of times, with two girls staying with their grandmother." She started laughing. "I *knew* you looked familiar."

My mouth dropped open. "You're serious?"

There had been a small group of kids that we'd hung out with, but I couldn't remember much about them. It was very possible Lauren had been one of them, since she was my age and a local.

"Yes. I remember being over there a few times," she said. "Your grandmother always had a freezer full of ice cream pops for everyone. Not the gross ones, either, but Klondike bars and stuff."

"Yes!" I was delighted at the memory. "I swear, that summer when I came to stay with her, I must have had the time of my life because she kept that freezer stocked and I couldn't stop eating them. That was before everything in my life switched to sugar-free."

On some level, I had always been grateful that the diabetes had waited to present until after that magical summer. I'd been able to eat whatever I'd wanted, whenever I wanted, without consequence. My grandmother would always tell us before she went to the store, and that summer had felt like a feast of ice cream, powdered donuts, and flavored potato chips.

"Does she still have the freezer stocked?" Lauren asked. "If she does, I'm going to have to stop by."

"My grandmother passed away," I admitted, wiping a spot of whipped cream off the side of my cup. "That's why we're working on the house."

Lauren frowned. "Jayne, I'm so sorry."

"Thanks." We sat in silence for a minute. "If you want to know the truth, I'm a little embarrassed about inheriting something so grand."

"Don't be." She shook her head. "I'm sure your grandmother wanted the best for you and your sister. But I get it. Every time something good happens here at the business, I have a week of panicking about it. Like, we were featured in a national magazine spread—"

"Congratulations," I said.

Lauren's dimple deepened. "Well, the entire time up until the interview and photo shoot, I was convinced that they'd made a mistake, and they'd meant the coffee shop down the road. Then, once they'd done an interview with me and the article was scheduled to print, I kept waiting for them to call and tell me they'd made a mistake, and they really had meant to talk to the coffee shop down the road. Even as I'm telling you about it, I'm half expecting them to walk in the front door and tell you that they—"

"Made a mistake and meant to talk to the coffee shop down the road," we chorused, and then laughed. "It's nice to know I'm not the only one who thinks like that."

"It's fear," she said. "I can't tell you how many relationships I've ruined with good guys, because on some level…" She paused. "Sorry. I don't mean to get so heavy."

"No," I said, thinking of my most recent relationship. "I had a breakup recently and I'm still not quite sure why I did it. He was a great guy."

I'd first met Daniel at an art exhibit in town. He stood to the side, looking befuddled, and when I struck up a conversation, he admitted he knew nothing about art. His neighbor was the painter and had been worried about low attendance, so Daniel had made a point to show up.

It was a quality I admired. I'd gone into our three-year relationship planning to show up for him, but as time marched on and he started to bring up marriage, I started to pull away. He deserved so much more and I kept hoping that he'd meet the right person soon, someone not afraid to trust that love could last forever.

Lauren gave a sage nod. "Sometimes, it's hard to believe that we deserve good things."

I fiddled with my straw. "That's true."

"Sorry." She gave a little laugh. "You didn't ask me for my philosophy about life, you asked me about things to do around here. So. There's a great yoga class on the beach. It's at six in the morning and right before sunset, depending on what time of day appeals. I do the night class because I'm here in the morning. Hit the Salty Slice for pizza. You can't miss at any of the seafood restaurants, but my favorites are Plankton and Hooked." She held up her hands. "I swear I didn't make those names up."

"That's so helpful," I said. "I'll put them on the list." It was getting close to ten, and I imagined Ken and my nephews arriving. "I should head out, but do you have any tips on where to buy a cheap bicycle?"

"Check the board in the hallway by the restroom," she said. "It seems like there's always something up there. If that fails, the bike shop can be a lot cheaper than you'd think. The bike rental place unloads its used inventory there, so they have some good deals. Tell them I sent you. It's right up the block."

"Thank you." I held up my empty drink. "This was delicious."

"No problem." She powered up her iPad. "Will I see you at yoga?"

"One of these days," I said, wondering if I'd be able to afford it. "It sounds fun."

The bells gave a friendly jingle as I walked out of the shop. I was glad I'd come to talk to her. Six months was nothing in the grand scheme of things but, considering Charlotte seemed determined to make it as difficult as possible to connect, it would be nice to have some sense of community while I was here. I couldn't help wishing that my interactions with Charlotte could be as easy as talking to Lauren.

The idea of meeting my nephews had me on edge. I took a walk along the Row to calm my nerves, and it left me hot and sweaty. There was a strange car parked in the driveway once I arrived back home, a black Lincoln Navigator, and I let out a breath.

Quietly, I opened the door to the house. No one was in the living room, but I heard laughter out on the back deck. I headed up the stairs to take a shower and hoped everyone would have moved on by the time I was out, but the back deck was still bustling.

Swallowing hard, I crossed through the living room towards the kitchen, hoping that no one would notice me. Their backs were all turned. Charlotte was sitting at the table with her arm around one of her boys, and the other was sprawled out in the deck chair Charlotte had set out for sunbathing. There was a man wearing what looked like golf clothing, and I assumed that had to be her husband.

I had finished putting together a sandwich and was reaching into the fridge for an apple, when someone burst into the kitchen and stopped short. I turned and blinked in surprise. My nephew, the absolute spitting image of me, stood in front of me like a mirror. Well, a mirror reflecting a boy who was much taller, skinnier, and had dark hair cut close to his head, and a healthy sprinkling of acne all over his face. "Whoa. You look like me," he blurted out. "The girl version. Woman? The woman version."

"I'm Jayne." His awkwardness was endearing and my heart immediately went out to him. I stepped forward and held out my hand. His hand engulfed it and gave me a firm shake that he must have been taught.

"Evan. It's nice to meet you," he said. "I wondered if we'd get to see you today. We rented some Jet Skis, and you can use them. My dad rented them because he's addicted to adrenaline-rush things." He stopped talking, and his face turned red. "I mean, if you want to."

"That is such a great invitation," I said. "But I think your mom is so excited to see you guys that she's going to want to have time with you all on your own."

He bobbed his head. "Probably. Do you like Airheads?"

"Airheads?" I echoed.

The name sounded familiar but I couldn't place it. I half wondered if I was setting myself up for some joke or something. It had been a long time since I'd been around teenage boys, but I did remember that part of it.

Evan pulled out a handful of shiny candy wrappers from his board shorts. "It's candy. They're chewy but I can polish them off pretty fast. Want some?" He made a move to dump a red one in my hand.

"No, thank you," I said. "It sounds great, though. I used to like jawbreakers. I had this one that was the size of a tennis ball and it took me something like a year to eat it. My mom thought it was so gross."

He laughed, the sound almost like a donkey. "My mom would second that."

"Evan," Charlotte called. "We're about to head out to…" She walked into the kitchen and came to an abrupt stop at the sight of me chatting with her son. "Evan, this is Jayne."

"Yeah, we're old friends." He gave me a big grin and started rummaging through the cupboards. He grabbed a bag of popcorn, and Charlotte said, "That's not mine, honey. The grocery delivery will be at the house in an hour. You should have some good stuff in there."

"You can have some," I said.

"No, he'll eat the whole bag." Charlotte took the bag of popcorn and put it back in the cupboard, shutting it firmly. "He's growing like a weed and I can't buy enough food to keep up with him."

Evan gave me a pathetic look. I wished I could grab the bag back out of the cupboard and give it to him, but of course I couldn't.

"You ready, doll?" The gruff voice of a man rang through the living room and my cheeks heated, knowing that I was about to meet her husband.

It was one thing to meet the kids, because I doubted they knew much about my history with their mother, but her husband was a different story. Straightening my shoulders, I turned to face the entrance with a bright smile fixed to my face. Sure enough, Ken strode into the kitchen.

I'd seen him before on Charlotte's social media pages, but he looked different in person. He was shorter than I'd pictured and solid. It looked like he spent a lot of time at the gym, but also appreciated a good meal. Sure enough, the first thing he did after introducing himself was invite me to dinner.

"One of the best things about this town is the food," Ken said, still shaking my hand. "I'm going to get us a table at Crane tonight. On the water, great seafood… I insist you join us."

Ken had one of those friendly faces that made him likeable right away.

"That's so kind," I said. "You all need to catch up, though. We can do it another time."

"You won't be interrupting a thing," he said. "Listen, we need an outside buffer because otherwise, these boys of ours will spend the entire dinner trying to convince me to get Jet Skis for the whole summer instead of the week. Dinner's my treat, Jayne. It's a big moment that we finally get to meet, and I say we make the most of it."

The sentiment was kind and I appreciated the effort he was making.

"Sure," I said. "What time are you thinking?"

"What time works for you?" Ken asked.

"Depends on the wait," I said. "I usually eat around six thirty."

"Then we'll leave at six. It's a Monday, but the season's started, so there's no telling." He gave an easy nod and ruffled Evan's hair. "Come on, son, let's get out of her way."

I gave a quick glance at Charlotte, but she was already heading towards the front door.

"Come on, Josh," Ken called, sounding jovial. "Get off the phone and get a move on. We're outta here!"

Even though no one was paying attention, I gave a perfunctory wave and headed upstairs. I wanted to meet her other son, but I could tell Ken was in a hurry to get somewhere, maybe to pick up the Jet Skis, so I figured it could wait. Josh walked by with his face buried in his phone, but I could already tell by the way he carried himself that he didn't have a confidence problem.

Standing at the top of the stairs, I watched as the boys clambered out the front door. Ken took Charlotte's hand and pulled her in for a kiss. Quickly, I turned away, fighting off a wave of jealousy at yet another perfect piece of my sister's puzzle.

Ken was caring, attentive, decisive, and charming. She didn't run away from those qualities the way that I had. Instead, she had the common sense to marry them. It made me feel a pang for the relationship that I'd left behind, because Daniel would have been nothing but supportive throughout all of this.

The moment I was in my room, I pulled out my phone and looked up Crane. It was the restaurant on the water with the low roof and black windows. It looked incredibly elegant, and the prices weren't listed on their sample menu. It seemed like a place that would have a million different pieces of silverware and desserts that would be lit on fire at the table.

Even though I had no idea what I was getting into, I had to admit that I was curious. The dinner would give me a glimpse into Charlotte's life, an opportunity to see behind the curtain and learn more about who she might be.

*

My grandmother was adamant that my sister and I belonged together and was furious that my father and mother couldn't work something out. She came to Ireland for a visit, and one night I heard her and my mother arguing about it.

"You need to bring Jayne home," my grandmother insisted. "Bring your father. He won't even know at this point."

Daideo was so close to death that my mother refused.

"You're making a big mistake keeping them apart," my grandmother said. "I hope you'll figure that out before it's too late."

Daideo died two months after my grandmother's visit, and I had high hopes that we would return to the States. My mother kept dragging her feet, and soon I realized that she didn't want to leave because she'd grown close to Rory, one of the homecare nurses who had worked with Daideo. I had noticed their relationship for the first time at the funeral, when he sat next to us and held her hand tightly.

It all moved quickly, and within a few months my mother came to my room and rested her hand on my forehead.

"I've made the decision to marry Rory," she told me. "We're going to stay in Ireland. The three of us."

"What about Lottie?" I demanded. "You said we were going to go back! Grandma says we should be together."

My mother pressed her lips together. "Well, your father won't let her live here with us, so what can I do?" She fiddled with the hem of the pillowcase. "Besides, Lottie doesn't want to live with us. She wants to stay with your father."

"That's not true," I said, sitting up. "I told her we'd get bunk beds. She wants the top. She likes the pictures of my school uniform and—"

"Jayne." The pain in my mother's voice silenced me. "Lottie has refused to speak to me for the past three years. I have done everything possible to fix the situation, but I can't force her to come here, especially not without your father's permission."

"Then we need to go back," I said.

"Rory is here." My mother showed me her new ring, the one with two hands holding a diamond. "His job is here, his house—where we'll live—it's all here. If Lottie changes her mind, I would like her to come visit as much as possible, if your father will let her. But I have to live my life. I have the right to be happy, Jayne."

"You're not happy, though," I grumbled. "You're always crying about Lottie."

I pulled the quilt tightly against my chin, thinking about what my mother had said. Living in Rory's house sounded okay because it was much bigger than Daideo's and had a fountain in the backyard.

"Did you see Charlotte?" I asked. "When you went back?"

Right after Daideo's funeral, my mother had taken a brief trip to the States. I'd begged her to let me come but she refused, since she was only going for two days to handle some clerical issues.

"Nope." Her voice was short. "Charlotte refused to see me. Now, it's time for you to get to bed."


My mother finally agreed to let me return to the States to stay with my grandmother the summer I turned twelve. By that time, she'd obtained her degree in archaeology and had gotten a job with a research team at one of the big museums in Dublin. Her

team had been awarded a fellowship for research in Egypt during
the summer and Rory planned to join her. My mother needed
someone to watch me, and my grandmother was the only option.

My mother's one condition was that I was not to have contact
with the other side of my family. My mother feared seeing
Charlotte would be too hard, especially when it was time for me
to go. My grandmother agreed and came to Ireland to get me.

The first few days at the house by the beach were exciting but
strange. I loved being at the ocean and it was fascinating to be
back in the country that I remembered in some part of my brain
but had not experienced. The food was different, the people were
different, and I was interested in all of it.

About a week after my arrival, my grandmother took my hand
and said, "Sometimes, Jayne, it's important to do the thing that
you know is right even though it may make other people angry.
Do you understand?"

I nodded, not quite sure what she was talking about.

"Good," she said, patting my cheek.

That afternoon, my grandmother encouraged me to sit in the
living room to draw with oils, which was something that I was
getting good at. I was hard at work on a picture of a unicorn
flying past a rainbow when keys jiggled in the front lock. My
grandmother had been busy setting up floral arrangements and
washing the windows, and she had been fidgeting ever since lunch.
Now her face brightened and she practically ran to the door.

A young girl stood next to my grandfather, holding a pink
suitcase. Her hair was long, dark, and shiny, and she was incredibly tan. She wore a blue sundress and a pale blue necklace made
of seashells.

"Lottie?" I whispered.

My grandmother squeezed my shoulder tight.

Charlotte must have known that she was coming to see me,
because she didn't look surprised. She looked scared, though. Shy.

"Hi." She gave a little laugh and waved with her free hand.

My grandfather kissed Charlotte on the head and then headed back to his study. My grandmother, Charlotte, and I stood there, looking at one another.

My mouth was dry and my heart, pounding. The idea that my grandmother had broken my mother's rule was shocking to me. I didn't know that adults did that.

"I have to call my mother," I said.

My grandmother's face fell. "No, no. Let's not. Take some time with this. It's a shock, I know."

Charlotte set down her suitcase and perched on the edge of the couch. "Can we swim?"

"Great idea!" My grandmother smiled. "Why don't you go up to the room you'll be sharing with Jayne and change into your suit?"

"What?" I asked. "How long is she staying?"

Charlotte smiled at me. "For the summer. You are, too, right?"

Her smile melted my heart. I'd had lots of best friends over the years, but this was different.

"You're my sister," I whispered.

Charlotte gave a silly shrug. "That's me," she said, before scampering up the stairs.

My grandmother pulled me in for a hug. I was stiff in her arms, torn between my loyalty to my mother and an intense need to know everything about my younger sister.

"Sisters belong together." My grandmother's voice was firm. "This summer will be the most magical time of your life."

"It will end," I said.

"Everything ends," my grandmother said. "Except love."

The words made me cry and she held me tight. It embarrassed me because I didn't like to cry, and I didn't want to act like a baby because I didn't know her that well. But I was scared, and I didn't know what else to do.

"Ready," a voice called from the stairs.

The joy I felt at the sound of my sister's voice made the tears stop.

"Go get your suit on," my grandmother said. "The ocean's calling."

I raced up the stairs, hiding my tearstained face.

Having Charlotte show up was not what I had expected, but deep down, it was exactly what I'd hoped for. I could hardly believe my wish had come true.

# CHAPTER EIGHT

Ken's black Lincoln Navigator gleamed like it had been washed. I headed out, feeling glamorous in a fitted black silk dress I'd worn to a friend's wedding in Europe. I'd brushed my hair with gel to give it a wavy look and had put on makeup for the first time since I'd come to town.

Evan climbed out of the side of the car to open the door for me, something I had no doubt Ken had instructed him to do. He was dressed in a pair of khakis, a salmon-colored shirt with a tie that his parents had probably forced him to wear, and a pair of bright blue sneakers that he must have negotiated in exchange for the tie. Pretending to bow like a chauffeur, he ushered me into the car.

"Take the seat by Josh," Evan called. "I'll get in the back since I'm not wearing a dress."

I laughed and settled in next to my other nephew. He was dressed like his brother, in a pair of khakis and a pastel plaid shirt, but he managed to look like he was modeling the preppy gear instead of serving out a punishment. He was texting something and didn't look up.

"Put your phone down and say hi," his father ordered.

Josh let out a hearty sigh and regarded me with cool blue eyes.

If I looked like Evan, he looked like Charlotte. He had the same slight upturn in his upper lip and the tip of his nose as she did, a smattering of freckles, and honey highlights in his hair. The kid was already polished and good-looking in a way that didn't seem fair for a kid only in high school.

It occurred to me that Josh was pretty old, considering Charlotte was only thirty-six. Now that I had stopped to do the math, I realized she'd started having kids in college. It made me wonder if she'd completed school while raising a child or if she'd gone back later or not at all. There were so many things I didn't know about her but couldn't ask.

"I'm Jayne," I said, holding out my hand.

He gave me a fist bump. "What's up, Auntie?"

Charlotte shot him a look and he gave her a slight smile, before returning to his phone. It looked like he was texting someone, probably in a group, based on how the pings kept rolling in.

"I don't think I've ever gotten that many texts in my life," I said.

Ken gave a hearty laugh. "Me neither, Jayne." He pulled out of the drive. "I can't imagine having cell phones back when we were kids, but now they can't live without them."

The scenery blurred by as he drove, a blend of green trees, beautiful homes, and the gray-blue view of the ocean. The restaurant came into sight, a striking emerald on the water with its sleek black windows. The parking lot was full as we pulled in, but Ken found a spot right away.

"Nice moves, Dad," Evan called out from the back.

"It's what I do," Ken responded. Looking over his shoulder at me, he said, "I never valet. I have a gift for finding the best spot in the house."

"Well… if his passengers are willing to walk," Charlotte corrected. "Sometimes, I'm tempted to bring my tennis shoes with me when we go out and change into my heels in the restroom."

This relaxed version of Charlotte was so nice to see. I hoped that she'd stay in good spirits throughout dinner. It seemed impossible to be in bad spirits, though, as we walked through the balmy night towards the high-end restaurant.

It was gorgeous on the outside, with its clean lines and deep-green paint, and that same elegant feeling followed us in. The entire vibe of the place was low-key with soft lighting and smooth jazz that crooned through the speakers without disrupting the low hum of conversation. The back wall was made of glass, allowing for a spectacular view of the water. The staff wore black dinner jackets and were all good-looking. I couldn't help but think that Charlotte's oldest son could probably get a job as a busboy with no trouble at all.

"Enjoy your evening," the host said, leading us back to a table in the corner.

The host distributed menus and the wine list. Ken ordered a bottle of Cabernet from the waiter, as the busboys set us up with sparkling water and a loaf of bread. It appeared to be fresh from the oven and was served with a side of truffle butter.

When Evan reached for it, Josh blocked him. "I'll take that."

Josh swiped the bread board, giving his brother a superior look in return. After picking through and taking what he wanted, he passed it back to Evan.

The exchange made me sad. Evan seemed like such a sweet kid. I didn't get the same impression from Josh. It wasn't fair to think that way, since I hadn't spent any time with him, but he looked so much like Charlotte and had that same cool arrogance that it was hard to be objective.

Evan was busy stacking pieces on his plate when his father boomed, "That's enough! Leave some for the rest of us."

The poor kid quickly returned the piece he'd been about to add to his tower before handing the nearly empty board to me. The busboy whisked it out of my hands before replacing it with a fresh one. I handed it to Evan with a smile and his eyes lit up.

When the wine arrived, the waiter poured and Ken made a toast.

"To family," he said, clinking his glass all around. "So, I can't begin to tell you ladies what a hardship it has been feeding these boys with Charlotte away."

Josh and Evan groaned, then gave each other fist bumps. It was the first moment of brotherly unity I'd seen and it was sweet. It made me feel better about what I'd seen with the bread board.

"The first night she was away, we did pizza," Ken said, swirling his lush Cabernet in the glass. "Easy, everyone's happy. Next night, Mexican. Then I get the idea in my head that these boys deserve better and I need to make them a homecooked meal."

"Ken, that's so nice," Charlotte said.

He gave a vigorous nod. "Yeah. So I rushed out to the grocery store and bought a twelve-pack of hot dogs."

I appreciated Ken and his kindness already, but his sense of humor was really growing on me.

"The package said you could microwave them, so I did."

Josh and Evan burst into laughter.

Hooking his thumb at his father, Josh said, "That guy didn't know enough to take them out of the package. The microwave started popping and hissing like a volcano—"

Evan hooted. "Hot dogs were like, shrieking, trying to get out—"

"So, Chef Pierre over there grabs the fire extinguisher," Josh said, "douses the dogs in this nasty white foam and tries to convince us that, since they were in the package, they're perfectly safe to eat."

Evan practically jumped up and down in his seat. "He's begging us not to call Mom, bribing us with extra screen time, and he tries to eat one on his own—"

The boys start laughing hysterically.

"I ran into the bathroom and spit it out. Into the..." Ken leaned in and mouthed, "Toilet. It wasn't good."

Once we'd stopped laughing, the boys moved on to Ken's attempts at breakfast, and we were all in stitches by the time the appetizers arrived. He had ordered an assortment of oysters Rockefeller, fried calamari, and stuffed mushrooms. Looking at it all, I was convinced I'd be full long before laying eyes on the entrees.

The food was decadent and Ken kept the conversation flowing. The thing that impressed me about Charlotte's family was that everyone got involved, even Josh, telling stories designed to make everyone laugh. Even Charlotte spoke up, making Ken, the boys, and even me laugh at the imitation of the sound the pipes in the house made the first time she used the water.

Ken laughed the loudest of all, splashing more red wine into our glasses. It was clear he was happy to have his family back together again and that he was one of those guys who wanted everyone to have a good time. I covered my glass with my hand when he tried to split the final drops between me and Charlotte. I didn't want to waste the wine, and I didn't want to risk drinking more than I should.

When Ken ordered another bottle, Charlotte gave him a warning look.

"It's fine," he said, waving his hand. "We're celebrating!"

"Boys, have you heard yet about how your grades will look this semester?" Charlotte asked, turning her attention back to them.

Evan had been busy chowing down on the calamari. He made a big deal out of pointing at his mouth, as if indicating it was too full for him to answer. His father squeezed his shoulder.

"Evan's set up for straight As in math and science, as always," he boomed. "Josh got straight As in anatomy, if you know what I mean." He held out his hand for a fist pump.

Josh gave a triumphant smile and bumped knuckles with his dad.

Charlotte pressed her lips together. "Let's keep it appropriate, shall we?"

"You asked," Ken said.

The waiter returned with the wine. Ken winked at me before telling him, "Keep the food coming, please. This one's never been here and I'm trying to impress her."

"Yes, sir," the waiter said. "I'll do my best."

Charlotte laid her hand on Ken's as he went to take another drink of wine. He brushed her hand away in annoyance but took a drink of water instead. Then he served himself up a hearty plate of appetizers and dug in, giving us all a momentary rest from his intense performance.

The silence was uncomfortable after the previous chatter, so I smiled at Evan.

"It sounds like you enjoy school," I said. "What's your fav—"

"He lives for school," Josh interrupted. "He's a total dork."

"That's enough," Charlotte said, her tone light.

"I liked school, too," I said, irritated to see Evan's ears turn red. "Evan, what's your favorite subject?"

"I don't know," he mumbled through a mouthful of stuffed mushrooms.

Ken had ordered a lot of food, but at the rate Evan was putting it away, I realized I'd better fill a plate like Ken had if I wanted to get a fair shot at everything.

"Josh, how about you?" I asked, spooning up some calamari. "I heard you play sports."

"Yes, ma'am." He gave a cool nod. "I'm a starter for the varsity squad in soccer, basketball, and I run track."

"That must be why you run," I told Charlotte. "So you can keep up."

"Pretty much." She smiled. "Josh has kept me on my toes since the moment he was born."

She beamed at him and he gave me a smug glance, as if to make sure I knew how much his mother adored him, but my mind had switched back to the idea of family. In particular, the fact that I'd missed the birth of my nephews. I'd missed seeing my sister pregnant, birthday parties, and every second of their lives. The thought made me take a long drink of water, to hide the emotion that threatened to come out.

"Charlotte is a great mom," Ken said, giving a sage nod. "Everything she does is for those boys. Jayne, what was your mother like?"

"Ken." Charlotte's voice was sharp, and the boys looked up as if something interesting was about to happen.

"Oh, relax," Ken said. "The fact that you're such a great mom impresses me, since your mother wasn't so great."

Immediately, I stepped in. "That's not true. She was very smart and incredibly loyal to her parents. I think the way she and my father settled on the custody arrangement was a horrible choice, but that didn't make her a bad mother. It was just the circumstances of the situation."

"Yeah." Ken popped a piece of calamari in his mouth. "I'm only saying the boys have a great mother. I had a decent upbringing and try to be a good dad, but I gotta tell you, there are days I fall short."

Josh rolled his eyes. "Nah, you're good."

"I'm fine. I'm okay. Your mother, though…" He took a long drink. "She's the good one."

Charlotte looked cautious, but she smiled at him. "Thank you."

The topic switched to the things the boys wanted to do this summer, like deep-sea fishing and learning to sail.

I pretended like I was listening, but instead I was watching Ken drink. He'd polished off his second glass of wine by the time the food runners arrived with our meals and poured another when Charlotte wasn't paying attention.

"Pepper?" the waiter asked, and I nodded.

I'd ordered a skirt steak with a rosemary marsala sauce, and it was served with tiny potatoes and creamed spinach. It smelled incredible. Ken made sure we each had what we needed, and thanked the waiter.

Once I'd brought the first, perfectly cooked bite to my mouth, Ken said, "Look, I like people. I like seeing what makes them tick."

His expression was earnest and he sawed away at his porterhouse steak. "You're not married, right, Jayne?"

There were two ways to answer his questions: Shut them down or make my responses as uninteresting as possible. I opted for the latter.

"Nope."

He peered at me. "You never see your father, right?"

"Ken, that's enough." Charlotte's blue eyes flashed. "Let's discuss something else, please."

Evan started to shovel mashed potatoes in his mouth and looked around the room, as if trying to figure out whether or not anyone else had noticed his mother's tone.

"I'm trying to get to know your sister," Ken said, looking wounded. "That's what this dinner is all about."

For the first time since we were kids, Charlotte reached out and touched my arm. "I'm sorry," she murmured. "This is not appropriate."

"It's okay," I said.

"It's perfectly appropriate," Ken said, starting to get louder. He repeated himself, saying, "Look, I love people. I love knowing that the people that I care about are doing well and, Jayne, now that I have the chance to know a bit more about you…" He shot his wife a look, and she took a deliberate bite of fish. "I want to take advantage of the opportunity to make sure everything's all right."

"Everything good with you, Dad?" Josh asked.

The question was said with enough snide teenage anger that I wondered what type of drama went on with this family behind closed doors. The perfect image they'd projected at the beginning of dinner was not holding up. I started to feel sorry for Charlotte.

"I'm only asking about your father because I wonder if that affected your relationships," Ken said. "Not having him around."

"I don't know how to answer that," I said.

Ken waited, as if expecting me to say more, but I didn't. Finally, he said, "I think those things make a difference." Then he picked up his fork and knife, digging back into his steak.

Charlotte rested her chin on her hand and stared out the window. The sun had started to set in pink and gold streaks across the sky. Josh and Evan were busy with their food, and since it was much too quiet, I considered the fact that everyone at the table knew my father better than I did.

Once we had finished our meals and dessert had arrived—a sampler platter with flourless chocolate cake, mini crème brûlée, and a bowl of fresh berries with cream—Charlotte and the boys got into a deep discussion about beach rules.

Since no one was paying attention, I looked at Ken and said, "Do you spend time with my father?"

He was spooning up a chocolate crème brûlée and paused. "We moved to Florida a few months back, down the street from Graham."

I didn't know that they'd moved. In my mind, Charlotte still lived in the house with the iron gates that she'd posted on social media.

"Graham and his wife had moved there to be closer to Iris, and we were looking for a change," Ken continued. "It felt like as good of a place as any."

The words twisted in my heart. "So, you see him all the time?"

"We do." Ken peered at me. "Look, I know that the way you and Charlotte were raised wasn't easy, but you're still young and there's still time. We just met, so I don't want to speak out of turn. I'm only going to say this: I'm a father. I can tell you right now that your father wants to be a part of your life."

"That's a little presumptuous," I said.

Ken looked at me in surprise. "Darlin', that's my middle name."

# CHAPTER NINE

The next morning, the sun was bright on the yellow walls of my room. Outside the window, the low foghorn of a ship wailed. It was accompanied by a warm breeze from the window, tinged with the scent of salt and the flowers blooming on the crape myrtle tree. The morning was quiet, and once the ship had passed, I listened for the ocean down below but couldn't hear anything.

Getting up out of bed, I stood in the window and stared out at the water. It was a beautiful day. The water was practically aquamarine, the beach was already dotted with a few people enjoying the early morning rays, and it was starting to feel like we were moving into the long, lazy days of summer.

I went down to the kitchen to cook breakfast. Charlotte was already at work out on the deck by the time Ken and the boys got up. The pounding of footsteps across the living room and the squeak of the deck door meant they were headed straight outside. I was relieved that I wouldn't have to chat with them until I'd had some coffee.

Dinner had been fine, but I was still adjusting to all of this. The idea that my nephews were here—an entire family that I hadn't known at all before this—was a lot to take in.

It was one thing to spend time with Charlotte, but we had a history that had separated us. These boys... well, I could see wanting to be a part of their lives. That worried me, because it was likely that this summer would be it for us and the thought was upsetting. There was no reason for me and Charlotte to be this far apart, and I wished we could find a way to resolve our issues instead of letting them continue to define us.

I had just taken the carton of eggs out of the fridge when Ken strolled into the kitchen. He wore another golf outfit, this one with bright blue shorts and a polo with bright blue stripes, and his face looked ruddy and tired.

"Good morning," he boomed, spotting me. "I'm going to help myself to some coffee." Once Ken had made a cup and had put the cream container back in the refrigerator door, he turned to me with an apologetic look. "Listen, I'm sorry about last night."

"What about it?" I cracked two eggs into the pan. "Thank you again for dinner."

"You're welcome, but hear my apology. Please." Ken wasn't at the same level of confidence and swagger he'd had the night before. I might have been wrong about my assessment that he was a seasoned drinker. "It wasn't right for me to ask those questions. I crossed a line and I'm sorry."

The dinner had ended with Charlotte driving us all home. It was obvious that she'd been incredibly embarrassed about the whole thing, and I hadn't tried to offer her comfort. Instead, I'd stared out the window of the car, trying to work through my feelings.

"I appreciate your apology." I watched as the eggs sizzled. "Can I ask why you felt the need to question me about those things?"

"Because I don't think that Charlotte will," he said, leaning against the counter. "The fact that the two of you never had the chance to become family seems wrong to me." I glanced at him and he shrugged. "I'd hoped to open the door to a discussion she'd feel comfortable walking into. It turned out not to be the best approach."

My whole-grain toast popped up, so I buttered it and set it on a plate.

"Look," Ken said, "I don't want to step in the middle of all this. The two of you have a history that I wasn't a part of. I also jumped in last night because I'd had too much to drink, so I apologize for that."

"No worries." I pulled an orange out of the fridge and sliced it up, the sweet citrus tickling my nose. "Would you like something to eat?"

Ken winced. "No, thank you."

I realized the smell of the egg might be too intense after all the wine he'd consumed. Moving the pan from the burner, I covered it with a lid. He laughed, as if noting the effort.

"Well, let's keep the lines of communication open," he said. "You and me."

In spite of his apology, it was clear he wanted to do what he could to make things okay between me and Charlotte, but things hadn't been okay for years. It wasn't like he could step in now and fix everything. Rather than explain that, I decided to keep the conversation light.

"Interesting," I said. "The last time a married man said that to me, he cornered me at an office party and tried to put his hand up my skirt."

Ken grimaced. "Would you believe the same thing happened to me?"

I laughed. There was something about Ken that I really liked. He was personable, and he had a great sense of humor.

"What are you up to today?" I asked.

"If I can shake this headache, I'll probably hit the greens later." I took the lid off my eggs and he winced. "I'm definitely not staying for that smell. See you later, Jayne."

"See you," I said, carrying my breakfast to the table.

No sooner had I sat down to eat than Evan came thundering in. "Hey, do I smell food?"

He wore a navy-blue T-shirt and a pair of bright orange swim trunks. His hair was sticking up in all directions and his smile was bright and friendly.

"Have a seat." I grabbed my toast and brought it with me to the stove. "I'll make you something."

Evan grinned and plunked down in a chair. "Cool. Dad's been pulling out the box of Lucky Charms all week and the way he was grunting and groaning about it, you'd think he made a five-course meal."

I whipped him up some scrambled eggs with cheese and two pieces of toast. It took all of five minutes, and we sat down together to eat.

"Do you have any orange juice?" he asked, wiping the back of his mouth with his hand.

"No, I need to go to the store," I said. "Do you want coffee?"

His eyes went wide. "No way," he practically squawked. "That would stunt my growth."

Considering Evan was already six feet tall, I didn't think he had much to worry about. His response told me a lot about him, though. The kid was not a rule breaker.

"So, what are your plans today?" I asked.

"Loafing." He gave a serious nod. "Followed by a good nap." He ate for a minute, then looked at me. "Do you think any of this is weird?"

I swallowed hard. "Any of what?"

"I mean, I'm sitting in this big house on the beach with an aunt that I didn't even know I had. I'd never even heard of you until all this happened. Turns out, you're super cool."

The words made my stomach turn.

Evan must have realized I was upset, because he said, "Wait, are you mad? That was supposed to be a compliment. I'm sorry."

"No." I took a drink of coffee to get rid of the lump in my throat. "Surprised, I guess."

"Because you didn't know about me, either?" he asked, ripping off the crust on his bread.

I hesitated. It wasn't like I could tell him that the only way I knew he existed was because I'd stalked his mother on social media. On the other hand, I didn't want him to assume that I knew about him but made the choice not to be around.

"It's complicated," I said.

"Did you guys have a big fight or something?" he asked. "You and my mom?"

"You should talk to your mom about all that."

His curiosity was innocent, and probably stemmed from all of the questions his father had asked the night before, but I didn't feel comfortable discussing it with him.

"She told me to butt out." He picked at something on his arm, then went back to inhaling his eggs. "I get it, though. Sibling relationships are hard."

I laughed at the gravity of his statement. "Sorry," I said, when he looked hurt. "You're just so grown-up."

"Okay, it's official—I like you." He gave a vigorous nod. "I'm getting you one of those #1 Aunt coffee mugs for Christmas. You don't have to get me anything, but I love video games. Like, a lot."

"Good to know, because I probably would have made the mistake of sending money."

He laughed out loud.

Charlotte walked in and looked back and forth between the two of us. "Evan, I hope you're not bothering Jayne."

"How could I bother her?" He hopped up to help himself to another piece of toast. "I'm her favorite nephew."

# CHAPTER TEN

The moving company that Charlotte had contacted showed up promptly at ten thirty. There were two college guys who wore cargo pants and black tank tops and made the whole house smell like sweat. The roofers were also here to repair holes and various bits of structural damage. The steady sound of hammering, stomping, and music from the roof above made the house feel busy.

Ken and the boys had gone out for a day on the Jet Skis and Charlotte worked. I stayed inside in case the movers needed help with anything. Since it's always been physically impossible for me to watch people work without pitching in, I offered them water so many times that they probably thought I was trying to score a date. They finally said yes, probably to get me off their back.

The movers tracked back and forth and up and down the stairs for the morning and well past lunch, until everything but the basics was out of the way. Charlotte and I had planned to only leave a bed and a dresser in each of the bedrooms, but I had them leave the blue wingback chair in my room. The conversation Charlotte and I had shared in my room had been stunted, but it was the longest conversation we'd had. Leaving the chair felt like leaving the lines of communication open.

Charlotte worked well past noon. She was seated out on the deck but underneath the sun umbrella. When the movers were nearly done, I poked my head out the door and waved at her.

"They're close," I mouthed, in case she was in a meeting.

Charlotte shut her computer and came inside, tossing her hair as she surveyed their work. The guys hung out by the front door, sipping on sports drinks and waiting to call it a day. She went out to the back deck without a word and my cheeks flushed.

"Okay. I guess that's it, then," I said. "Thank you for your—"

The deck door slid open and Charlotte sailed back with four crisp twenty-dollar bills.

"Thank you for all of your hard work," she said, tipping each of them forty dollars.

The smiles that they gave her were a lot brighter than the ones I got for offering them water. They left and Charlotte brushed off her hands.

"This looks good," she said, sounding pleased. "This house has great bones."

I nodded. "It opened up the space in a big way."

We both stood in silence, looking out over the living room. I got hit with a wave of memories: pushing back the coffee table to learn dance routines in front of music videos; ice-cream-cone-eating contests until we rolled on the floor with brain freezes; and the time the entire house lost power because of a bad lightning storm and we had a sleepover with our grandmother in the living room with all of the couch cushions and blankets.

I wondered if Charlotte remembered any of those things.

"You know…" She drummed her fingers against her lips. "We have to work our way through the list, so we wouldn't get to this for some time, but Ken and I were talking about some remodeling ideas. What would you think about putting in a gigantic picture window right there?"

She pointed at the two plain windows on either side of the room. They were small and old, but they faced the ocean and offered a decent view. Putting in a picture window would open it up, but a different image popped into my head.

"I see where you're going with that, but what if we put in three huge windows that stretched up, like eight feet?" I suggested. "It would look great from the outside and also give an unbelievable view in here."

Charlotte wrinkled her forehead.

"Picture it," I said, before she could protest. "This is such a tall ceiling and it feels big in here, but the lighting does it a disservice. That's why it felt small with all the furniture."

Charlotte gave a slow nod. Pivoting, she pointed at the wall that led into the dining room. "I'll raise you. Structural repairs are first on the list. Some of the plaster looks like it's bubbled up from the moisture in the air. It's not that bad but it's crumbled a bit down here. What if we knocked out the wall instead of repairing it? It would open up the room and we could do the windows you're describing all along the stretch."

My heart started to pound. "Yes! *If* we could do it. If the wall isn't…"

"Load-bearing," Charlotte finished, because I didn't know the term.

"How do we find out?" I asked. "We don't want the house to fall on top of us."

"Ken took a look and doesn't think that it is. The home inspector should be able to confirm that," she said, walking over to tap on the wall. "It's not hard. He can look up in the attic and down in the crawl space, and if the wall's holding up the house, he'll know. We'll also have to deal with the electric." She pointed at an outlet towards the floor. "Plus, the light switch. It will probably come down to cutting the breaker and confirming the power's off so that we don't run into a problem. I think it's a great idea."

"Me, too," I said.

"So, moving on from the wall, the windows are not something we need to decide about now, but I'm glad we're on the same page."

I pulled out my phone to review the list. "Agreed. Windows are eleventh on the list. It will give us plenty of time to think about them."

"There's so much to do." Charlotte shook her head, taking in the room. "It could take a lifetime to remodel this place."

We looked at each other.

I was thinking about our grandparents and the sense of fun they must have had making a purchase like this. They would have gotten into the repairs the same way my sister and her husband had at the beginning of their marriage, flipping houses. I wondered if she was thinking the same thing.

"Well, we need to decide on a carpenter, since the sunroom is a structural issue. I grabbed a list of recommended locals from the hardware store…" Charlotte pulled a folded piece of paper from her notebook and handed it to me. "We probably should have booked them a few weeks ago like I did with the roofing company but it should be a relatively quick job. Maybe we'll get lucky."

I skimmed the list of names and stopped. Logan was the second name on the list.

"I know one of the guys on here," I said.

"You do?" Charlotte wrinkled her brow. "How?"

"He works at the blacksmith shop downtown and his sister owns the coffee shop next door. She actually recommended him to me for carpentry work."

"The guys at the hardware shop said we can't miss with anyone on there," she said. "Find out his rates and see how soon we can get him in here."

Logan's number was on the paper and I stared down at it, wondering whether to call or text. The thought of calling him made me nervous for some reason, so I decided to text.

*Hi Logan. It's Jayne—we've met at the coffee shop, and at the fire at the bed-and-breakfast last month. Both Lauren and the hardware shop recommended you for carpentry, so can you tell*

*me your earliest availability to rebuild a hole in the wall caused*
*by a fire? (Not joking.) Thanks!*

"There," I said, pressing send.

"You didn't buy enough cleaning supplies," Charlotte said,
jolting me back to reality.

"Oh?" I said, but that wasn't news. I'd known since I'd returned
from the grocery store that what I'd picked up wouldn't cut it.

Cleaning supplies for a whole house were substantially more
expensive than supplies for a one-bedroom apartment, and I'd
found myself in over my head. I'd deposited the two-thousand-
dollar stipend, but the check needed a few days to clear. The
amount that was immediately available was little more than what
I'd need for groceries. I was not about to put cleaning supplies
on a credit card, because I'd get stuck with the interest, so I only
bought what I could with the cash that I had.

"Sorry," I said. "I'm used to apartment living."

Charlotte nodded. "That's fine. I'll revise the cleaning appointment so that it includes supplies. The confirmation email said
that was an option, but I didn't see that when I booked them
online originally."

"Perfect." I hoped she hadn't guessed the real reason I hadn't
bought enough. I didn't want her to know that I had financial
problems, since she seemed to have it all together.

"Well, since that's done, I should probably get back to work,"
she said, and headed back out to the deck.

The exit was abrupt but I felt good about our conversation.
It had been fun imagining what we could do to the house and,
for a moment, it had felt like we were in this together. My phone
chimed. Logan.

*Yes, Jayne of the Fire Safety fame. Fascinated to know how*
*someone with that distinction put a hole in a wall with fire. I had*

*a cancellation, so I can be available later this week depending on the size of the project. How about Thursday?*

He went on to include a list of his rates, and I headed back outside to show Charlotte.

"More than fair," she said. "Book him for the morning, if you don't mind handling it."

The idea of trying to tell Logan what to do left me feeling flustered, but I texted him back.

*Thursday would be great. #7 at the Row, 9 a.m.*

The remainder of the day stretched in front of me, so I decided to take a walk on the beach.

Once I'd applied sunscreen, I gave Charlotte an awkward wave before heading down the steps to the shore. The ocean stretched out in a sea of dark green with small streaks of aquamarine rolled in between the waves. As the water tumbled closer, they seemed to change into a burst of gold right before tumbling into a white froth over the pale blonde sand. I walked along the edge of the water, my heart beating with the rhythm of the crash of the waves.

When I stopped to take a sip from my bottle of water, I enjoyed the feeling of the sun on my face, the smell of the brine of the air, and embraced the silence of the day. It was hard to believe that this type of relaxed life existed, compared to the crunch and press of the city where I had lived for so long.

My hair whipped in the wind and I could already feel it stiffening with salt. In my heart, I wanted to shout out *thank you, thank you, thank you* as loud as I could but the beach was not empty, and everybody would stare. Still, I felt so full of gratitude that I wanted to let it out.

For a split second, I imagined that my life was different. That Charlotte and I had remained close after that summer and that somehow, we were back, living here together as a happy family. It wasn't realistic, of course, but it made me feel like I had stepped into a rare moment of perfection.

# CHAPTER ELEVEN

Thanks to the excellent work of the movers, there was a clear path for the cleaners the next morning. They arrived first thing with a team of six people, a collection of mops and brooms, and buckets of industrial cleaning supplies. Instead of age and mildew, the house started to smell like lemon Pine-Sol and bleach.

Thursday morning, Logan rang the bell at 8:55.

I wanted to beg Charlotte to answer, but she was out back working. The roofers were still going at it, so I wasn't sure how she could concentrate with all the noise. Her earbuds had to be blocking it out, but either way, her focus was impressive.

Clearing my throat, I threw open the door.

"Morning." Logan greeted me with the scent of sandalwood aftershave and a cheerful smile. "I'm here to fix a sunroom?"

I smiled back. "Thanks for coming."

The cleaners hadn't touched the sunroom since the wall needed to be rebuilt and that would make a mess, so I felt a little self-conscious to show it to him. He must have seen much worse because he barely blinked, taking in the damage.

"It's amazing how quickly something like this can happen."

"Were you here for this?" I asked, and he gave me a confused look. "The fire. Did you help put it out?"

"No, not this one," he said. "I'm part-time, so I miss out on a lot. Some of my buddies probably helped out, but it was a while back, right?"

"Years." I nodded. "That door was shut at the time, so there wasn't smoke damage to the rest of the house, just in here."

Logan removed the tarp and considered the wall. The boards were charred and the smell of soot, intense.

"Sorry," I said. "It's pretty bad under there."

Looking over his shoulder, he grinned. "You think that's going to stop a firefighter?"

"No." I watched him for a moment. "You said you were pretty booked up. What do you think?"

He pulled the tarp back across, thinking. "It's a relatively big project. Like I said on the text, I had someone cancel out, so I have today and tomorrow free, but I'd have to get going now or I wouldn't be able to get back here for a few weeks. I imagine you want to get quotes from some of the other guys?"

"I don't think so," I said. "You come highly recommended."

"From my sister?" His voice was dry.

I laughed. "Yes, but also the guys at the hardware store. So, if you can get started today, that would be great."

"Sure," he said. "Let me do some measurements in here. I'll run out, get what I need, and get it taken care of in no time."

"Thanks."

Our eyes met. For some reason, I felt embarrassed.

"Well, I'll get out of your way. Call if you need anything."

Logan lifted his hand, and I headed out, confused by my desire to stay.

I was loading dishes into the dishwasher from lunch when Logan poked his head into the room.

"Hey, Jayne?" He held out a small box. "This was in the sunroom."

I studied it in confusion. It was made of metal and about the size of a shoebox. It wasn't heavy, but I could tell there was something inside it.

"Where?" I asked.

"That was the strange thing." Logan ran his hand through his dark hair. "It was tucked into the space between the boards, like someone had left it there."

I was about to open it when I realized it wouldn't be right to do that without Charlotte. "If it's treasure, I'll let you know," I told him. "Thank you."

Charlotte was sitting at the table outside, reading a book and finishing up a sandwich. "I have to show you something," I said. "Logan found it in the wall of the sunroom."

Charlotte's blue eyes widened. "What is it?"

"Let's find out," I said.

I pushed the metal button and the box popped open. There was what looked like a paper-wrapped book down below, but on top there was a small envelope that contained a letter.

It read:

*My Dear Girls,*

*I do hope you are enjoying the task of remodeling. This house has incredible potential to be something special—even more so than it already is. I must ask that you remember that the true joy of life is the trip. The days will go faster than you can imagine, so take the time to enjoy the mundane. And in the moments when you're looking for something to remember your time together here, I have something for you to see.*

*The reason I wanted the two of you to have this book is so that you could better understand the hurt and heartache that both of you experienced. I don't want to bring up bad memories, but I do think that it's necessary for you to consider all sides of this. The story that Jayne wrote makes it clear that she wanted to be with you, Charlotte. And, Charlotte, the things that you wrote show me how angry you were that the two of you could not be together. I would like you both to discuss two things:*

*Charlotte, why did you destroy the book that you created together?*

*Jayne, please discuss the story that you wrote and the meaning that you see behind it now.*

*Here's the reality—your parents made a bad decision separating the two of you. They did not do it out of malice or a lack of love, but it wasn't the right choice. Please work together to recognize that the choices that were made were not your fault.*

*Hugs and kisses,*
*Your grandmother*

"What on earth?" Charlotte unwrapped the book and immediately dropped it. Then she stared at it with a look of disbelief on her face.

"What is it?" I asked, squinting in the sun.

Without a word, she picked it up and handed it to me. I took in the front cover of the book we'd made. The mermaid and the rainbow, drawn in glitter glue with such cheerful colors. The sudden flood of memories nearly knocked me down.

It was a book Charlotte and I had written together that summer. It was about two magical sisters who had never met spending the summer together. We'd written it in a notebook, passing it back and forth, picking up the story where the other had left off. The entire book had been written in pink and purple ink.

"Summer Sisters," I said slowly. "I had forgotten all about it."

I sank into a chair at the table, the book in hand, and began to read:

Rainbow and Mermaid held hands tightly as they stood at the shore.

"I don't want you to leave," Rainbow said, starting to cry. When she cried, the whole sky filled with silver water and rained down.

"I have no choice," Mermaid said. "I have to go back to my mother. I have a secret to tell you. She's your mother, too. Come with me, Rainbow."

Rainbow smiled. Slowly, her body transformed into a mermaid and together, the summer sisters dove into the sea.

I turned the page and drew back. There was a black X over both characters' faces. As I looked through it, I realized nearly every page had been vandalized.

"Why did you do that?" I asked.

"I have no idea." Then she sighed. "Why do you think? It was something you and I created together. To be quite frank, I think I was mad we wrote a book about friendship when we didn't have the first clue what we were talking about."

"I think we did." I reread the part where Mermaid and Rainbow said goodbye, then slowly flipped through the book. "This book is about two friends who loved each other and couldn't be together. When I read it, that's what I see, and that's what we felt back then. It must have been so frustrating to know that we didn't have the freedom to make our own choices. Or we would have had them stay together."

Charlotte considered the book once more, then shook her head. "Such a strange thing to show us."

"I don't think so," I said. "It's a piece of our history. Do you mind if I hang on to it?"

Charlotte flipped her ponytail. "You can burn it. I'm going for a jog."

"Wait," I called.

She rested her hand on the railing of the stairs that led down to the ocean.

"I'm wondering…" The small metal box sat on the table. The sun seemed to glint off of it and an idea took root in my brain as certain as if my grandmother had whispered it. "I think I know why she wants us to work in a certain order. I bet she hid stuff like this for us to find."

Charlotte shook her head. "I don't think so."

"Why not?" My heart started to pound with possibility. "This was hidden in the wall of the sunroom. If she wanted to give us the book and the letter, it would have made sense to do it when we received all the other paperwork. Instead, she hid it in the wall for us to find. I bet it's going to keep happening."

"Grandma hasn't lived here for years," Charlotte protested.

"She had Martin do it." I pulled out my phone. "Should we call him?"

Charlotte hesitated. She came back to the table and touched the book. "Yes."

Once Martin came on the line, I put him on speakerphone. Charlotte gestured at me as if to say, *This is your theory. You do the talking.*

"Yes, hi," I said. "Martin, we have a question for you. Do you know whether or not our grandmother left items around the house for us to find as we go? Sentimental-type things?"

There was a pause on the other end of the line. Then he said, "It's possible."

"It's possible, or she did?" Charlotte demanded.

"She did." Martin's voice sounded cheerful. "It sounds like you've found one, then."

I patted the book in triumph, but one look from Charlotte wiped the smile off my face.

"One last thing your grandmother wanted to do was to connect with the two of you on a personal level," he said. "I admit that I did help orchestrate her wishes, but it was her idea."

"This stresses me out," Charlotte said. "How are we going to know if we've found the things she wants us to see? What if we miss something?"

"There's not many," Martin assured us. "Just a few things designed to spark a conversation."

Charlotte turned away from the table and stared out at the water. By the rigid way she held her shoulders, it was obvious that she was upset.

"Thanks, Martin," I said. "We appreciate your help."

Once I'd ended the call, I walked over to her. "You okay?"

Charlotte's blue eyes were stormy. "Fine."

The waves churned below, the sun hot on my shoulders. The idea that my grandmother had done this made me feel nervous but also intrigued. The book she'd left was a piece of history from one of the turning points in my life. The idea that Charlotte had nearly destroyed it hurt but at the same time gave me a deeper glimpse into what had happened between us.

Part of me had believed that she'd cut off contact because she didn't care. Now I understood that she had felt just as hurt and angry at the situation. It gave us a common ground, one that I hadn't been certain that we'd shared.

"I'm sorry if this upsets you," I said.

"I don't understand it." Charlotte flipped her ponytail. "Why didn't she do all of this when she was alive?"

"Would you have been open to it?" I asked.

She didn't respond.

Quietly, I said, "That might be your answer."

"I'm going for a run."

Charlotte headed for the steps. I walked back to the table and picked up the book that we'd written so long ago. The mermaid and rainbow glittered from the front cover, and my heart ached. Slowly, I flipped through the book and considered the heavy black marks Charlotte had used in an effort to erase our history.

My grandmother had wanted to show me how angry Charlotte had been at our separation. It was something that I hadn't realized at the time. To me, the summer that we'd shared had felt like a time of hope and a time of healing. I'd been heartbroken when

Charlotte cut me off, but based on this, I could see how some hurts might feel beyond repair.

The sky was gray when I woke the next morning. The waves looked larger than usual, as if gearing up for another storm.

I trudged down into the kitchen and stopped short to see Charlotte standing in front of the open door of the fridge, her shoulders tense. She was bent over, studying something in her hand.

My insulin pen. I didn't want to startle her for fear she'd drop it, but I didn't want her touching something that held my life in the balance.

"Please be careful with that," I said, taking it back.

"Sorry." Charlotte studied me. "I didn't know what it was."

"It's an insulin pen." I placed it carefully back in the fridge. "I need it, and I can't have it broken."

I was not about to tell her what a financial hardship it would be to try to replace it or how unfair it felt to need it in the first place. Through no fault of my own, I had to factor in hundreds of dollars per month just to stay alive. For me, medicine wasn't optional, it was the equivalent of buying food.

"You have diabetes?" Charlotte asked.

"Yes." It was a change since we were kids, as I hadn't been diagnosed until I was nearly fourteen. I poured the coffee into a filter and started the pot before getting some eggs out of the fridge. True to the topic, it was time for me to eat.

"My college roommate had diabetes." Charlotte watched me closely. "It can be serious. It's important for you to tell me things like this, Jayne, since we're living together. If something happened, I wouldn't have known how to help you."

"It didn't come up." The idea of eating anything didn't appeal, but I cracked eggs into a bowl with the precision of a contestant on a cooking show. "Do you want some eggs?"

"No." She gave an adamant shake of her head. "Thank you."
She started to reach for the coffee, but it was still trickling away,
the steam hissing in angry bursts. Turning on her heel, she left
the kitchen. Moments later, she returned. "If something happens
and you need help, ask."

We looked at each other for a long moment.

"Thank you," I said quietly.

"You're welcome. Let me know when you're done eating and
we can get started."

I stood at the stove, staring down at the thin skin of the eggs
in the pan. It surprised me that she'd gotten frustrated that I
hadn't told her I was a diabetic. She'd been almost... protective.
Like she cared if something happened to me.

Such a small thing but, after years of assuming the opposite,
it felt like everything.

*

That summer when Charlotte and I had stayed at the beach, I'd
been obsessed with the seashells on the shore. I collected them in
a little blue pail and brought them back up to the house to wash
them. Grandma was always wringing her hands at the idea that
I was carrying a bucket up and down the steep steps, because she
was scared I'd trip and fall. She told me not to do it several times,
but it was the only way to transport so many shells.

One day after low tide, my bucket was so full that the plastic
handle was about to snap. I walked up the stairs holding it tight
in my arms. Halfway up, I slipped. The seashells shattered across
the steps and the bucket thumped its way down as I fell forward,
splitting my knee.

The cut was deep, and blood ran down my shin.

"I'm going to get Grandma." Charlotte's face was horrified,
her blue eyes filled with worry.

"No," I pleaded, grabbing my leg. The blood wouldn't stop. "She'll get so mad. Please, stay with me."

Charlotte had sat down next to me and wrapped her favorite pink towel tight around my bloody leg. Then she put her thin arms around my shoulders and held me tight. I'd nestled into her warmth, crying harder at the reality of who I was sitting with and what my mother would say about it than the fact that I'd split my leg open.

"Are you terribly hurt?" Charlotte asked.

There were so many things inside of me that hurt. The idea that my family was broken, that my mother would be devastated when she learned the truth about this summer, and the idea that I lived thousands of miles from my sister. But in that moment, none of it mattered.

"No, I'm not hurt," I said. "Because you're here."

This time, Charlotte started to cry, too.

# CHAPTER TWELVE

Logan completed the repairs on the sunroom late Friday night and it looked great. He'd fixed the damage to the wood, rebuilt part of the wall, and then drywalled it. The only thing left to do was paint, which wouldn't be for a few months, based on the order we were expected to work in.

Since structural damage was at the top of the list, Charlotte enlisted her family to help us knock out the wall between the living room and the kitchen early Monday afternoon. The boys scampered off to change out of their beachwear while Ken cut the power, and the three of us stood around in hard hats like some sort of a wrecking crew.

"My real estate buddy loaned me the hats and the sledgehammers," Ken told me with a grin. "It's not worth it to buy all that for a little job like this but I was not about to say no to some extra power."

Josh and Evan came back down dressed in worn shorts and T-shirts, but instead of joining the rest of us, Josh sat on one of the folding chairs in the living room. He pulled his baseball hat low over his eyes like he'd rather be sleeping on the beach, while Evan bounced around like a large puppy.

"Put on your hat." Charlotte ruffled Evan's hair. "Josh, honey. Come get your hat and we'll take a picture."

"I'm good over here," he said.

Charlotte gave Ken a frustrated look and he shrugged.

"Okay," she said, setting it on the floor. "If you change your mind, it's right here."

Josh nodded but didn't look up.

We took a group selfie without him, and Charlotte sent it to me. I saved it right away, delighted to feel like part of their group.

"Well, we've got one man down but two ready to work," Ken said, rubbing his hands together. "Ladies, let us know what you need."

Charlotte pulled out her iPad. "Ken, this is for the rest of us. I know you've done this before, but I want Jayne and Evan to take a look at this video on YouTube. It walks you through how to do this."

Charlotte was such a planner, I'd learned, that she made sure to talk to the guys at the hardware store for each new project and then she'd watch a bunch of video tutorials on YouTube until she'd gotten a handle on it. Then she'd plan to make me watch the one that she found the most helpful. I was grateful because I learned much better by listening to a real person walk me through it.

The four of us settled onto the ground to watch. I felt struck once again at the ease of the situation, that we were all sitting together like a family during movie night.

"Cool," Evan said, as the guy in the video swung away at the wall. "I'm going to hit a homer with this."

"You couldn't hit a home run if you were batting in the house," Josh called.

"That's enough," Ken said. "I'd like to see you try it when the time comes."

Listening to the video must have piqued Josh's interest because he came over to us, chomping away on a piece of bubble gum. "This must be our baseball bat," he said, picking up a sledgehammer and trying to give it a swing.

"Hey," Ken barked. "Put that down. That's dangerous."

Josh gave it one more try, getting a little too close to Evan and bumping it into the wall. "Sorry," he mumbled, dropping it with a clatter.

Evan's eyebrows shot up and he looked at me in alarm.

"It's okay," I said. "The only one who's getting taken down today is the wall."

If Josh's performance unnerved Charlotte, she didn't comment. Pulling on a pair of safety goggles, she said, "Jayne and I are going first."

"Hey, batter batter batter, swing. Hey, batter batter batter, swing!" Josh called, shoving his hands in his pockets.

I appreciated the fact that he was involved instead of spending time on his phone, but I could have lived without the commentary. The safety goggles were tight on my temples, the dust mask hot, and the sledgehammer heavy, but I was ready to open up this room. There was a small possibility that it would be too big once we were done, but it would be so bright.

Taking a breath, I looked at Charlotte. "Ready?"

With a shout, we both drew back and attacked the wall. My hammer got stuck in the plaster right away and, laughing, I tried to dislodge it, with no luck.

"Let a man do the work!" Josh strode forward and yanked the handle out of my hand, the smell of bubblegum strong on his breath. He gave the hammer a reckless tug and it jerked out of the wall.

I leapt back just in time. Josh lost his balance and fell, bumping the back of his head on the ground. The metal part of the hammer landed on top of his leg and he yowled in pain.

"Josh," Charlotte cried.

Ken grabbed the hammer, then checked him for bruises and breaks. "Bend your knee, son."

Slowly, Josh bent his knee and sat up. "Bummer. That didn't go as planned," he said, laughing. He was limping when he got up, and he rubbed the back of his head.

My mind kept replaying the uncontrolled moment when he yanked the hammer out of the wall. It could have hit me, smashed into his face, or caused damage a million other ways. It probably wasn't the best idea to have the boys helping us. It was unfortunate because Charlotte seemed so much more relaxed when they were around.

"I'm going back to the safety of technology," Josh said, in a sports-announcer voice, and returned to his place on the folding chair with his phone.

I let out a breath and caught Charlotte's eye. "You okay?"

She lifted her chin. "I swear, it's a million moments like that, raising boys, but it guts me every time." Pulling her hat back on, she said, "You ready?"

Gripping the sledgehammer hard, I made a point to be extra controlled in my hits this time around. The hammer did not get stuck. Ken, Charlotte, and I took turns, finally switching to crow bars to dislodge the remaining lathe boards. Evan did well, with no mishaps, and I gave him a high five.

Once there was nothing left but the wooden frame, Charlotte set down her hammer and pulled out the reciprocating saw.

Spotting it, Josh leapt to his feet. "Sweet. I want a turn!"

"No chance," Ken said, stepping forward. "Back away from the saw."

We all laughed but Josh looked angry. He grabbed the bottle of water he'd been sipping on and slipped out to the back deck. It was a shame he'd jumped ship, but it was a much safer spot for him to be.

"You should probably go out, too," Charlotte told Evan, looping her arm around his shoulders. He was so tall that her small frame only made it up to his shoulders, and she beamed up at him with adoration.

"I'll stand back," he promised. "I want to watch. It's pretty cool."

Ken and Charlotte exchanged glances but nodded.

"So, we're only going to use this on the pieces at the bottom and then we should be able to pull them out." Charlotte glanced over at me. "If we cut it instead of breaking them, we won't have to worry about jagged pieces sticking up. It will keep it clean."

"You should have been a surgeon, honey," Ken said.

Charlotte got to work and soon the wood was loose. Slowly and carefully, Charlotte and I removed the boards. Ken and Evan worked together to carry them out front to the dumpster.

The bottom plate was the only thing that was left, so I handed off the crowbar to Ken. He wedged the bar under the thick piece of wood attached as a base for the wall and worked it until it pulled up.

Once all of the pieces had been removed, I couldn't believe the difference. Before, the living room had felt small. Removing the wall opened up the room in such a way that it was flooded with light. It was enormous, grand, and was a perfect fit with the overall look of the house.

"Great work, ladies," Ken said. "Evan, help me get the rest of these pieces out to the dumpster."

Charlotte and I stood in silence, considering the open space. Sunlight filtered into the room, dancing on the plaster dust that still floated through the air. I walked over to the entryway that led to the kitchen and the new light made it ten times brighter than it was before.

"I think it looks fabulous," Charlotte said, brushing plaster off her clothes. "Grandma would have loved this."

"It brightens everything." I considered the view of the ocean. "I know windows don't come until later, but now that this is open, it changes my suggestion. I wonder if we should try for windows across the entire room, like they had at the restaurant we went to. The view at night would be spectacular, and the light that would hit the room during the day would turn this section of the house into a work of art."

Charlotte gave a slow nod. "I think they should stretch up, though."

I shook my head. "I thought so before but now, I think it would be too much. That's to open up a room. It's already open. Let's use what we've got. Here's the difference."

I found a piece of paper and sketched both options for her. Slowly, she nodded. "You're right. That would look amazing."

"Thanks," I said, embarrassed at how much her approval meant to me. "I'm going to make some snacks. What does everyone like?"

Charlotte looked surprised. "Thank you. Maybe a cheese plate with crackers and cold cuts for everyone? I have a lot of cheese in there."

Collectively, we had the right ingredients. Charlotte had bought Brie, drunken goat cheese, and an aged cheddar, while I had a strong array of lunch meats, crackers, and a small can of olives.

"Yes, that's perfect," I said.

"Thank you." She nodded. "I'm going to go check on Josh."

Such an insignificant thing, sharing ingredients, but to me, it meant so much. Only a week ago, I never would have imagined that Charlotte would be okay with that. Now, we'd settled into a somewhat comfortable rhythm. Even though I'd been nervous about having her family here, I attributed my level of comfort to them. They were loud and funny and served as a great buffer to intimacy, which made my interactions with her less pressured.

When Ken returned, he and Charlotte headed out to the back deck to check on Josh. Evan followed me into the kitchen.

"Did you hear me say snack?" I teased.

"No, I need to talk to you." Evan's hands were in his pockets and his ears were red. He was so tall and thin that it seemed like he was all elbows and knees.

"Yeah?" I pulled out the collection of cheese and found a cutting board. "What's going on?"

Evan was quiet and when I looked up, his eyes were serious.

"Josh is being such an idiot," he said, in a low tone. "He's been drinking with his friends at parties and I think it's affecting his brain."

"He drinks?" I said.

The news surprised me because Josh looked so young. He and Evan were kids. Still, I remembered when I was in high school. I'd felt invincible and had experimented with alcohol, too. Nothing had ever happened to me, thank goodness, but it hadn't been the smartest move.

"Yeah." Evan bit off his thumbnail and spat it in the trash. "I mean… he was acting like he was drunk in there."

I set down my knife with a thump. "Was he?"

"He said no." Evan frowned. "I know a lot of kids do that stuff, but we always promised each other that we wouldn't. Now he barely talks to me. I think it's because he's embarrassed, like he thinks I'm judging him or something. I kind of am, I guess. I'm trying not to, but it scares me that he's doing this."

I pretended to focus on slicing the Brie. "How often is this going on?"

"He does it almost every weekend," Evan said. "Sometimes his friends have even come to school drunk. The teachers are pretty clueless—they just told them off for being loud. I don't think Josh has taken it that far, but his grades haven't been good this semester and my parents can't figure out why. I don't want to be a tattletale, but I don't want him to fall into a hole that he can't get out of, do you know what I mean? He's such a good athlete, and I don't want him to risk that."

My heart ached for Evan. He was such a sweet, earnest boy. I had no idea how to counsel him and I wondered why he was talking to me about this, considering he barely knew me. Probably because he thought I might tell his mother for him, but I wasn't sure I could do that.

"If you want my advice, which it sounds like you might be asking for…" I waited, and he nodded. "Talk to your brother. Tell him that you want to have a hard conversation and that you

love him and want to figure this out together. Then if he won't
listen, you should talk to your mother about it."

I knew Evan would feel better about giving his brother a chance
to figure things out instead of tattling.

"Could you talk to him?" he asked.

I opened the can of olives and dumped them in a small bowl
before answering. "Sorry, but I don't think that's the best idea.
I'd like to help you, but this is something to take to your mother.
It can be dangerous for him to be doing this, and it worries me
that you even thought there was a possibility just now."

"Yeah." He looked forlorn, scratching at a mosquito bite. "Do
you think you and Mom would've gotten us all together if this
house hadn't happened?"

"I don't know," I admitted. "Our parents kept us pretty far
apart, so I doubt either of us would have reached out. It's been
over twenty-five years since I've seen her."

"Maybe when you were older you would have," he suggested.

"No." I shook my head. "I don't think so."

"Oh." He swiped a handful of cheese from the cutting board.
"How do you feel about her now?"

"I don't know her as well as I want to," I said carefully. "That
takes time."

"I don't think many people know her," he admitted. "To me,
she seems lonely."

"What do you mean?"

"Since we moved—that's also when my brother started to hang
out with these party guys—my mother hasn't made an effort to
make friends."

It still surprised me to think that the image of the house I'd
seen posted so often on Charlotte's social media was no longer her
home. For so long, it had been the backdrop to my imaginings
about what she was like and what she might be doing.

"You don't think she likes Florida?" I asked.

He shook his head. "I think the move was hard on her. She was so worried about whether or not it would be hard for us, but we're fine. I don't know. She doesn't seem that happy."

This new perspective on my sister made me sad. I'd had an image in my head that she lived this fabulous life, but I'd also assumed she had a crew of friends to do it with.

I did have to wonder, given the way Ken had acted at dinner. Maybe they were in a bad place because of the stress and she was trying to hide that from people. One part of making new friends was hanging out with other couples, and if she was worried he might embarrass her... But no. He'd been perfectly lovely until he'd had too much to drink. I could tell he was one of those people who were good at putting others at ease.

"Why did you move?" I asked.

His ears turned red. "Dad probably got a good deal on our house. If he can save a buck when he needs to, he'll do it."

"Thanks for sharing with me," I told Evan. "It helps me see your mother in a new light."

"Is that a good thing?" He fidgeted. "I mean, I'd like it if you two stayed in touch after all this."

"I will," I told him. "Especially with you."

We sat in silence for a moment, then he looked at me.

"Can I eat that cheese?" he asked.

Pushing the tray towards him, I said, "I thought you'd never ask."


The things that Evan had shared with me weighed on my mind because I wasn't quite sure if I should tell Charlotte. Our relationship had enough trouble without me playing the role of the messenger. Nevertheless, it made me uncomfortable to keep the type of thing that Evan had said a secret, even though

he mentioned it again later that afternoon, once the group of us
had spent time at the beach.

"The stuff I told you," he said. "Please don't say anything,
okay?"

"I won't," I said. "But if things get worse, I want you to say
something to your mother."

He chewed on his upper lip and then nodded. "Deal."

I hadn't brought my phone to the beach and when I went up
to my room to check it, there was a message from a number I
didn't recognize on my missed calls. Probably a creditor, but I
listened to it just in case it was something important.

To my delight, Lauren had called. "Hi, Jayne, I'm going to go
out with some of the girls for trivia night by the water on Friday
and wanted to see if you and your sister want to join us. I'm sure
we are the only people on the planet who still go out and do this,"
she said, laughing, "so no worries at all if it's not your thing. I
just wanted to give you the invite."

Trivia night? I used to do trivia night all the time with my
girlfriends back home.

Even though it would be fun to do with Charlotte, I didn't
feel that our relationship was there yet, and I didn't want it to be
awkward around Lauren. So, I decided to go alone. Maybe there
would be another opportunity later to bring Charlotte but, for
now, I wanted to build a friendship with Lauren.

I fired off a text to her confirming and asking for the details.
I was already looking forward to the opportunity to make a new
friend and, to be completely honest, I couldn't help but wonder
if Logan was going to be there, too.

# CHAPTER THIRTEEN

One of the features of the house that had attracted me was the belvedere. I had been meaning to get up there ever since we'd moved in but, when I tried, the door leading up to it was locked. Later that week, I went to get Charlotte and she led me back up to find the key.

I followed, noting the muscles in her upper arms. She ran the beach every morning before work, I'd discovered, and once or twice, she'd come home with her hair wet. It was possible she was also adding an early-morning swim to her fitness routine. I had to admit, Charlotte could be prickly but she was incredibly driven.

Now I watched as she reached up and ran her hand over the top of the crown molding above the door and found a key. Without a word, she opened the door and headed up there with me.

"Why is it locked?" I asked as we climbed a steep staircase up to the top.

"Liability, I think," Charlotte said. "Grandma probably didn't want the risk of anyone wandering up here, like a kid or something, since it's so dangerous."

The moment we walked in, I knew Charlotte wasn't talking about the stairs.

The belvedere was a small room on the roof of the house surrounded by four glass walls. They were windows, yes, but also walls since there was only about four feet between the glass of the windows and the floor. It was like standing at the top of a lighthouse and the view seemed to stretch on forever.

"This is beautiful," I breathed.

Down below, the ocean was a color palette of blue. Dark navy, cobalt, aquamarine, and light blue water mixed with the gold of the sunshine as far as I could see. Our neighbor's roof with its ornate trim was right across the way, with a few browned pine needles scattered across its rust-colored tiles. There was also the view of the flowering crape myrtle trees, so soft and gentle in the breeze.

"Pretty, huh?"

"It's probably my favorite room in the house," I said. The sun made it unspeakably hot, but I could have stood there all day.

"Grandma felt that way, too. She used to sit up here and write letters," Charlotte said, resting her hand on top of the small antique desk that, along with a matching chair, was the only piece of furniture in the room. "Whenever I got a letter from her when I was back home, it would transport me to this room."

The moment the words left her mouth, she seemed to regret letting me in on the memory, because she said, "It's hot up here. I'm going to head back down."

"I'll be down soon," I said. "I just want to take a look."

The desk was made of cherrywood and had a lift-up top, a middle drawer below, and three drawers on each side. I peeked in the drawers, but they were all empty.

I pulled out the chair and sat at the desk, thinking of my grandmother and wondering who she might have been. I remembered bits and pieces from that summer but wished I'd taken the time to get to know her better when I'd come to the States for college. I'd been so worried about hurting my mother's feelings, but really, there was no excuse. I should have made a greater effort to stay in touch.

Of course, I'd tried that with Charlotte, and it had caused me years of heartache.

Staring out at the crashing waves, I thought of the letter that I'd received from her, two months after our summer together.

*Dear Jayne,*

*I've spent the past few weeks thinking about the summer. It makes me sad, not happy.*

*I missed out on so much back home. I don't want to be pen pals, so you don't have to write me.*

*Charlotte*

That letter was the last one I'd ever gotten from her.

I'd tried. My mother did, too. We sent birthday cards, Christmas cards, presents, all of it, but Charlotte refused to stay connected.

It was ironic to think that we were here together now, after so many years. It was hard to wrap my mind around. We'd been children when all of this had happened. Wasn't it time to let it go? I wanted to, and for all of the pleasant moments we'd shared so far, she didn't seem ready.

Getting to my feet, I took one last look before turning and heading back down the stairs. I considered replacing the key, which Charlotte had left on the desk, back in its hiding place. Instead, I left it where it was. There was no reason that I could see to keep the belvedere locked any longer.

Charlotte and I were so busy with the house that Friday trivia night rolled around faster than I would have expected. I had taken a shower, gotten dressed, and was headed out the door when Ken called from the back porch, "Hey, where you headed?"

Charlotte and the boys were seated around the small umbrella table eating salads and Ken was working away at the grill, which was sending all sorts of smoky and delicious smells of roasted meat into the evening air. I hadn't eaten dinner with their family other than that first night, even though Ken had asked once or twice. I would have been happy to if the invitation had come from Charlotte, but until then, I wanted to give her space when we weren't working.

"You're all dressed up," Evan said. "Do you have a date?"

Charlotte shot him a look. "Evan."

"What?" He grinned at me. "She looks like she has a date."

"Thank you." I'd taken extra care to pick out a cute outfit just in case Logan would be there. The navy-blue romper brought out the blue in my eyes and I'd always loved stacking jewelry, so I wore a collection of colorful necklaces to brighten it up. "I'm going to trivia night."

"On a date?" Josh drawled, and Evan snorted with laughter.

"Boys," Ken scolded. Holding up the grill spatula, he added, "I will have to meet him first, if it is indeed a date."

Charlotte tsked but gave me a slight smile. My heart swelled a little to think that her family cared enough about me and my whereabouts to even make it a thing.

"It's *not* a date," I said. "It's a girls' night."

Charlotte wrinkled her brow. I suddenly felt guilty for not inviting her.

"You'll have to come next time," I told her.

She raised her eyebrows and turned back to her salad. I headed out feeling confused about the interaction.

On the one hand, I'd never dreamed Charlotte would agree to a trivia-night outing, but the real reason I hadn't invited her was because I was afraid. I wanted the night to be fun and easy. As much as we had gotten along when her family was around, I wasn't confident we could do that on our own. Her reaction made me feel guilty to think that I'd excluded her.

The small bar on the water was about a mile away, and once I'd arrived, I let out a pent-up breath, determined to enjoy the night. The bar was adorable, designed like the inside of a ship, with wooden floors and sailors' knots hung strategically across the walls. Each table was equipped with the wheel of a ship.

"If you want a drink, you turn it." Lauren tugged the pegs. "It calls the waitress somehow. Isn't that fun?"

"I love it," I said, giving it a hearty spin.

The women at the table laughed. They introduced themselves one by one as I settled in.

"I'm so glad you came," Lauren said, once the waitress came over and I placed an order for a vodka soda. It had been ages since I'd had a real drink, and it was the cheapest thing on the menu. "Everyone here is super competitive about our trivia."

"I love trivia," I said. "I'm not going to claim to be good at it, but I love it."

"I don't love trivia, but I love the prizes," said the woman who'd introduced herself as Maggie. She had tortoiseshell-framed glasses and a strikingly pretty face. "There's always a gift certificate to a fabulous coffee shop…"

Lauren fanned herself in exaggerated delight.

"One of the jewelry shops always puts up a piece," Maggie continued, "and of course, there's the week's worth of pizza."

"Week's worth?" I echoed. "Okay, I want to win that."

The women laughed. "It's actually a gift certificate to one of the local pizza places where the pies are the size of the planet Earth," Lauren said.

It would be nice to win a prize, but at the same time, the house I'd inherited might have put me over my luck quota for the year.

"How's the remodel going?" Lauren asked, as if reading my mind. "Logan told me it's beautiful up there."

"Yes!" The redheaded woman—Jessica, I think she'd said—put down a menu. "Tell us everything."

The waitress dropped off my drink and I took a quick sip before answering. The vodka was smooth and sharp, and the lime gave it a splash of summer.

"It's been interesting," I said. "It turns out my grandmother left a scavenger hunt for me and my sister. Not a scavenger hunt, exactly, but little things that we're going to find in the house as we go."

Maggie's mouth dropped open. "What a perfect idea. What did you find?"

"Family history, so far." I kept it vague. "I don't know whether to be excited or scared at what's coming next."

"If this was my family, I'd be scared." Jessica made a silly face. "I feel like there would be scandals. Like, endless scandals."

I laughed. "No scandals. Not so far."

Well, other than the fact that my sister and I had practically been separated at birth.

"How's everyone doing tonight?" a loud voice rang out over the speakers.

Everyone in the bar jumped to their feet, applauding and whistling. I looked around in confusion, then spotted an older man strolling to the front area of the bar, holding a mic. He had a deep tan, wore a button-up Hawaiian shirt, and sported a head full of silver hair.

"For those of you who don't know me, I'm Mickey Marlson and… this is trivia night!" his voice boomed.

The crowd cheered again. I imagined Mickey worked on a cruise ship or something before settling in for the summer.

Lauren grinned. "The older women in town line *up* to get his number."

"I'll bet," I said, laughing.

"I'm going to pass out the cards," Mickey said, "and we'll get started here in a minute."

Lauren took a deep drink. Then she stretched her arms up over her head before folding her hands in front of her chest in an exaggerated move reminiscent of a yoga pose.

"No cheating," she told her friends. "No peeking. It's fair and square."

"Of course." Maggie gave me a conspiring wink. "Lauren's very serious about her trivia."

Once everyone was set up, the bar went silent. Mickey stood in the center of the room like a preacher gearing up to start a very high-energy wedding.

"First question," he shouted, making me jump. "Category: Entertainment. What is the highest box-office grossing comedy of all time?"

Even though I loved attending trivia nights, the actual trivia part was not my specialty. There were days I couldn't remember why I went to the next room, let alone how many years cicadas stay underground. Still, I made my best guess at the best comedy and gave Lauren a high five.

"Next question: Which president was the youngest to ever take office?"

Lauren lit up. "That's an easy one."

"*Is* it?" I said, laughing. "Who knows this stuff?"

"Lauren," the women at the table chorused as she quickly jotted down an answer.

"Next up: What fruit contains the highest amount of vitamin C?"

The questions came hard and fast. They were a lot harder than I'd expected for a bar setting, but it seemed like there was a good bit of people getting them right. No one was trying to sneak and pull out their cell phone, either. It was nice to know that, if the world went offline, there would be a handful of people who could help me survive.

Finally, Mickey ended the round and had us score our cards. "If you don't achieve fifteen or higher, you're out until the next game."

I made a decent showing with an eleven. Maggie and Lauren each got eighteen and could progress to the next round, but Jessica and I were done.

"Let's head outside," Jessica said. "There's a nice area on the sand."

I followed her into the balmy night and she led us over to a small group of people. While she chatted with them, I looked around, enjoying the evening. The area was cozy, with hanging lights, wooden benches, and an area to play games like croquet and lawn darts next to the sand. Rock music played quietly over the speakers, the stars sparkled overhead, and I felt like a part of the town in a way I hadn't before.

Logan walked up, dressed in a pair of fitted jeans and a weathered T-shirt. He had day-old stubble on his face and was chewing a piece of mint gum. "Hi, Jayne," he said, giving me a charming smile. "Jessica, you got knocked out?"

She gave him a playful swat. "Please don't rub it in."

Everyone in the group seemed to know each other as they laughed and joked. Once there was a break in the group conversation, Logan turned to me.

"Look," he said, slowly chewing his gum in a way that brought my attention to his lips. "I've had a drink or two and I have to tell you something. That stunt you did with the coffee made me feel like a jerk for days."

I grinned. "We've moved past that, haven't we?"

He scratched his head, and a lock of dark hair fell over his eyes. "I'm just telling you that you left an impression."

"I try." I clinked my glass to his. "But the real impression was the fire safety award."

"The robe," he said, nodding. "That robe did leave quite an impression."

My mouth dropped open. "No, I meant *you* left an impression by giving me the..." He winked, and I realized he was joking. Nevertheless, my cheeks were warm from the comment. "There's another trivia game after this one. Are you going to do it?"

"Nah." He looked up at the stars. "It's too nice of a night. I also have to get up for work in the morning. The boss gets cranky if I don't show up on time."

"Crankier than you?" I teased.

"Well, considering I'm the boss..."

Our eyes met.

"Do you want to sit for a minute?" he asked.

"I thought you were leaving."

"I am," he said. "But we can sit."

We settled in on the bench and I dug my toes in the sand. "So, I'm curious about the shop," I admitted. "I thought that a blacksmith was for horseshoes and things like that."

Logan nodded. "It actually covers all types of metalwork. I do everything. Those metal-brushed tables in my sister's coffee shop were one of my favorite projects but my biggest moneymaker is wrought-iron gates. I ship them all over the country."

"Really?" I said, surprised. "How did you get into all of that?"

He squinted, considering the question. "It was by accident—or fate, I don't know. I didn't do well in school, so my mom tried to get me to work with my hands as much as possible. The hardware shop had a lot of classes on metalworking, so I was in there with these fifty- and sixty-year-old guys who were trying to learn a hobby and they all took a shine to me and pushed me to get good at it."

He paused as if surprised that he'd said so much.

"I love that," I said. "There are so many times that the older generation doesn't connect with the younger one. I actually..." It must have been the drink, because it wasn't something I usually confessed to people. "Whenever I'm having a bad day back home, I stop by the old folks' home that's in my neighborhood. The ladies there like to play cards and tell stories and I like to sit there and listen."

He gave an eager nod. "That's exactly it. I'd keep my mouth shut and listen to these older men talk to each other about what was going on. Gave me a different perspective than I would have had at that age. It was good for me because it's a small town and there was not a lot to do around here. Some of my friends fell into trouble because there's a lot of privilege and not many positive outlets for them to channel that into, but my parents kept me on a close leash. They got me into the metalwork. That was also also the summer that I got into firefighting."

"Yeah?" I said, sifting some sand through my fingers. "Why, what happened?"

"I was starting to look for trouble and, as a lesson, my father made me choose between volunteering my time at the animal shelter or the fire department. I started at the animal shelter but…" He lifted his hands. "I wasn't brave enough. It broke my heart to see the animals aching to have a home. Three days of that and I was washing fire trucks. It was ten times easier."

My heart swelled at the admission. "I hear that. I wouldn't be able to leave the shelter without bringing an animal home."

He started laughing. "My father had no choice but to welcome in this beagle that was fifteen, incontinent, and bayed every time I left the house. She was my first true love. I'll never forget her."

The idea that this handsome, dog-loving firefighter was chatting with me on the beach under the stars was starting to have an effect on me. No sooner had the thought crossed my mind than he said, "I should probably head out." He rubbed his hands against the dark stubble on his cheeks. "I have a project that I've been thinking about and I need to get started."

"What kind of project?" I asked, lulled by the sound of the waves crashing to the shore nearby. The moon was out, and I felt like I could sit here all night.

"A sculpture." Logan rested his hands on his knees. "I can almost see it and I can't stop thinking about it, which means I need to get to work."

"You do the sculptures in the shop, too?" I said, surprised.

For some reason, it hadn't occurred to me that he was the artist. Some of those sculptures had been brilliant. Knowing that he was the one behind them impressed me even more and it also made me feel foolish for not figuring it out in the first place.

"They're amazing," I said.

"Yeah?" He looked down at the sand, as if embarrassed. Then he smiled at me. "Thanks."

Something about his smile made me feel like we were the only two people on the beach. Hoots and hollers from inside interrupted the moment and Jessica came bounding over.

"Come on," Jessica said. "There's a new game. We're back."

Logan laughed and helped me to my feet. "Have fun."

We were eye to eye for a moment and he gave me a half smile.

"Good talking to you," he said, and headed up the path along the side of the bar that led to the parking lot out front.

I followed Jessica back into the bar, taking one last look up at the glittering night sky. That conversation with Logan had been unexpected, and so was the way I'd felt when he smiled at me.

I hadn't expected that at all.

The next round of trivia had started by the time Jessica and I sat back down at the table.

"Hey, I need to tell you something." Lauren looped her arm around my shoulder as I settled in. She passed me a new trivia card and I smiled to see she'd answered the first two questions for me. "My brother is a good guy."

My cheeks went hot. I wondered how she knew I'd been talking to him. It was such a small town. Someone had probably reported back to her.

"Yeah, he's nice," I said.

"No." Lauren took my hand and squeezed it tight. "I'm telling you. He's an incredible person and his ex-wife totally did a number on him. It wasn't fair."

"Next question." Mickey flashed his bleached smile. "How many miles is the moon from the Earth?"

"That's not even a challenge," Maggie shouted. "Is this amateur hour?"

Everyone laughed, including Mickey. Our group chewed on the tips of their pencils, each of us working our way through the options.

Turning back to me, Lauren said, "So, I know he was rude to you that one day in the coffee shop."

Logan again.

"It was one moment." I doodled a smiley face on my answer sheet. "He was having a bad day. We're all entitled to a bad day or two, right?"

"Yes." Lauren took a French fry from the appetizer platter someone had ordered and dipped it into some barbecue sauce. "I'm glad you think that way. I'm just protective, you know? I don't want people to think badly of him. He's already gone through so much. His ex-wife moved across the country when they split and she takes the girls each summer. He has two."

The picture of Logan was becoming even more complex. The firefighter sculptor with two daughters. I wouldn't have guessed that about him, but for some reason it made perfect sense.

Lauren pushed her hair out of her face. "They leave next week and I already miss them, so I can only imagine how he feels. I don't understand how someone could do that with kids. Keep them away from one parent for so long. I mean, their mother chose to move across the country. How could you even do that?"

I swallowed hard. "It's awful."

"It's going to affect those girls for the rest of their lives." Lauren frowned. "I'll never understand it, but I'm going to do my best to forgive her. For their sake, you know?"

"I do." I blinked against the sudden sting in my eyes. "Believe it or not, I really do."

# CHAPTER FOURTEEN

The outing to the bar left me feeling emotional, and when I got back home, I wasn't quite ready to call it a night. The shore was bathed in moonlight. It might not have been the safest choice to go down to the beach by myself at night, but I needed to feel the power of the ocean, to understand that there were things bigger than my heartache.

Pulling on a sweatshirt, I turned the flashlight in my cell phone on and made my way down the rickety steps. The waves were loud in the dark and I stood in silence, feeling the cool breeze on my cheeks. I slid my shoes off, hoping there wouldn't be too many creatures crawling in the sand.

I walked along the water's edge, far enough away to prevent a wave from pulling me in, but close enough to feel the occasional brush of foam against my feet. Eventually, I sank into the sand and looked up at the sky. The stars were out, their bright lights shining through the dark.

My mind shifted to the moment Logan had sat down next to me. He was so much more complicated than I'd given him credit for, and Lauren had made a point of letting me know that. She must have noticed I couldn't stop looking at him, which was embarrassing. I was attracted to him, no question, but considering the fact that I'd walked away from something perfectly good with Daniel, I didn't fully trust myself. Besides, I would only be in town for six months. There was no point in starting something new.

Charlotte jumped to mind.

I wanted to build a relationship with her, but even that scared me. Yes, we were family, but that hadn't made a bit of difference up to this point in our lives. What if we worked through everything and became close, only to have our relationship fall apart? It wasn't like we'd have the opportunity to see one another after this unless we made a point to spend time together.

Time was such a tricky thing, though. Charlotte had been on my mind my entire life, so in some ways she'd always been with me. Not the real-time version of her but the memory of the younger sister who had copied my words, actions, and games. The time that we'd spent together had carried so much more weight than so many other moments in my life that maybe it didn't come down to the actual number of days we'd been together. It had come down to the amount of heart that had filled the time.

I stretched back in the sand. For a split second, my eyes got heavy. It was tempting to doze off right there on the beach. Reluctantly, I got to my feet.

A few yards into my long walk home, I picked up the sickly-sweet smell of marijuana. There was probably a group of teenagers somewhere on the beach. It made me think of the issues Evan had brought to me about Josh. It wasn't my place to say anything, but I wondered if Charlotte had any idea what was going on with her sons.

I headed back to the path that led up to the house and, once I got to the top, I stopped to look up at the moon. It was covered in clouds that floated over the stars, making the night silver in its faded light. I sat in a chaise longue to catch my breath, wondering if everyone else in the house was asleep.

The thought had no sooner crossed my mind than I heard footsteps coming up the stairs, along with the rustle of the brush. Was it one of the boys? I'd heard Charlotte discussing a curfew with them, so they weren't allowed out after ten.

It wasn't like I would tell Ken or Charlotte that they were out late, but I didn't want to be in the position of keeping secrets. I decided to try to make it inside before whoever it was spotted me, but stopped dead as the thick scent of marijuana wafted across the breeze. The back door creaked open.

The dim light from the dining room illuminated a small figure as she wandered into the house. I had to blink at least three times to bring my mind to accept what I had seen. It wasn't the boys at all—it was Charlotte.

My uptight, perfect sister. The realization made me want to scream and burst out laughing all at once. Where was that side to her when she was around me?

I couldn't believe that she would take that risk. Where did she even buy it from? She must have traveled here with it in her fancy Range Rover, tucked away in her expensive suitcase.

It hit me that Charlotte might be more receptive to me if she was high. It might not be a bad idea to talk to her right now, while I had the chance. Quickly, I got to my feet, the questions I'd hoped to ask her pounding in my head.

The light in the kitchen was turned on and I walked in. Sure enough, there she was, pouring a bag of tortilla chips into a baking pan.

I hid a smile. "What are you doing?"

Charlotte looked at me as if confused. Then she considered her hands, which were poised to distribute shredded cheese over the chips.

"Nachos. What about you?" She set down the cheese and fumbled through the cupboard. There, she found a jar of jalapeños and held it up. "Necessary."

Popping the lid like the cork of a champagne bottle, she scooped a few of the peppers in the pan, followed by the cheese. She slid it into the oven and stared at it for a moment.

"Are you going to turn the oven on?" I asked when she didn't move.

Charlotte turned to me, her eyes wide. "I don't know how." I started to laugh and she looked surprised for a minute, then started laughing, too. We both giggled, and gently I stepped in front of her.

"Let me do this." I hit broil. "Or you might burn the house down."

"You mean the rest of it?" she said.

We both looked at each other and burst out laughing again. This time, we laughed so hard that tears came to our eyes.

"Shh," I said, still laughing. "We have to be quiet or we'll wake your family."

I peered through the oven door. We waited, giggling all the while, until the oven started to smell like smoke and I hurriedly turned it off.

Charlotte opened the door, oven mitt in hand. The cheese had melted and the nachos were only slightly charred. "Want some?" Without waiting, she used a spatula to scoop a serving onto two plates and handed one to me. It smelled delicious but I could only eat a third of what she'd given me, so I put some back in the pan when she wasn't looking.

"This looks great," I said. "Let's sit outside."

Charlotte frowned and for a split second, I was afraid she'd say no. Then she nodded. "Okay."

I grabbed two glasses of water for us and we settled in at the table on the back porch. The frogs were loud in the nearby trees, singing into the night. I bit into a cheesy chip. They were spicier than I was used to and I chugged some water.

Charlotte put her hand out for a fist bump. "My husband can't eat them like this."

"Must be in our blood," I said.

The words hung in the air. "Yeah." Looking back down at her plate, Charlotte suddenly seemed very young. I felt the strangest urge to wrap my arms around her and hold her tight. "If you would have told me even two weeks ago that I'd be sitting here with you…"

I set down the chip that I was about to eat. "What would you have said?"

Charlotte shrugged her thin shoulders. "Did you know that you left a dress hanging in the closet back then? When you left?" She plucked a jalapeño off of her plate and ate it. "I wore that thing so much. For two years straight."

My breath caught. "Which dress?"

"Blue and white stripes. Pink bow on the back. Mom used to think you looked so pretty in it. Maybe I hoped she would see me and think, *Oh, I should take her with me, too.*"

My breath caught. "Charlotte, I—"

"Don't." She ate a nacho. "My kids are everything to me. Did you know that?" She gave a firm nod. "Everything. I think about that a lot, though. That dress. I don't know what happened to it. There was a point that I just stopped wearing it."

My appetite was gone. There were so many directions this conversation could go and I didn't know if I should be the one to lead it. But I had some things to say, and right now, I could.

"You know, it wasn't like Mom was always there with me. There were so many times I felt like I didn't have anyone at all. Mom was busy with Daideo like, all of the time." The surprise on Charlotte's face made me keep talking, even though it wasn't something I liked to remember. "Once he started to get really sick, she was always busy."

Charlotte sipped at her water. She seemed to be struggling with my words, but I kept going.

"When Daideo died, I thought, okay, this will be my time with her. But then she had to get Daideo's house cleaned out and sold, and she started seeing Rory—he'd been one of the nurses at the care facility. Apparently, their relationship started months before

Daideo passed away. I thought we'd move back, but instead, she married him and we stayed in Ireland. I don't know how you pictured my life, but she wasn't there like you think she was, Charlotte. I wished you had been, though."

The words caught in my throat. The years in Ireland remained in my memory as a happy time because I had so many friends and the freedom to play with them whenever I wanted. Even so, I had longed to spend more time with my mother and I had never stopped missing my sister.

Charlotte took a bite of chips. "Dad told me she was like that."

"Like what?" I asked.

"Selfish."

The word made me wince. My mother wasn't selfish; she'd been busy. It would have been impossible for her to care for Daideo and be with me at the same time. She'd done her best.

"That's not true," I said. "She devoted herself to caring for her dad. There's nothing selfish about that."

Charlotte shook her head. "Yes, there is. She should have left you with us. Why did she take you there if you never got to see her?"

"It wasn't like I never got to see her," I insisted. "I'm only saying that it wasn't like she was braiding my hair every second and pushing me on swings at the park."

The idea that my mother should have made a different choice didn't seem fair, given how hard she'd worked to keep Daideo happy and how often she'd cried about Charlotte.

"Daideo might have been the selfish one," I admitted. "He could have come back with us to the States, but he refused. He made her stay there."

Charlotte looked at me with wide eyes. "Her father didn't make her do anything. She made the choice to be there with him. She was a *mother*. She shouldn't have separated us to do that."

I stared down at my hands. "You're right. It wasn't—"

"She could have visited him," Charlotte said. "She didn't have to be his caretaker!"

"Flying to Ireland would have been expensive. She only could have done it once or twice. She'd already spent so much of her life away from him, living in the States, and she hadn't been there when her mother died. Once she realized he was terminal and, given the timing of the divorce, I think—"

"Stop making excuses for her." Charlotte pushed away her nachos. "It was selfish to abandon her kids. Period."

"Dad wouldn't let her take us both," I said. "What, she was supposed to choose between her kids and her father?"

Charlotte glared at me. "She did choose between her kids."

Flipping her hair, she looked out over the darkness of the water. It loomed beyond us, the waves reshaping the shore in a never-ending rhythm.

"I'm going to bed," she said, pushing back her chair.

"Charlotte, wait." I struggled to find a way to bring the conversation to a place where we could connect. "Please stay. It's such a nice night."

Charlotte's buzz must have faded because she looked tired. For once, her posture wasn't pert and perfect. "Jayne." Her voice was quiet, and a little scared. "You have to understand that it's incredibly hard for me to talk about all of this. Give me time."

I thought of the angry marks in the book our grandmother had left for us to find and I knew better than to push it. We had months to go; it could wait.

I gathered our plates and pinched the water glasses together. Back inside, she crossed the living room and headed for the stairs while I headed for the kitchen. Even though we hadn't lived there long, it still surprised me to see that the wall was down. The house had changed.

"Charlotte," I called, turning to her.

She was halfway up the stairs. Her silhouette turned to look at me through the dim light.

"Thank you," I said. "For talking to me tonight."

For a minute she looked uncertain. Then she nodded and headed back up the stairs. My heart ached because our conversation had not brought us closer. If anything, it had merely emphasized how far apart we were.

# CHAPTER FIFTEEN

The next morning, I half expected some sort of look or acknowledgment from Charlotte that we'd talked late into the night, but she just nodded at me when I walked past the living room and waved at her out on the porch. Ken and the boys weren't up yet, either, so I ate breakfast alone before heading back to my room to shower.

I realized that it was a luxury to shower in my own room, since the bathrooms were fourth on our list of repairs. Once we had to start ripping out fixtures, we'd have to share the bathroom in the main hallway. Five people sharing one bathroom sounded like a recipe for disaster, and I resolved to take an extra-long shower while I still could.

My phone started ringing as I was getting out and I ignored it. Ten minutes later, I'd finished drying my hair to hear it ringing once again. Rushing back into the room, I grabbed for it. "Hello?" I demanded.

"This is Wayside Credit Delinquency. You are on a recorded line." The line clicked as if to emphasize that point before the woman on the other end continued. "We have attempted to contact you several times and at this point, we have no choice but to move forward with filing a judgment to remove funds directly from your bank account."

Quickly, I rushed to the bedroom door and shut it. I felt lightheaded. "You can't do that. I'd like to set up a payment plan and—"

"You've ignored our repeated notifications." The woman sounded firm, like she'd heard it all before. "We will request the full amount of your delinquent payments to be withdrawn as soon as the funds are available. Do you have any questions?"

"Yes. I—" I stared at myself in the old-fashioned mirror over the dresser. It had been so easy to get lost in remodeling the house and the freedom of not struggling for every dime that I'd managed to push my debts out of my mind. "Would it be possible to do that without a judgment? I would be willing to set up direct payments from my bank account."

That meant that the creditors would take my stipend the moment I deposited it. There was the option of cashing it instead, but most places charged a percentage for that. I couldn't afford to lose money for being broke and, besides, it wasn't like ignoring the problem had made it go away.

"Funds must be deposited by the first of the month to meet the minimum payment." The woman read off the numbers. It was the majority of my stipend and I winced. "Yes," I told her. "I can do that."

The woman's tone changed. "In that case I will need an authorization to the bank by the end of the day. If you are unable to complete it, we'll have no choice but to move forward with an injunction."

Feeling defeated, I gave her my current information. The creditor ended the call and I sank down on the bed, considering the room with its cheerful yellow wallpaper.

There was no need to panic. This was a challenge, but I had so much to be grateful for. I had a place to live and money that could be removed from my bank account. However, I wouldn't have enough to buy food or my medication without getting a job.

I would have to wait tables. This was a resort town, so there should be plenty of opportunity to get a job where the tips would be quick and, hopefully, generous. And if there was anyone in town who would be able to point me in the right direction, it would be Lauren.

Lauren was hard at work when I walked into the coffee shop later that morning. As soon as the line died down, she slipped out to join me. "Trivia was so much fun. You have skills."

I laughed, thinking of my inability to get more than a few questions right on each sheet. "The skill to know that I have no business doing trivia?"

"How's it going up at the castle?" she asked.

"We've been working hard. I can see some progress, which is good." I paused. "So... I wanted to talk to you about something and it's a little embarrassing."

Concern crossed her face. "What's going on?"

"The terms of the will require Charlotte and me to be here for six months. My grandmother left us money to survive each month but, to be perfectly frank, I can't make ends meet without getting a job." The shop was crowded and I kept my voice low. "Can you recommend a place where I could wait tables, bartend, or cocktail?"

"It would be hard to find something at this point in the season. Most places hire in April." She drummed her fingers on the brushed-metal table, thinking. Her face brightened. "Wait! My friend owns a restaurant on the water. One of his summer girls just decided to go back home to her boyfriend and left him in the lurch. How much experience do you have? Because this place is super busy."

"I've waited tables on and off since college. High volume, and I know the computer systems."

She nodded. "Perfect. Let me call him."

Lauren picked up her phone, and I stepped out to give her some privacy. The sun was shining as the tourists strolled, enjoying their day. It was such a cute street, with high-end olive oil shops, homemade bread shops, antique shops, and art galleries. I could see why so many of the locals had stuck around and opted to build a life here.

"Great news," Lauren called, and I headed back in. "He needs someone to start, like, tonight. Could you do that?"

Relief cut through me. "Absolutely. I can't even tell you how much I appreciate it."

"Of course." She beamed. "I'm texting you the address right now. He wants you to come by to train or, at the very least, grab a copy of the menu so you're not walking in helpless. He's going to throw you into the fire, but it's a nice place, so there's great money potential."

"Thank you," I said again. "You have no idea how much this helps me. If I can do anything to repay you…"

"Invite me to your house soon," she said. "I want to see it."

It would be fun to show Lauren the house. It also felt completely strange to think that she'd said "your house." It didn't feel like mine yet, not at all, but maybe time would change that.


That night, I tried to be grateful as I reported for my first shift at Plankton. I had to admit, it was tough. I'd worked at several restaurants in my life, starting back when I was in college and up until I'd started my business. Walking right back into a waiting-tables job when I was in this beautiful resort town reminded me how badly I'd failed at my effort to succeed in the real world.

So much had been going on with the house and Charlotte that I'd managed to push the topic out of my mind. Now, however, I couldn't help but think what a mess I'd made of things. I never should have failed. There had been a market for the children's art studio and plenty of opportunity. There were so many people who had been willing to answer questions and help me out, but I'd been determined to do it on my own, which had been a mistake.

Now, I looked around at the restaurant, grateful that I'd been brave enough to talk to Lauren, because this was not a job I would have gotten on my own. The restaurant was hopelessly hip, right on the water, with a big patio and ample foliage lining its iron gate. Based on the menu and what the manager had told me during training, there was potential to make good money every night.

The waitstaff were all gathered at the bar in the back for the nightly meeting and I went over to join them. The thing that struck me was that they were all young college kids. Feeling my cheeks get hot, I pasted on a smile and walked up to join the group.

"Hey, I'm Jayne," I said, giving a half wave.

There was a chorus of hellos. Rob, the night manager, launched into a speech about specials and new wines. Then he said, "Everyone, work with Jayne tonight to help her out. We're a team."

Rob handed me a black apron after the meeting. "Do you think you can handle getting right on the floor?"

My mouth was dry, but I said, "Yes. The menu is pretty self-explanatory and I've used the same computer system you have, so it should be great."

"Excellent." The chef was beckoning from the back so Rob gave me a friendly nod. "If anything goes wrong, give the table a free dessert. Good luck."

It all seemed like smooth sailing until the doors opened. The moment the clock switched to five, every single table in the restaurant was full. It was as if I'd blinked and every vacationing family in Woodsong Harbor took a seat in my section.

I was not prepared to take on four tables at the exact same time with no experience with the menu, but I reminded myself of those calls from my creditors, put my head down, and got to work.

Somehow, I was successful getting everyone drinks, appetizers, and bottles of water. I only messed up one order, switching the baked grouper with the baked sea bass, which set back one family's dinner by thirty minutes.

"It's fine." The mother gestured at her kids. "They're happy, so we're happy."

Her children were coloring away on the paper menus.

"Can I bring them complimentary cookies after your meal?" I said quietly, so the kids wouldn't overhear.

The mother nodded. "They'll be thrilled."

It was such a fast pace that I remembered about fifteen minutes too late that someone had asked me for a fork, and I'd jostled a tray and nearly spilled a martini on someone's head. Other than that, I did surprisingly well for my first night, and walked out with a pocketful of tips.

I sat in my car and counted the cash at least three times, startled at my good fortune. The money was excellent, and it would make it possible for me to start putting a dent in my debts. For the first time in ages, I fell asleep the second my head hit the pillow.

# CHAPTER SIXTEEN

The mold and mildew had been an issue that Charlotte and I had wanted to attack since the first day. We were finally at that point on the list, and I woke up feeling excited that we could finally eliminate that musty smell from the house.

The home inspector had said in his report that it hadn't gone farther than the drywall in the ceiling and walls. The fact that we could handle the problem on our own would save us major time and money, since we only needed to cut out the drywall and replace it. The hardware store had recommended wearing masks to protect ourselves from the mold spores. We also put on the hard hats Ken had borrowed to protect our heads, me in yellow and Charlotte in red.

"We really need to take more selfies with these things on," I said, catching sight of myself in the mirror.

Charlotte ignored the suggestion, opting instead to thumb through the book-sized report from the home inspector. "They used moisture-resistant greenboard in this bathroom—that's why the mold didn't get very far. So even though we had some wood in the roof that needed to be torn out and rebuilt, we're in a good spot."

I nodded, feeling awkward standing in the bathroom with her in my big hat. Her family had been around nearly every day since our talk on the porch and I'd been busy with work, so we hadn't had a chance to discuss anything since. Today, they were on a deep-sea fishing excursion with a friend of Ken's who lived in the area, so it was only me and Charlotte. I found myself unsure what to say to her.

"Let's watch the video," Charlotte said, pulling out her iPad.

Once the video was finished, I said, "I have to be done by four today. Is three hours enough time to do this?"

"It'll take as long as it's going to take."

I hadn't told Charlotte that I'd taken a job, because it hadn't come up. Now, I cleared my throat. "I'll need to head out then. I have a job waiting tables at a restaurant on the water. I needed something to do and a way to meet people."

Charlotte wrinkled her brow. "We're here to work on the house."

"I typically won't be in until six," I said. "I had to cover for someone today. Look, I work around you in the mornings, so you'll have to work around me."

She regarded me with a cool stare. "Then you should have gotten something in the mornings."

"That would make sense, but this is what was available," I said. "Sorry. I'm not good at just hanging around."

I didn't want her to know the real reason I had to get a job, because she would never understand. Besides, we had a thousand other things to discuss that were more important than my financial status.

"Let's get started," I said.

"Sure." Charlotte shook her head and climbed up the stepladder. "Now, I'm going to need you to hand me—" Her phone rang. "Hold on. It might be the boys." She pulled her phone out of her back pocket, bracing herself against the wall with her hand. "Dad! How are you?"

I drew back, and she said, "Hey, let me call you later, okay?"

Charlotte hung up and we looked at each other in silence. "He would have wanted to talk to you if he knew you were in the room. I'd like to call him back so that you—"

"No," I said quickly. "Thank you for not putting me in that position."

Charlotte climbed back down the ladder and sat on the lid of the toilet. Removing the hard hat, she regarded me with her cool gaze. "It makes me frustrated to hear you say that, because Dad is a good man, Jayne. It would mean so much to him if you'd give him a chance."

The bathroom felt stuffy and I opened the window. "How is he?" I took a drink from my water bottle, wincing at its sudden chill.

"He'd love to talk to you."

"It's kind of pointless," I said.

"He's your father," she said quietly.

I wanted to remind her that she was my sister and she had refused to talk to me for years. That she wouldn't be talking to me now if our grandmother hadn't set this up. Instead, I said, "True, but he's not a part of my life. He sends me birthday cards and we talk a couple times a year, but it's all... disappointing. I don't feel like I know him, or that I ever will. I know he lives down the street from you, but for me, he may as well still live on the other side of the country."

Charlotte fiddled with the strap on her hat. "What would you think about having him come to visit?"

"Here?" My heart started pounding. "No. I don't want that."

There were enough ghosts in this house already. We didn't need to add my father to the mix. Even though our relationship had been polite but distant, I still harbored a lot of resentment towards him.

For one, he was the one who'd had the affair that had ended my parents' marriage. He went along with the plan of separating me from my sister and did nothing to stand up to my mother when I told him that I wanted to come back to live with him and Charlotte. He could have stepped in at any point when

Charlotte refused to get on the phone with me, but he'd allowed her to cut me off.

Daideo had filled the need for a father figure in my life, and once I was older, my stepfather, Rory, had done the same. I didn't need to spend time getting to know someone who hadn't been there and, truthfully, had only made my life harder.

"He's a good man," Charlotte said.

"That might be true, but he didn't support Mom when she was stuck in Ireland to care for her father. He could have worked harder to bring the two of us together, and instead he kept us apart. Not to mention the fact that I never had a real father."

There were times I had wanted that connection so badly. Like when the girls in my fifth-grade class all went to the father/daughter dance or the career days at school where the dads were encouraged to talk about their jobs. I'd wondered in those moments what it would be like to have my father come to school and if he had done all of that for Charlotte.

Based on our conversations, I knew Charlotte had dealt with the same issues regarding our mother, and it wasn't like my father had chosen to leave me behind. But at the same time, he hadn't done anything to stop the situation. He had broken up our family to begin with and that had led to all of this.

"Jayne." Charlotte seemed to be weighing her words. "Dad had a very good job with a high level of responsibility. It wasn't like he could pick up and go to Ireland whenever he wanted. It wasn't his fault."

"He had a family." I took off the hard hat and smoothed my hair in the mirror. Charlotte watched, her look intent. "He decided to throw it all away by having an affair that destroyed their marriage. If that hadn't happened and they had stayed together—if he had loved our mother—he would have supported her in caring for Daideo."

If my parents' marriage hadn't fallen apart, my father could have tried to step in and convince Daideo to migrate to the United

States, so that we could all be together. My mother hadn't been able to do that because she'd been too close to the situation, but an outside push could have changed things, especially with Daideo being so rigid about upholding the sacred bonds of marriage.

None of that had happened.

Instead, I had always been cordial with my father, exchanging birthday and Christmas cards and enduring the occasional, painful "happy birthday" call, but that's where it ended. I hadn't seen him since he came to my college graduation. He'd made attempts here and there to get together, but given the fact that Charlotte had refused to be a part of my life, it was hard to get past the fact that I held him to blame for the choices he'd made and how they'd affected our family.

"I'm just not interested in dealing with the hurt and heartache that comes with that relationship," I told Charlotte.

She jutted out her chin. "How do you think he feels, being rejected by his oldest daughter?"

Exasperated, I said, "Probably about the same as Mom felt about being rejected by her youngest daughter. I didn't see you racing to be with her. You didn't even show up at her funeral."

I hadn't meant to bring it up, but Charlotte had put me on the defensive. Here she was, trying to convince me to have a beach vacation with our father, when she'd never made a single attempt to get to know our mother or, at the very least, honor her memory.

Charlotte's face went pale. "It was in *Ireland*. Besides, the woman left me behind because she thought I would need her too much. Well, guess what? I was a kid. If she didn't want me to need my mother, she shouldn't have had kids."

The words hurt because I knew how much my mother had wanted her to be a part of our lives. I wished Charlotte could understand that.

"She didn't have a choice," I said. "There was no way Dad was going to let her take both of us—"

"So, she chose you—"

"Because I was older," I insisted. "That was the only reason. You would have ended up in daycare practically seven days a week if she'd brought you instead of me, because Daideo took up her full focus there at the end. You would have been in a strange country with people you didn't know, missing your home and your family and…" My throat went tight, and I took another drink of water. "It wasn't easy on anyone."

Outside the window a bird chirped and I looked outside, breaking our tense eye contact.

"You know," I said. "We could spend the rest of our time together fighting about who hurt who the most, or we can make an effort to let it go. Personally, I think it would serve us better to let it go."

Charlotte let out a forced laugh. "Our history isn't like brushing off the fact that someone cut me off in traffic. Sorry, but it goes a little deeper than that for me. It does for you, too."

"That's true," I said. "It does."

The thing that went the deepest for me was the idea that Charlotte had cut me out of her life. We could talk about our parents all day and dance around the issues between us, but Charlotte had cut me out of her life for over twenty-five years. The fact had simmered beneath the surface from the moment we'd moved into this house and, even in the rare times we'd connected, I knew we could only go so deep because that truth was always lurking down below like a poison that could destroy both of us. Yes, I understood that she was angry about the way things had happened, but I was angry, too. It wasn't like bringing our father here was going to change that.

"We need to get started." I pulled on my hat. "There's a lot to talk about, Charlotte, but I don't think this is the time or the place."

Charlotte tugged on her own hard hat and climbed up the ladder. Face cold, she said, "Of course. Let's get to work."

*

I had been waiting tables at Plankton for a week when Logan walked in. It was about thirty minutes before the restaurant was due to close and the host seated him in my section. Right away, I started to worry that I'd do something embarrassing, like spill water on him.

"Hi." I put on my friendliest smile. "What can I get you to drink?"

It was good to see him simply because he was a familiar face. He looked sun-kissed, like he'd spent the day out on the water, but he also seemed troubled.

"Hey, Lauren told me you might be here." He smiled, but there was sadness in his eyes. "Did she tell you this is my spot? Best food in town."

"No, but I'd agree with you."

One of the perks of waiting tables was that the workers received a free meal each night. I took mine home with me to save for lunch, since I had to eat before I came to work. My favorite so far had been the salmon salad with jicama, pomegranate, and oranges. I could have eaten that for days.

"What can I get you?" I asked.

"The dover sole with the lemon orzo."

"That's one of my favorites," I said, and he smiled. "See you soon."

I wanted to stay and chat, but four of my tables were about to order dessert. It would be a crunch to do all the coffees, desserts, and checks at once. Logan's fish came out when I was in the back making cappuccino, so another waiter served it to him and, since he was only drinking sparkling water, the busboys kept his glass full. Finally, once the restaurant had closed and he was my only table left, I had time to talk to him.

"So, what's going on tonight?" I rested my hand on the back of the chair he wasn't sitting in. "You seem kind of subdued."

"Meaning?" He regarded me with his dark eyes.

"You don't have your typical spunk."

He sighed, rubbing his hand over the stubble on his cheeks. "It's been one of those days. My wife has custody of my two daughters for the summer, and today is my youngest's birthday. The house is too empty with them gone. It makes everything feel… pointless. You know?"

My heart went out to him. Lauren had told me at the bar that night that her nieces were six and eight, both girls. It must have been awful to say goodbye to them, and I felt for him about the birthday.

My mother had made a cake each year, this elaborate chocolate marshmallow layer cake with pink sprinkles on top. I never thought to wonder about it. Eventually, I figured out that it was in honor of Charlotte's birthday and then I couldn't bring myself to eat it.

"I'm so sorry," I said quietly. "My sister and I were raised separately. It's always hard when your family isn't what you hoped it would be."

I typically didn't share my history with people, but I felt safe telling him.

"You guys were separated?" His face darkened. "That's awful."

"Yeah." I looked down at my hands, thinking of all that had been left unsaid. "I don't have kids, but I know a bit about what you're going through. It's not easy."

"It's not." He fiddled with the check folder. "I would move to be closer to them, but it wouldn't matter. My wife gets them for the summer and she would hold tight to that. I get them for the school year. Her job is more demanding and she travels all year so she can be available during the summers, so I guess I got the longer straw, but I have the hardest time letting go. This is my second round with this, the second year." He shook his head. "Every day, I wish we would have worked out our problems instead of letting things fall apart, because I just want to be with my kids."

There had been so many times I'd wished my parents had made that choice. That we all could have moved to Ireland as a family to care for Daideo. Maybe a change of scenery could have helped my parents to be happier, or at least helped them to manage without putting us in the middle.

"I'm so sorry," I said. "It's hard, I know."

Then, because he looked like he might start crying right in the middle of the restaurant, I added, "Listen, I am not an expert on kids. But the thing that I always wanted was some sort of connection, a way to feel close to this family that I'd lost." I took a deep breath to steady my voice, careful not to get too emotional about it all. "It might help you to do something while they're away so that you can feel like you're somehow with them. You like to work with your hands, so maybe..." Inspiration struck. "Do the girls already have a playhouse? I watch a lot of those home shows, and it seems like some of the most outlandish playhouses in the world can be built without too much trouble if you know what you're doing. Rumor has it you know your way around a measuring tape and a wood cutter."

Logan ran his hand over his face. "The sunroom wall hasn't fallen apart yet?"

I laughed. "Your sister said you built your own house. I trusted her."

"Why does my sister feel compelled to tell everybody everything about me? Living in a small town, I tell you." He thought for a minute. "That's actually a great idea. I'm not sure I'd know how to pick something they'd like, though. I mean, I know it would have to be pink, but from there..." He held up his hands.

"You could work on it together," I suggested. "Video chat with them, show them as you go. It would be a way for you to stay connected while you're apart."

He nodded, starting to look cheerful again. "Yes, they'd love that."

"Do you want some suggestions?" I pulled a sheet off my order pad, set it on the table, and began to sketch. "I saw something like this on one of these shows and it caught my eye. I thought, if I were a little girl I would adore to have a place like this to play with my friends." My pen ran over the page in smooth clear strokes. "What do you think?" I said, sliding it over to him.

He stared at the drawing. "That's amazing." Slowly, he traced his thumb across the page, as if lost in thought. "I could actually do that. It would be a challenge, but I could do that." His eyes were bright when he looked back up at me. "Can I keep this?"

"Of course."

"This idea is extraordinary, really." He studied the paper. "The girls have been asking for a playhouse. They would be thrilled to come home to this." Turning his attention back to me, he said, "I didn't know you were an artist."

His admiration was so apparent that my cheeks went hot.

"Don't be fooled," I said. "I copied this house design from the show I saw. It is not my idea. It seems pretty cool, though. Plus, you'd be thinking about them the whole time you're building it. It would be a win for all of you."

The other servers had started the closing tasks, things like cleaning the coffee machine and rolling silverware for the following day.

"I should get back to work," I said.

"Here—" Logan handed me his credit card. "Thank you. Seriously."

I ran his bill and handed it back to him. He signed with a flourish and stood up, putting us at eye level like that night at the bar. We stood for a moment, looking at each other. Then he smiled.

"Have a good night," he said.

"You, too," I said, trying to maintain eye contact without blushing.

It wasn't easy. There was something about Logan that made me blush, and the more I talked to him, the harder it was to ignore it.

Even though I knew I wouldn't be in town long enough to justify getting involved, I couldn't help but look forward to seeing him again.

# CHAPTER SEVENTEEN

The next morning, the boys were hanging around and the house felt crowded. Charlotte came into the kitchen while I was cooking breakfast and the tension remained thick between us.

"We made good progress yesterday," Charlotte said, pouring herself a cup of coffee. She was dressed in workout clothes and smelled like a lilac body spray. "Can we move on to your bathroom later this afternoon?"

"Mom," Evan said. "Can I have toaster pastries?"

Charlotte nodded and pulled the box out of the freezer. Like she'd done it a thousand times before, she laid them out on a plate, defrosted them for a second in the microwave, and lined them up to toast.

"Yes, that's fine," I said.

I'd enjoyed pulling out the drywall yesterday and working to rebuild the water-damaged ceiling in the master bath. The work we'd done was still drying, so it was time to move on to my bedroom, where there had been similar damage on a much smaller scale. Part of it was up over the linen closet, though, so it was going to be harder to access.

"Did the ceiling collapse in the master bath?" Josh asked. "You guys tried to drywall, right?"

"It might have," Charlotte said, adding some protein powder to her coffee. "I haven't been in there. Have you, Jayne?"

I chuckled. "No." It was good that she was being somewhat sarcastic. It was much better than being cold and removed. "Your bathroom is after mine, Josh."

"Great," he said, his voice wry.

Josh swiped the frosting packets off the counter, along with the batch of pastries that popped up.

"Hey," Evan barked, but Josh had already run out with them to the back porch.

Charlotte ruffled Evan's hair. "It's not like you didn't know he was going to do that." She dropped his pastries into the toaster, and I got to work making a big pan of eggs.

"These are for whoever wants them," I said.

Ken rushed into the room in a waft of cologne. He was dressed up, wearing a button-up and pair of navy slacks instead of his signature golf gear. "Morning, all," he said, grabbing some coffee to go. "Evan, I'll be back at ten thirty. Be ready to bust a move out of here."

"They're going camping for a few days," Charlotte told me. "I figured it would be good to get them out while we work on the bathrooms."

"Camping?" I said. "That's fun."

"You like camping?" Ken sounded impressed. "Charlotte hates it."

"I don't hate camping," she said. "I dislike sleeping in places that do not have beds."

"Right there with you," I told her.

Evan rubbed his hands together. "I'd sleep in a tree if there were roasted marshmallows. It's going to be epic. I'm going to find a snake and put it in your sleeping bag," he told his father.

Ken laughed. "I'll probably deserve it after putting honey in your hair and leaving you out for the bears. See you at ten thirty," he said, and rushed out the door.

"Where's he going?" Evan asked, practically diving for the pastries as they popped up.

"Don't eat those yet or you'll burn your mouth," Charlotte warned. "He has a meeting with one of the real estate guys here in town."

"I have a meeting with the beach." Evan headed towards the door, but paused to look at me. "Will you bring the eggs out?"

"Sure," I said, putting some bread in the toaster.

He headed out to the porch. Josh was sitting on the back deck, playing a video game. Evan biffed him in the back of the head when he sat down and Charlotte shook her head.

Turning to her, I said, "Listen. Yesterday was a little heavy."

"Welcome to our lives," she said, sipping at her coffee.

"Thank you for trying to get me to talk to Dad." I turned off the burner and moved the pan before turning to her. "You're right, it's important."

The words were hard to say but, if anything, the conversation with Logan had me thinking in that direction. It was obvious how much he was hurting to be away from his daughters, and even though I was angry that my father had not done much to change our situation, I knew he cared.

"I'm not ready to spend time with him," I told her. "But I've been thinking about what you said, and one day, I'll get there. Okay?"

Charlotte looked surprised. "I'm glad to hear you say that."

I turned back to the eggs, spooned some onto my plate, and put the remainder in a serving pan. "Do you want to take these out to the boys?"

"Thank you." She gave a quick nod and headed out to the porch with the pan, plates, and silverware.

Now that the wall had been knocked down it was impossible to hide in the kitchen. Buttering my whole grain toast, I added it and some sliced oranges to my plate. Then I headed out to join Charlotte and her family.

The morning stretched in front of me. I needed something light and fun to do, so I texted Lauren on the off chance that she wasn't working.

*Hey, do you want to go for a quick hike?*

Response bubbles popped up:

*Hold on. Calling.*

My phone rang and eagerly I picked it up. "Hey, good morning. I figured you'd be working but thought I'd give it a try."

"I am working," Lauren said, sounding reluctant. "I'd love to get out of here today, but I can't. I'm calling, though, because Logan's here and he was literally trying to convince me to do the same thing. Why don't you guys go together? Here, hold on."

My mouth went dry as she passed the phone to her brother. "Jayne?"

"Hi." I leaned against the counter, fighting back nerves. "You're going hiking?"

"Trying. I put on a sun shirt and everything, but Lauren is letting responsibility get in the way of fun. Ouch!" I could practically picture her swatting him as he said it. "Do you want to go? No pressure. I know you called looking for her, not her annoying older brother."

I laughed. "Yes, I'd love to. Where do you want to meet?"

When we hung up, my heart was racing and it wasn't from the coffee. Spending the morning hiking with the hot firefighter had not been on my to-do list but now that it was, the day definitely seemed a lot brighter.

Logan and Shamrock were waiting by a bench at the edge of the forest trails when I arrived. This time, I'd ridden the bike that I'd purchased in the discount section at the bike shop, thanks to the extra money I'd made waiting tables. Logan lifted a hand in greeting and I rang the bell.

He was indeed wearing a sun shirt, a light green fabric that made his dark features stand out. Shamrock was on a leash but Logan let her go so that she could run up and greet me. Laughing to hide my nerves, I bent down and hugged the dog, pressing my face into her warm fur. She licked my arm.

"I've always wanted to have a dog," I said, smiling up at him. "I've lived in the city my whole life, in apartments, so it's never been practical."

Logan shrugged into a backpack that showcased his broad shoulders. "Where do you live now?"

"Raleigh," I said. "I went to school there and before that, I lived in Dublin."

"Ireland?" He raised his eyebrows. "Well, Shamrock approves of that."

Logan and I headed down the trail as if we'd done it a million times before. The birds were singing and the sun and shadows played chase along the forest floor. The patterns made me think of the wrought-iron gates Logan had been talking about.

"Does nature ever inspire you with your work?" I asked.

"Definitely." He reached up to grab a leaf off one of the dogwood trees. Handing it to me, he said, "Summer is the greatest sculptor."

I ran my fingers over the smooth silk of the leaf. "It's beautiful." Hesitating, I admitted, "I used to paint forest landscapes. I'd spend hours studying leaves, sticks, bark—you name it—trying to capture what it was that made the forest so mysterious. I never could figure it out."

"So, you are interested in art," he said. "I suspected as much, given your drawing of the house. Right?"

I liked the way he looked at me when he asked questions, as if he was genuinely interested in what I had to say.

"Yes," I said. "I did an exchange program in high school where I studied art in Italy. It was a pretty incredible experience.

My mother also made it her life's work to show me all the art museums in Europe."

Some of my favorite memories had been the times we'd take long weekends to explore our new corner of the world. She'd made a checklist of all of the different countries she wanted to see with me, and each year we managed to visit a handful of them by rail or a cheap flight. These trips were an opportunity for us to finally spend time alone together because Rory didn't come, as he wasn't that interested in art. By the time I'd left for college, I had so many stamps on my passport that it seemed like it could have been framed and displayed in any one of the museums we'd seen.

"She gave you a gift," he said.

I nodded. "I tried to do the same. When I moved to the United States for college, I got a job waiting tables and used every spare penny to surprise my mother with a trip so that we could see the museums in New York." The memory of her arms around me at the train station made the trees look brighter around me. "It was special."

"Do you still paint?" he asked.

"I mean… I'm going to paint my grandmother's house," I said, laughing.

A light breeze passed through, drawing my attention to the fact that Logan smelled like metal and musk. It made me more aware of his body than I wanted to be and I tried to focus on the forest.

"Look, I loved art," I said, "but I never quite managed to become a good artist. My passion shifted into teaching kids, and I opened an art studio in town for kids to create. My mother left me a good sum of money when she died, enough to make me overconfident.

"I thought it would be smart to take out a small business loan and use her money for emergencies. Of course, I didn't have a handle on so many different aspects of running a business, so I ended up relying on that reservoir more and more—until it had dried up. Then the competition came in. This sleek franchise opened up across town, and even though I was the shop-local option, the franchise had a better location. I kind of knew it was the end when…"

"What?" Logan prompted.

My cheeks burned at the memory. "I was friends on social media with several of the moms who came into my place. One of my favorite, most loyal families posted pics of their daughter's birthday party, and it was at the franchise shop. I 'liked' the pictures—even gave them a smiley face."

He winced.

"I know," I said, groaning. "Ten minutes later, she sent me this long message full of apologies and excuses, saying her daughter had been to a birthday there and refused to have her party anywhere else. It was awkward, I'd overstepped, and it was the moment I realized that things had stopped being fun."

Shamrock tugged at the leash, trying to smell a patch of ivy.

Logan was quiet for a moment. Then he said, "You know, I had no clue what I was doing when I opened the blacksmith shop. I made a lot of mistakes. Lauren helped me move the business in the right direction because she has a head for that. I don't. It must have been hard, to let that go."

"It was," I said. "I had this vision in my head of what it could be, and I kept thinking it would get there eventually. But before I knew it, my time was up." I took a drink from my water bottle and, after glancing at my watch, pulled out a protein bar. "I'm going to have a quick snack. Would you like a bar?"

He shrugged out of his backpack and rummaged around before holding up the same one. "Yes, but I have my own."

We exchanged a smile and sat down on one of the many wooden benches off the pathway. He pulled a portable bowl for Shamrock out of his backpack and filled it with water.

"How are you feeling about your daughters?" I asked.

He slid on his sunglasses. "Same."

"Sorry." I regretted bringing it up. "I imagine you're trying to forget about all that."

"It's okay," he said. "They're on my mind every second, so there's no forgetting about it. I miss them. It's such a long period of time when you only get a certain amount of time with someone anyway, do you know what I mean?"

I nodded, thinking of Charlotte. "I barely saw my sister growing up, and now I only have six months with her. I'd give anything to have a relationship, but she's not interested."

"How do you know?" he asked.

"That's the vibe I'm getting from her. We can only get so far with things, when we talk."

"Did you consider that she might be scared?"

The idea surprised me. "I doubt that."

"I don't know much about your situation," Logan said, his voice gentle. "But you're the one who told me that you never know what someone's going through. I can't imagine it was easy for either one of you to deal with a trauma like that. People handle things differently."

The words hurt, because they made me feel hope. I didn't want to feel that, unless there was a reason.

"I keep wishing I could go back to who we were when we were little," I admitted. "There wasn't this history between us, this wall that keeps us apart."

"On the inside, we're the same people we've always been," Logan said. "Our baggage just makes us look bigger. It might be easier to talk to her if you try and see her as she was back then. It might be easier to accept that she's scared, too."

I considered his words.

"Thanks," I said quietly. "It's a different way to look at things. Did you decide whether or not to do the playhouse?"

He nodded. "Yes. I planned to surprise them at first, then I decided it would be more fun to get their input, like you'd suggested. So, I texted them a picture of your design and asked them to add to it. They printed it out and with the assistance of markers and glitter, they have reshaped your vision into one of their own." He pulled up a picture on his phone and showed it to me. Sure enough, my drawing had been turned into something reminiscent of a pink palace with several turrets and a moat. There was also a sticker up in the one of the turrets and I leaned in to squint at it.

"Is that a princess or a fairy?" I asked.

"Fairy." He gave me a perplexed look. "Right? It has wings."

I laughed. "You're a good dad," I said, and he gave me a grateful look.

"Thanks," he said.

Our eyes met. Quickly, I took a drink of water.

"What are you going to do about the moat?" I asked.

He considered the drawing. "Flood my backyard?"

"Try hard plastic," I suggested. "White on the bottom and cover it with a transparent blue. Build a cute little white—sorry, pink—bridge over the top?"

"That's great." He ran his hand through his hair. "You are quickly earning the title of assistant architect."

Shamrock rested her face on her paws and let out a huff.

"Poor thing," I said. "It's hot."

Logan grinned. "Clearly, you haven't run into a burning building weighted down with fifty pounds of fire gear."

It was something I'd never considered.

"The coat's heavy," he explained. "It's not something that you think about but, man, when I first started I had to run with weights because I got tired out too easily in the gear. Now, it's no big deal."

"When did you make the switch from washing fire trucks to riding in them?" I asked, thinking about the story he'd told me that night at the bar.

"Adventure seeking, I think." He draped his arms over the back of the bench, and his hand accidentally grazed against my shoulder, sending a jolt of electricity through my body. "Civic duty, wanting to contribute to my town. Lots of reasons."

"Well, good," I managed to say. "That's admirable."

His eyes met mine once again. "Thanks."

The sudden chatter of a squirrel crashed through the silence. It jumped from branch to branch, chased by another squirrel. We both watched it, then turned back to one another.

"How long are you in town?" Logan asked.

"We'll be done with the remodel at the end of November."

He raised his eyebrows. "Then you leave?"

"Yeah."

He nodded, then got to his feet. "I should probably head back. There's a couple of orders that I should be working on."

The walk back was silent. I couldn't help but wonder if his question about how long I planned to be around had any significance. Once we got to my bike, Logan rested his hand on the handlebars. He rang the bell and I laughed.

"This was fun," he said

"It was. Thanks for coming with me."

"Any time." Logan sauntered to his beat-up truck and Shamrock jumped in next to him, ears flapping in the wind as they drove off.

The time on the walk had flown by. Logan felt like one surprise after another and I had enjoyed every second I'd spent with him. Much as I wanted to focus on the conversations we'd had and our shared interest, I couldn't get the moment his hand had brushed against my shoulder out of my mind.

# CHAPTER EIGHTEEN

The next morning, I met Charlotte in the living room, ready to get started on the wallpaper removal. We'd been successful with the drywall in the bathrooms and entryway, so I felt confident moving on to our next task. I was less confident with our relationship, as Charlotte had spent most of our time together yesterday with earbuds on, listening to an audiobook.

I'd let it go because I figured she was still annoyed that I had been unwilling to talk to our father and I also had Logan's advice about the situation fresh on my mind. Today, though, I hoped she and I would do a better job of connecting.

"There's a lot in front of us," she said. "Let's start in the dining room."

"That sounds good to me." I patted the wall. "Shouldn't be too hard, right?"

Charlotte let out a little snort. "Sure. Simple. I had to buy a bunch of tools, but I think I got everything. Do you mind helping me bring in stuff from the car?"

In preparation for the job, Charlotte had purchased supplies from the hardware store, including a roll of plastic, knives, a drop cloth, sprayers full of wallpaper removal solution, and a variety of tools to help. We hauled them in, and then she set them all up in the dining room, laying them out in a neat row on a sheet of brown paper. We unpackaged everything and took the trash to the dumpster.

"So, we have to start by covering up the baseboard with this," Charlotte said, once we were ready to go. She plucked a large roll of plastic out of the supplies. "It's not going to matter so much in some of the other rooms, but I assume we're leaving this floor, yes?"

"Yes," I said. "I think it's lovely."

The hardwood floor in the dining room was a beautiful pine color that was in great condition for its age. The rest of the floors in the house were hidden beneath a somewhat dingy-looking brownish-gray carpet.

It was tricky to line up the drop cloth to stick to the wall and roll it out, but soon, we were in a steady rhythm of pressing the tape against the wall and unrolling. Finally, we were back to the part of the wall where we started. Charlotte used a pair of scissors to cut the plastic before resealing it on the roll. Then we pulled it out in a smooth sheet, letting the thin pieces cover the floor.

"Careful, this is sharp." Charlotte grabbed a round tool and held it up, showing me a shiny underside complete with something that looked like miniature razor blades. "It's to weaken the paper and let the solution get in to loosen up the glue on the back of it. I'll take that wall and you take this one."

I got to work, and moments later she stood next to me, frowning. "You're supposed to go in a circle."

Surely she wasn't telling me how to use a tool neither one of us had ever used before. Then, like the star of some do-it-yourself program, Charlotte acted out a circular motion on the wallpaper.

"Thank you," I said, trying not to laugh. "Why don't you focus on your area?"

Once we let it sit, the wallpaper solution did its good work. It was quick and easy to peel back sections of wallpaper and dump the wet, crumbling mess onto the drop cloth. My clothes were damp, hands sticky, but it was fun. While I used the metal scraper to attack a small section that refused to come off, there was a sharp tap on my shoulder.

*I swear, if she's here to tell me that I'm doing it wrong again...*

"Yes?" I said, turning to her with exaggerated patience.

I dropped the attitude at the sight of her face. It was pale and she looked ready to cry.

"What happened?" I asked. "Did you get hurt?"

"No." She pointed at her area of the wall. "You need to see this."

I tensed. Judging by the expression on her face, the wall beneath the paper must be covered in black mold, or she'd unearthed a hole that led to a nest of mice. I strode over to the area where she'd been working to take a look.

A large piece of the wallpaper hung off to the side. Beneath it, there was a message. It must have been written in black Sharpie because the glue remover hadn't smeared it at all.

The date at the top of the message was from a year ago and it read:

*Welcome, girls. Please check beneath the loose floorboard.*

"What is this?" I said, baffled. Then I got it. "One of the items. One of the things she hid."

"Yep." Charlotte's voice was wry. "Let's find the floorboard."

We searched with cautious steps, testing each board to see if any of them were loose. Nothing. Finally, I peered at a vent. It didn't have a knob to open or close it. Cautiously, I reached down and tugged at its edges.

"Here," I called.

Charlotte hovered over me, a strand of hair falling over her eyes like when we were kids. She tucked it behind her ear and watched as I tried to pull up the metal grate.

"It doesn't open," I said. "I don't think it's real."

"Hold on." She grabbed one of the wallpaper scrapers. Using it as a lever, she pushed and cranked as I lifted the vent trap up and out of the floor.

It was indeed a fake, nestled into a small hole that held a flat box. We both lunged forward so fast that we practically knocked heads. I let Charlotte take it, since she'd found the message, and perched on my heels as she opened the lid. I had no idea what to expect. Money? Jewelry? A coupon to the ice-cream shop?

"It's their wedding album," Charlotte breathed.

She flipped through the pages and wrinkled her brow. Suddenly, she drew back her hand as if something had bit her.

"What?" I asked, leaning in.

"It's not Grandma and Grandpa," she said. "It's our parents."

The idea that my parents even had a wedding album was news to me.

I'd never heard a word of good about their relationship. My mother had said very little about my father at all. My grandmother had tried to talk to me about their marriage, back during our one visit, but the topic had made me so uncomfortable that I shut it down in the way that only a preteen girl could. She never brought it up again.

"I can't believe they were actually in love with one another," Charlotte murmured.

"Yeah." I squeezed my hands together, not sure what to say.

"I wonder why Grandma left this for us," Charlotte said, breaking my train of thought. "I understand the book, but this?"

"There must be a note or something," I said, reaching for the album. "Some sort of explanation."

I flipped through quickly, searching for additional guidance, but there was nothing there.

"I see it," Charlotte said suddenly.

The small piece of yellow paper must have fluttered to the ground when we first found the album, because it was halfway

across the room, wedged in the wrinkles of the drop cloth. Pluck-
ing it out, Charlotte handed it to me. I read the words out loud.

*My Dear Girls,*

*I found this album in a box in my garage at home. Your father
must have left it there years ago and forgotten all about it. Well,
I don't believe that love in any form should be forgotten.*

    *Your separation was caused by such strife between your parents.
I know you've heard the worst of it, but I wanted you to see this
as a reminder that there was a time where they loved one another.
And they never once stopped loving you.*

    *Please consider that when mistakes are made and hearts are
broken, the path to healing can still be found.*

*Your grandmother*

"I'd like to look at this in private," Charlotte said. "If that's
okay with you."

I wanted to look at it right then. Together. To pore over the
pictures and discuss them with the one person who had also
experienced the heartbreak of their divorce.

"Could we please look at it together?" I asked. "We both went
through it."

"Sorry. I'm not comfortable with that." Charlotte shook her
head. "You go ahead. Let me have it when you're done."

"I really would like to—"

The look on her face made me stop talking.

It was as clear as day. The divorce had hurt her as deeply as it
had hurt me. Maybe more, because she was the one my mother
had left behind.

\*

I went up to my room with the photo album. It had started to rain and I opened the window so that I could hear it pouring down. The wind was driving the rain against the sill so I sat farther away on the bed to make sure the album didn't get wet. Letting out a breath, I opened it.

Initially it felt like the wedding could have been anyone's. The church was small and pretty, with a cross that reached towards the heavens. Strangers who must have been bridesmaids and groomsmen wore lavender and pale blue as they lined up next to the altar. The reception had a gigantic cake, a dance floor, and based on the number of people with microphones, either a singing competition or a lot of speeches.

Then I looked at the pictures of my parents. My mother was absolutely radiant, her strawberry-blonde hair billowing around her face, the cut of her gown ideal for her thin shoulders. Her dress was woven through with shimmering beads and, in some photographs, it seemed to sparkle around her décolletage. There were photos of the two of them lighting a candle, sharing their first slice of cake, and locked in an intimate kiss.

I could see why my mother had been drawn to my father. He had deep green eyes and a strong jaw and regarded the camera with a confident, knowing smile. Like one of the heroes in a nineteenth-century romance, his hair fell almost to his shoulders, draping across both sides of his forehead. My mother looked completely different from how I remembered her, exuding an air of relaxed contentment as he held her close in almost every shot.

The wind rattled the eaves as I considered the fact that it was the first time in my life I'd seen so many pictures of my father. I'd looked him up online and had seen shots of him on Charlotte's social media page, but it was odd to finally see the type of pictures I would have had access to if she and I had been a part of the same family growing up.

I lay back on the bed, pulling the pillow close to my chest and letting the mist blowing in from the window brush across my cheeks. There were so many times I had screamed in silence into my pillow while growing up, wondering why my parents didn't just work through it. It was so selfish to separate me and Charlotte because they couldn't get along. It broke apart our family. Charlotte blamed me and my mother for leaving her behind, and I blamed her for being angry with us. We should never have been put in the position in the first place. We were kids, doing our best to survive a bad situation.

I wanted to step inside the photo album and convince my parents to make better choices, to think about how their actions would affect the people that they loved. There was no changing the past, though. It might be time to let it go and focus on the future.

Once Charlotte and I had finished our work, an idea was brewing. The rain had stopped and I rode my bicycle into town to the tiny grocery shop. I knew Charlotte was a fan of salmon, so I bought two salmon filets, asparagus, and some fresh raspberries. Logan had mentioned that Charlotte might be scared to move forward with our relationship and his words had stuck with me. More than anything, I wanted to try to work through the heartache that had kept me and Charlotte apart.

Back at the house, the flowers in the garden out front were a tangled mess of weeds and vines but they were still blooming. I broke off several and built a flower arrangement to set outside, then poured sparkling water, worried that she wouldn't want to join me with every step.

She was sitting out on the back deck reading, dressed in a pair of pink yoga pants and a black off-the-shoulder T-shirt that made her look strong but put together.

I poked my head out and gave her a tentative smile. "Hey. I wanted to make us lunch, if that's cool with you."

"Oh. That's really nice." She glanced at her phone. "I was planning to run some errands, though. Another time."

"Can you do your errands later?" I pressed. "I thought it would be good to catch up."

Charlotte slid on her sunglasses and stared out at the water. Her shoulders stayed squared, and her posture precise. Finally, she nodded. "Thank you. That sounds good."

I returned to the porch half an hour later with baked salmon, roasted asparagus, and a bright smile. It was obvious Charlotte wasn't interested in hanging out with me, but I was determined to push forward. When I set down the plates, she looked at them in surprise.

"Wow. That looks wonderful." She gave me a half smile. "It's not my birthday."

The comment made me think of how many of her birthdays I'd missed.

"Well, we can pretend," I said, settling in. "I was in the mood for a nice lunch. I thought we could do it together."

We ate in silence and she reached for the bottle of sparkling water. "Pellegrino?" she asked, holding it over my glass.

"Thank you," I said. "So, I wanted to have lunch because we haven't had much of a chance to get to know each other. It's been more about the house and our history, but I…" My cheeks warmed, and I took a drink of water. "I wanted to tell you a few things I've noticed that I admire about you now. I admire you as a mother. Ken said it that first night and he was right—you're a great mother."

Charlotte's eyebrows shot up and her water glass remained at her lips. "Thank you."

"I also admire your poise." It was hard to look right at her as I talked, so I focused on the flowering tree in the neighbors' backyard. "I noticed it right away when we were in the lawyer's office. It's the way you carry yourself, with confidence. I also admire your obvious commitment to fitness because most of the time, I find it hard to get motivated to work out at all. Finally, I admire your planning skills. That day at the lawyer's office when you thought to book the roofers was so impressive. Then you coordinated the furniture removal, house cleaning, and home inspection, and I was so grateful. I wish I was better at seeing the big picture instead of what's right in front of me."

"Goodness." Charlotte's smile was wide. "I wasn't expecting all of that."

"Well, you deserve to hear it," I said. "We were cheated out of our time together and I want to make the most of the time we have now."

Yes, there was hurt and heartache, and I would never understand why she'd cut me off for so long, but if this was going to be my one shot with her, I didn't want to spend it dwelling on the past.

"That... seriously. Thank you." Charlotte set down her fork. "You know, your kindness is one thing that I've admired about you, Jayne. Ken has commented on it, and the boys, and I feel it, too. In spite of all that's happened, you still go out of your way to be kind and it's—I appreciate it."

Her approval meant more to me than it should, but on the other hand, I'd been waiting for it my whole life.

"Thanks." I looked up at the house, fighting back a wave of regret. "I don't think I was as kind to Grandma as I could have been. I did go to her funeral. You asked me about it that first day at the lawyer's office. I went."

Charlotte's face darkened. "We don't have to talk about—"

I held up my hand. "No, hear me out. In spite of what you thought, I went to her funeral. I walked in right as it started, and left right before it ended, so that I didn't have to see the side of the family that I hadn't seen in so long. My actions felt a little extreme at the time. Now I realize they were self-preservation. Sorry, but it's true."

Charlotte picked up her fork and set it down again. "I'm glad to hear that you were there. I wish..." Her voice trailed off and she pushed a piece of asparagus around her plate.

"Say it," I pressed.

She adjusted her sunglasses and looked back out at the ocean. "Nothing." Then she said, "I wish we would have known that you were there. It would have helped in how I looked at things. How I assumed you cared or didn't care."

"Didn't care?" My mouth went dry. "Is that what Grandma thought?"

"No, I don't think so," Charlotte said. "Grandma was more understanding than most people. She was well aware that you and I were the victims in that whole scenario, growing up. I mean, I can see that with the things she's leaving for us. I remember she was always pushing Dad to find a way to move to Ireland so that we could be together, but it was impossible. He had so much responsibility at work. Grandma was frustrated by it all but there was nothing she could do, and she never blamed us." She paused. "Dad tried to make things work, though. I don't want to make it sound like he didn't. He was always on the phone with our mother, trying to get her to compromise, but she just wouldn't. She was in Ireland and if he wanted to come, that was fine, but she wasn't about to come back here."

"Grandma tried to bring us together even back then," I said.

The words were stilted, like I was reading from a script, but I had no idea how to get to the question I'd decided to ask. It would serve me better to move on, to make kind gestures like this lunch, and build a pleasant relationship with Charlotte as the months progressed. It's what I had intended to do; it was the purpose of this lunch. But as we talked, with the sun shining and the ocean crashing down below, it hit me that keeping our conversation on the surface wasn't going to cut it.

My grandmother had put us in this position for the very purpose of working through the obstacles that had kept us apart. I didn't want to disrespect her memory. I wanted to take the steps to move forward with my whole heart, and that meant addressing some of the harder topics.

"Do you think a lot about that summer?" I asked. "The one where she brought us here?"

"Yes." Charlotte's voice was terse. "Especially when I'd come back here to visit, once you were gone. It was hard for me to deal with, seeing you after so many years and then not seeing you again."

"That was your choice, though, Charlotte." I kept my voice gentle. "We could have stayed in touch. We could have stayed friends. Instead, you cut me off. Why?"

Charlotte looked down at her plate. "Because I was ten," she said quietly.

I stared at her. "That's your answer?"

"I don't know what else to say." She adjusted her sunglasses. "I'm sorry that I can't give you more, but yes. I was ten, I was stupid, and it was a bad decision."

Her aloof dismissal hurt. "There are bad decisions and there are life-altering decisions," I said, fighting the sudden tremor in my voice. "There's a difference."

"I know, and I'm sorry." Charlotte got to her feet. "Lunch was delicious. Thank you." Her tone was painfully polite. "Now I really must get to those errands." Turning, she went inside.

I sat for a moment in stunned silence. Then I grabbed my plate and followed her, but she was gone. Upstairs or in her car, I had no idea, and I was not about to chase after her. I stood in the kitchen in frustrated silence. My attempt at lunch felt so pathetic.

Nothing had changed. Nothing would change. It was ridiculous to try to fight for it.

*What am I doing here?*

I leaned against the counter. My grandmother might have had good intentions, but it was too late. If she'd wanted Charlotte and me to have a relationship, she should have stepped in years ago. Not pulled us into some house of memories, long past the time to heal.

I heard a sound upstairs. Charlotte was at the top of the stairs. Quickly, I headed out to the deck and down to the beach. I took the steps two at a time, stumbling once along the way, before making it to the shore. There, I sank into the cool sand.

It was a hot day but windy, so the ocean was rough. The stretch of sand by our house was nearly empty, save for a few pieces of seaweed. Waves crashed at my feet and I considered the dark shadow of the ocean, trying to remember that it was so much bigger than me, any of my problems, heartache, or fears. This time, the visualization didn't work.

The lick of the wind against my face did nothing to fight back my tears. They spilled down my cheeks, dripping off my nose, and I pressed my shirt against them like a tourniquet.

The sound of Charlotte's voice in the wind made me jump.

"Jayne!"

What was she doing here? Did she have to come to see me break down?

I swiped at my eyes, but the tears kept coming. "Please go away."

"Jayne, wait."

Turning, I saw that she'd changed into navy shorts and a button-up shirt, the wind whipping her precise ponytail around her face. "What do you want?" I demanded.

She didn't answer and I turned away, tempted to run. The waves were getting higher, crashing to the shore with fury. I wanted to dive into the water and swim as hard as I could to outrun this pain. Instead, I whirled on her.

"You cut me off," I shouted. "You hugged me goodbye that summer and made me feel like we were sisters again. My heart was broken when I had to get back on the plane, but the one thing that made it possible was knowing that you would write to me, that you would be there for me. The day you sent that letter…"

A sob escaped and I rushed for the water, scooping up a handful to splash on my face. The salt mixed with my tears, but the fury didn't stop. With a cry, I grabbed a fistful of sand and threw it against the roaring waves.

"Jayne, please listen to me." She grabbed my arm. "I'm sorry. I'm so sorry. I—I've spent so many years thinking you didn't care about me. Thinking that you wanted me as far away from you as possible, and you should feel that way. I did a terrible thing."

She pressed her lips so tightly they went white, then tears spilled down her cheeks. I stared at her, stunned to see her crying.

"Then why did you do it?" I demanded.

"Because Deidre had her baby." I drew back at the mention of the woman who'd married our father. "Bruno was born two weeks before I got home, did you know that?"

I had a vague memory of that. My grandmother had been so excited to go see him. I wasn't interested in babies and knew that I wouldn't get to see him anytime soon, so I hadn't paid much attention.

"Grandma flew home with me." Her fists were clenched tightly at her sides, but the tears kept coming. "We walked into our house, and I was so excited to see my father that I shouted *Daddy*. He shushed me and said, *Quiet, Charlotte. Your brother is sleeping.* That's when I realized he and Deidre were sitting on the couch together and there was no room for me, because she had this baby sleeping in her arms. I'd been replaced, again. I'd been left behind again." She rubbed her hands over her crossed arms. "The next few months, I did everything possible to get their attention, but it was all about the baby. I was invisible."

"That's awful," I said, stunned at the revelation.

Her stormy eyes met mine. "I blamed you."

"Me," I whispered.

"I kept thinking that if I'd stayed home, if I hadn't spent that summer with you, I could have found a way to stop them from forgetting about me. I blamed you because you'd started the trend of people leaving me behind."

My heart flooded with hurt on her behalf. "Charlotte, I—"

"It was wrong, but I was ten," she said, her voice shaking. "I didn't have the insight to realize that I'd made a huge mistake until college—that's when I got pregnant and I had Josh and then Evan, and for the longest time my life was about survival. I've wanted to reach out to you—there's been so many times I've looked at your social media account, started letters to you—but I wasn't brave enough to follow through. I assumed you wanted nothing to do with me."

A million thoughts, feelings, and images flashed through my mind. The half-finished letter in my mother's book. The iron gates. The moment I'd realized Charlotte wasn't with me and my mother on the plane.

"I'm so sorry." Charlotte's damp cheeks gleamed in the sunlight and the tip of her nose was bright red. "I can't tell you how sorry I am."

The words made me choke up so much that I couldn't speak. Instead, I held out my arms. She hesitated but then stepped forward. I wrapped her into a tight hug and we stood there in silence, the heartache strong between us.

The wave hit Charlotte first, knocking her off balance. I stumbled, losing my footing, and we fell into the water. The waves crashed over us, icy and relentless, but I didn't let go of her hand. We struggled to our feet, hands gripped tight, and found our way back to shore.

*

For the first time since we'd moved into the house, Charlotte asked me what I was planning to do that evening.

"Nothing," I said, cautiously optimistic that she'd ask me to hang out. We'd had a huge breakthrough on the beach, but I didn't know how it would translate to real life. "Do you want to find a karaoke bar? My friend Lauren was telling me that it's big around here."

Charlotte laughed. "I have a better idea. Meet me in the kitchen at eight."

When I walked in later that night, Charlotte had set up the kitchen like a salon. There was a paraffin machine at the table, manicure sets, and a small row of pink nail polish bottles. She sat at the kitchen table, waiting for me.

"I thought we would do manicures," she said.

My disappointment must have been apparent because she laughed. "You look like I suggested a round of home-taught acupuncture."

I grinned. "It's not that. It's because my nails always chip within two days when I try to paint them."

"I have an amazing topcoat," she said. "It will be fine."

Charlotte turned on her paraffin machine and as we waited for the wax to heat, I said, "I'm surprised you do these yourself. I would have pegged you as someone who would get her nails done in a salon."

She shrugged. "I do, but I like to do it at home too. I've always been into beauty treatments. I think…" Her voice trailed off.

"What?" I prompted.

"The girl that I played with when I was little, her mother was into this sort of thing." The hurt in her eyes was apparent. "It was the type of thing I imagined a mother would do, I guess, so

I latched on to it. Deidre wasn't like that, but I guess I chalked that up to her being a stepmother. I kept waiting to find out that she secretly loathed me."

Outside the window, the evening was quiet, and I could barely hear the shift of the ocean down below.

"Was Mom like that?" Charlotte asked, when I didn't say anything. "Into beauty regimens, I mean?"

I started, surprised that I'd missed the hint in her earlier comment. I was so used to Charlotte avoiding the topic of our mother that I hadn't tuned in to the nuances behind it. There was a sense of shyness in her voice, coupled with a hint of jealousy. The same tone I imagined I used when I spoke about our father.

"Yes, she was," I admitted. "That might be where you got it from, because I missed out on that gene. She didn't have the time to go to the salon or anything, but she always did this home treatment or that. Like, I remember when she decided she wanted a perm, she bought this boxed chemical, and the whole apartment reeked for a week. We're lucky to have made it out of that alive."

Charlotte beckoned me to the bathroom, removed the paraffin gloves and pieces of wax. "Wash your hands." I did and she applied a rose-scented lotion before saying, "Did she try to get you to do that type of stuff with her?"

"Sometimes," I said. "She was forever wanting to paint my nails, but then she'd spend the whole time scolding me about biting them. My cuticles were always a mess, too, so it wasn't fun for me."

"Well, I will make a point not to scold you. What color would you like?" Charlotte pointed at the five jars of perfectly pretty pink nail polish. They all looked the same; the only difference was the label on each jar.

"You pick," I said. "You know more about this stuff than I do."

Charlotte plucked a pink Chanel polish from the lineup, set it to the side, and attacked my nails with clippers and a cuticle stick.

"Ouch," I said.

"You okay?" she said quickly.

"Yes," I said. "I was being a baby. It's fine."

The thing that continued to impress me about my sister was her gentle heart. I'd seen it in small moments, like the time with the spider, but I'd also seen it so often with her sons. It wasn't anything loud but it was a sense that she was always watching, trying to decide where to step in and when to let the boys handle things on their own. I was tempted to talk to her about what Evan had told me, but I'd promised him that I wouldn't and I wanted to keep his trust.

"This looks beautiful," I said, when she was nearly done. "I heard that nails dry best during a late-night walk along the beach. What do you say?"

Charlotte glanced out the window. She finished my pinkie and capped the polish.

"I'll get my sandals."

We walked along the edge of the water in silence. For the first time, the quiet felt comfortable instead of cold and I looked up at the stars, breathing in the peace.

"This isn't going to be easy," Charlotte said.

"Trying to walk on the beach in the dark?" I asked, knowing full well what she was talking about.

"I think the best way to work through it is to be honest with one another," she said. "Mainly, about our feelings. That won't be easy for me, either, so I apologize in advance. I also want to apologize that it's taken me this long to stop being so rude. I know I come across that way and I'm sorry. You'd said something about self-preservation earlier, and I can relate to that."

The words felt like a warm hug. "Well, I'm sorry if I seemed rude in any way, and I also apologize in advance for the moments

that I'm going to overshare, so tell me if I need to tone it back."
She laughed. "For right now, though," I said, "I'm feeling really
cautious but really happy. I don't want to get hurt by all of this,
and I know you don't either. We both went through the same
thing, so I think we both get it."

In the dark, I saw her nod. "It's going to be a lot more fun
doing this if we can be friends and then start to address some of
the things that happened over the years."

"I don't know if I want to," I admitted. "I'd rather be your
friend and move on."

"That's a great idea in theory, but we'll both have questions."
Her voice sounded small. "I have a lot about our mother, and
you're the only one who can answer them."

The words nearly made me tear up. It would have meant the
world to my mother to know that Charlotte had cared so much
about her because much like me, she'd finally accepted the idea
that Charlotte didn't want to be around her. If we would have
moved back to the States, though, I had no doubt my mother
would have fought for her relationship with Charlotte. Those
hurts would have been healed, and they could have been there
for each other.

Of course, there was no changing the past, but I could do my
best to honor my mother's memory and to help Charlotte finally
get to know her and me.

"Ask away," I said. "I will tell you everything you want to
know."

Charlotte stopped walking. "Thank you for being brave enough
to push for this. Seriously. I would not have been strong enough
to make the effort the way that you did."

I was tempted to make a joke, to say something to lighten
the mood. Instead, I nodded. "You're welcome. You know, it
startled me when you mentioned that dress that I'd left hanging
in the closet."

"Why?" Charlotte took a seat in the sand, up away from the water, and I joined her.

"Because one of the things I missed about having a sister was not having someone to trade outfits with. The girl in the cottage down the way had an older sister and she was always dressed up in this or that, and I was jealous—not because of the clothes, but because I'd always wanted to do that with you."

Charlotte pulled her knees to her chest. "I know what you mean. It was the small things like that, as much as the big stuff, wasn't it? The first time I went out on a date, I kept wishing that I hadn't ruined everything with you because I needed my sister to tell me what it would be like to kiss a boy. I swear, I worried I was pregnant for like, that whole year, because he'd slipped his tongue in my mouth and I had no one to tell me the reality of the situation. I wasn't going to ask my friends, because they'd think I was an idiot."

"So many things like that," I agreed. "I had lots of girlfriends, but I didn't want to talk to them about the real stuff, like when Daideo died. I wanted to talk to you."

"What was he like?" she asked. "I don't remember much about him."

"Daideo?" I thought for a minute. "Solid. He'd never met a stranger. He always had a great sense of humor and kept things light. I think that time would have been a lot darker if he hadn't brought a sense of steadiness to it."

"How old were you when he died?" she asked.

"Ten." I shook my head. "He started to decline shortly after you and Dad visited, but he hung around for years. Mom managed to care for him up until about a year before he died, and that's when she had to put him in a facility."

Charlotte wrinkled her brow. "Why was she so committed to him? I mean, I know he was her father, but that's pretty impressive."

"She was like you," I said, and Charlotte winced. "I mean, she had a kind heart. The idea of leaving him like that was too much for her to take. I think that it really hurt her when her mother passed away. Mom was here, in the States, and she was caught up in her own life when it happened. She'd wanted to take me to visit her parents, but Dad could never get away from work. Then her mother got sick. She died before Mom could make it over there to see her. Part of her devotion to Daideo was probably guilt because she didn't want the same thing to happen."

"I don't agree with her choices," Charlotte said. "That helps shed some light on them, though. Thank you."

Picking up the sand, I let it sift through my fingers.

"You know, I was devastated when I learned you'd had kids," I said quietly. "I wanted so badly to be a part of that. To throw you a party, to be there in the hospital to meet them. It sounds ridiculous, since we don't even know each other, but..."

Charlotte rested her hand on mine. "No, it doesn't." She sat in silence then let out a breath. "I felt the same. That was another time in my life where I'd really wished you were there. The pregnancies were so hard for me. I was so young. Ken and I were not expecting to have a family until we were out of college, established, and had a big, beautiful wedding."

"You weren't married?" I said. Quickly, I added, "There's nothing wrong with that, you just come across so..."

"Uptight?" Charlotte said, watching me with a wry smile.

"Perfect," I said. "The word I was looking for was 'perfect.'"

"Far from it." She laughed. "We got married at the courthouse. It saved Dad a ton of money. He's liked Ken ever since."

"I like him, too," I said. "What do you mean, the pregnancies were hard?"

Charlotte shrugged. "I'm tiny. The boys were big. I had to do C-sections with both of them, which was not what I'd planned."

She paused. "I'm seeing a theme with everything I'm saying. My life hasn't gone according to plan. I'm not complaining, because it's a great life, but it would have been better to have you along for the ride."

"You, too," I said, fighting back another wave of emotion.

"What did you do after college?" she said. "Did you start working right away?"

"No." I dug my toes deep enough into the sand to cover them. "I had no idea what I wanted to be, so I actually started college, dropped out to see the world, and then started back up again once I figured it out."

"Where did you travel to?" Charlotte asked, her eyes shining. "I always wanted to do that."

"Everywhere. It was amazing," I said, thinking back. "I was engaged to this guy and he'd just graduated, so we decided to travel together. We didn't have any money, but he was ridiculously talented on guitar, so we traveled through Europe and he'd set out a hat and perform everywhere we went. Later, once we'd broken up, I decided to teach English as a second language in South America, so I got to see another part of the world. I spent most of my time when I wasn't teaching riding the bus, exploring the mountains, and painting. It wasn't a bad way to live."

"You'll have to show me pictures," Charlotte said.

"No one wants to see pictures of someone else's vacation," I said. "Well, maybe one at a time, but—"

"Pictures of your paintings," she said. "I bet you're so talented."

"Why?" I said.

She nudged me with her knee. "Because you're my sister, silly," she said, and I smiled.

Charlotte yawned. "It's getting late."

I could have stayed out talking with her all night, but she was right.

"Let's head back," I said, brushing sand off my legs.

We walked in silence. When we got to the steps, I said, "You mentioned earlier that we need to keep being open and honest about our feelings. I'm scared, Charlotte. This has felt like a dream; it's the kind of thing I've wanted to have with you my whole life. I don't want it to come to an end."

"It's not going to." Charlotte's blue eyes were bright. "This is only the beginning."


The next morning, Charlotte was working and I headed down to the beach. The warm sand welcomed my feet and the air smelled fresh. I made my way straight for the water. It was chilly and I stepped into the ocean, feeling the salt sting the dry skin on my legs before welcoming me into its fold.

The water seemed to surround my body and bring it new life. I sank down into the ocean, barely feeling the cold seep over me. Soon, my arms pushed me through the waves and I couldn't remember the last time I had actually gone for a swim.

I started to laugh, tasting the salt on my lips and wiping it out of my eyes to see the gentle waves and the tourists back on the shore. I had not felt the sense of happiness that threatened to overtake me in years. Everything around me seemed alive. I was out far enough that I couldn't see the golden sand and I had a brief moment of delicious terror, wondering if there was a shark down below. I decided that it didn't matter, because I would fight off anything that threatened to take this joy from me.

It felt like miles away, but as I treaded water, I peered through the sun at my grandmother's house perched on the edge of the hill. If I squinted just right I could practically see me and my sister racing each other down the steps, the future bright ahead of us.

# CHAPTER NINETEEN

The next morning, Charlotte and I were ready to start tearing up the tile in the recreation room. The room was down the hallway by the storage room and it had a decent view of the ocean, but so far, we hadn't spent any time in there. I had a feeling it had once been used as a ballroom of sorts.

"Whew," I said, when we walked in.

I could see how the deep-blue tiles coupled with a swirling purple floral pattern had once been beautiful, but now the tiles were faded and cracked and gave the room a kitschy feeling that didn't fit with the rest of the house.

"I have been waiting to tear up this floor," Charlotte muttered.

"It sounds like you have a vendetta against it," I said.

"Well..." She tucked a strand of hair behind her ear. "Grandma and I used to spend time in here because it had a lot of space for me to run around and pretend to dance and all that. One summer, I came up from the beach and my suit was still soaking wet. I had left the book I was reading on a table in the corner and I went to grab it. Grandma called me from the kitchen with ice cream so I went running, slipped, and broke my wrist."

"Ouch," I said, wincing. "No wonder."

"Yep."

"Well, that does not look like a joke," I said, indicating the huge machine she'd hauled into the room. "So you'll get your vengeance."

Charlotte laughed. "Ken is ridiculous. This is probably the biggest hammer drill you can get. He borrowed this from the same friend that loaned us the sledgehammer. It's actually going to save us a lot of time because the tile is really old and thick. That is, if we don't cause damage to the floor. We'll just have to be careful."

"Of course," I said.

Charlotte laid down the machine and pulled out her iPad. She pulled up the tutorial we'd watched a few days prior on tearing up tile. It seemed pretty self-explanatory; there was just no telling how taxing it would be.

The video ended and she got to her feet. "Okay," she said, brushing off her hands. "Let's give it a try."

I picked up the hammer drill. "Let me go first. I've always been kind of fascinated with heavy machinery."

"Please be careful," Charlotte said.

I set it down to put on safety goggles, a dust mask, and earplugs. Charlotte did the same. I was about to turn it on when I paused.

"Where's the spot you fell?" I asked her.

Looking puzzled, she pointed to a spot in the corner.

I headed over there. "Here's your vengeance," I said, and switched it on.

It shook in my hands, vibrating my arms down to the bones, but I held on tight, determined not to let it go. The tile started to crack, falling away in small chunks and pieces. It was precise work, as I had to slide the chisel underneath the edge of the next tile that I wanted to break, but the moment it shivered and broke off, my sense of accomplishment was grand.

Charlotte stood off to the side watching and when the pieces started to give, I saw her applaud. There was so much dirt and debris that came up that a thin layer of dust covered those that were remaining, and I wiped the back of my sleeve over my sweating forehead. It wasn't easy but it was satisfying. The faded tiles finally began to clear away, leaving a dark-gray concrete exposed below.

We used a hammer and chisel to get up the last pieces. Once everything had been removed, we swept up the broken bits and dumped them into the garbage cans, puffs of dust welling up into our hair. Even with the assistance of the mask, my mouth felt chalky. The debris gone, I realized there was still plenty of grout remaining and attacked it again. Finally, the area was clear, swept, and perfectly flat, ready for the new flooring.

My arms ached and my whole body felt exhausted. I was grateful the room wasn't bigger because it had taken us hours. There was a small section of tile still left in the guest bathroom and we'd planned to tackle, it but now I wasn't so sure. I had to get to work in an hour, and it would be necessary to take a shower before then.

"Let's do the bathrooms tomorrow," I said. "It's going to take time and I have to get to work."

"Whatever you need," Charlotte said. "We're in this together."


Working and remodeling the house with Charlotte was fun but exhausting, and the nights I didn't work the closing shift, I was in bed by ten o'clock. My muscles ached with the effort from both sides, but life was starting to feel like it was on an upswing. Things almost felt like they were under control.

My relationship with Charlotte was the biggest improvement. We settled into a comfortable rhythm of sharing coffee in the morning until she went to work, eating lunch together, and then tackling the house. There were moments of laughter and, of course, moments with tears, but the one thing that stood strong was our desire to work through the hurt feelings and missed opportunities that had shaped our relationship for far too long.

It was also such a relief to stop worrying about money. The monthly stipend from my grandmother, coupled with what I was making at the restaurant, gave me enough to make a payment large enough to get the arbitration department at the credit card company to take me seriously. They finally agreed to work with me to set up a reasonable repayment plan, which I appreciated.

So far, we hadn't found anything else hidden by my grand-mother, which was also a relief. The constant threat had kept both me and Charlotte on edge, wondering when something else would crop up. Neither one of us said it, but I think we were both afraid that the introduction of another piece from the past could threaten this new hope we had for the future. Thank goodness, nothing turned up and I did my best to stop worrying about it.

On top of that, the house was starting to shape up. So many of the rooms that had been cluttered and dingy to begin with, thanks to the old wallpaper, ancient carpet, and faded paint, were beginning to look like clean slates ready to be renewed. It had only been a short period of time, but it felt as though Charlotte and I had moved mountains.

The true work was yet to be done, as there were tile replace-ments, electricity concerns, the plan to add windows, as well as the need to replace all the toilets and deal with some of the plumbing issues. Most days, though, it felt manageable. I was relieved at the sense of peace but at night, right before I fell asleep, I couldn't help but worry that things were too good. That there was still a chance everything could fall apart. Then the rational part of my brain would push those thoughts away, and I'd fall asleep to the sure and steady sound of the ocean waves crashing to the shore.

The leaves in the trees danced a bright green as I walked down the block towards the blacksmith shop. My palms were damp. I wiped them on my pale-blue sundress and focused on taking measured breaths.

I hadn't expected to feel so nervous. I was seeking Logan out for the first time and that made me uncomfortable. I didn't want to send any type of message that could be interpreted as flirtatious, but I did want to thank him for the advice that he'd given me that day on the walk.

Logan had helped me to see my relationship with Charlotte in another way by suggesting that maybe she was as scared as I was to take those steps to reconnect. If he hadn't said that, I might not have found the courage to push for a reconciliation. He might not have realized it, but his words had made an impact on me and I wanted to thank him. So, there was nothing wrong with bringing him a box of chocolates from the local candy shop, was there?

I hesitated at the shop door, wondering if I was being too bold.

My lingering must have gone on a moment too long, because someone behind me said, "You going in?"

"Yes," I said quickly.

Opening the door, I walked in without giving myself another chance to change my mind.

My eyes adjusted to the dim lighting as the person behind me headed straight for the counter. It was a mail delivery guy and the store itself was empty, which was a welcome surprise. Every time I'd poked my head in the window, someone had been there, studying the sculptures or talking over a project with Logan at his desk. I took advantage of the silence to take a quick look around.

Each sculpture was impeccably crafted. Logan had mentioned that he'd had a passion for this type of work since he was young and I could see that, because the level of skill in each design could not be learned overnight. I was glad that he had some sort of an outlet to escape from the stress and loneliness of missing his daughters and could easily imagine him losing himself in the creation of these pieces for hours—if not days—at a time.

"Hey, what are you doing here?" Logan's deep voice echoed from the back, and I jumped.

He walked towards me with a pleased smile on his face, wiping his hands on the apron hung loosely over his jeans. He wore a gray T-shirt, dirty with what looked like grease and sweat, and his hair appeared damp, so he must've been working near the flame. In short, the man looked hot. My cheeks turned red with the knowledge that I was seriously attracted to him.

Up until this point, I'd convinced myself that my feelings for him were casual, but seeing him in his element, taking in the raw talent that came from those hands, left me feeling unsettled. My legs felt weak as I held up the box of candies.

"What's that?" he said.

"I brought you a thank-you," I said, hoping my voice didn't sound as nervous as I felt inside. "It's for the advice you gave me about my sister on the walk that one day. You offered a new perspective. I'd never considered the fact that she might be scared, too, because she seemed to have it all together. We've finally started dealing with our issues and this past week has been so much fun. For the first time in years, I feel like we're sisters again."

The words almost brought me to tears, so I looked down at my feet. Thanks to Charlotte, my toenails were painted a striking pink that looked amazing.

"Anyway." I cleared my throat. "The thing you said made all the difference. So you get candy."

I handed him the box and a slight smile crossed his face. "Lauren is telling my secrets again, isn't she? These are my absolute favorites."

I widened my eyes. "No way. Lucky guess, huh?"

He tore the ribbon off the box, opened it, and offered one of the chocolate-covered creams to me.

"You go ahead," I said, and he popped one into his mouth. The look on his face was pure ecstasy, and I couldn't help but shiver at the thought that I'd made him feel that way.

Our eyes met and electricity seemed to cut right through me. Logan must have felt it, too, because his gaze darkened and he took a step towards me. The door opened at that very moment and abruptly, he turned away.

"Welcome," he called, his voice huskier than usual. "Take a look around and let me know if you need anything." Turning back to me, he said, "I'm glad you stopped by."

"Me, too."

Surprised to feel the pounding of my heart, I headed for the door and stepped out of the shop. My breath was coming too fast because I couldn't get past the look he'd given me right before the door opened. There was no denying the chemistry between us, but I had to try to keep it in perspective.

Nothing had happened; there was nothing to get worked up about. But riding my bike home, the breeze cool in my hair, I couldn't stop thinking about him.

Charlotte and I had gotten into the habit of cooking dinner for everyone on the nights I didn't have to work. It had started to feel like second nature for the five of us to sit down at the table together. Tonight, we'd planned for a salad with fresh vegetables, dinner rolls, and grilled chicken breasts, and she was already hard at work chopping vegetables when I arrived home.

"Right on time to taste the magic," she sang, slicing in time to salsa music.

I'd learned she loved to eat raw vegetables as an appetizer as we prepped our meals, dipping snap peas or carrots into hummus.

"It's radishes tonight," she said, holding one out. "I'm telling you, it's fifty times better than a potato chip."

"But it's a radish," I said, sipping at a bottle of water.

"It's heaven."

She refused to drop her arm so, reluctantly, I reached for it. I hadn't eaten a radish in years. Popping it in my mouth, I crunched down. The texture was harder than a pickle but not as crunchy as a carrot, but I could see why she liked it.

"It's bitter in a good way," I said, chewing. "I don't hate it."

Charlotte peered at me. "I don't think you could hate anything right now. You've been grinning ever since you walked in. What's going on?" she asked, pulling out the bags of chicken breast she'd had marinating in the fridge.

There were only two, and I said, "Ken and the boys aren't eating?"

"They went to an early movie," she said. "They're going to grab a bite on the way. Now, tell me why you're giddy."

I had been putting ice in our water glasses but at her words, I pressed the glass to my cheek instead of filling it. "What do you mean?"

Charlotte studied me for a minute. Then her eyes widened. "It's a guy!"

"What?" I sputtered. "What are you talking about?"

The smile on her face could only be described as knowing. "Tell me who it is. Someone you work with?" She snapped her fingers. "Wait. It's the tile guy."

I snorted. "The tile guy." He had chiseled good looks, bright green eyes, and had gone through all of the tile samples with us at the store. "I bet there are a lot of houses around here that have been tiled to excess for no reason."

Charlotte laughed, poking me with a pair of grill tongs. "Tell me, then. Who?"

"Logan. The sunroom guy." Quickly, I added, "I can't believe I just said that. It hardly sums him up."

"Yes, it does." Charlotte put her hand to her heart. "He's gorgeous. Ken actually told me that I needed to focus more on the house and less on that guy's upper body."

I laughed. "Let's get these on the grill," I said, indicating the chicken breasts, "and I'll tell you all about him over the salads."

Once we were seated on the deck, the chicken smoking on the grill as we sipped on sparkling water, I gave her the update, probably talking about him longer than necessary.

"It's not anything serious." I watched as the waves splashed against the sand and retreated, then splashed the sand once again. "Nothing's even happened yet."

Charlotte got up to check on the chicken. "It's not ready." She sat back down. "Ten minutes." Squinting at me, she said, "Would you be interested in something with him long-term?"

"I'm here for six months," I said. "That makes it tricky."

"True," she mused, tapping her fork against her upper lip. "The world's a lot smaller, now, though. You could do long distance, see where it goes."

"I don't know. It's not that big of a deal."

"Mmm-hmm." She took a sip of sparkling water. "That's why you turn red each time I mention him. I think you should see where it goes." She paused. "It's so nice to see a relationship in the early stages, before all the mistakes set in."

"What do you mean?" I asked, squinting through the evening sun.

"Oh, you know." She took a bite of salad. "There are times I wish Ken and I could go back to the start, to that time when anything was possible."

It concerned me to hear that, because Ken seemed so good for her. "Why? What's happening with you guys?"

Charlotte set down her fork. "Let me check on the food again."

It had not been ten minutes, but I waited while she opened the grill, stuck in the meat thermometer, and nodded. Plating it, she brought it over to the table and squeezed fresh lemon on top. The chicken was covered in herbs and smelled delicious.

"Perfect timing, actually," she said, passing me a piece. "It was right on the edge of getting overcooked."

I cut into it and took a bite. The contrast between the spices on the chicken and the fresh lemon was delicious. "This is amazing."

"Thank you." Charlotte waited as the steam from her food rose into the night. "So, Ken." She sighed. "Ken is a great guy. He's given me a wonderful life, has been a wonderful husband, and an even better father. But this has been a hard year for him. He's had to struggle a lot, for the first time ever." She held up her hand. "He's a self-made man. He's very smart and very good at what he does. He didn't grow up rich or anything, but he made some lucky investments in the beginning of his career—right out of college, actually. And last year was… well, different."

"How so?" I asked.

"He stretched himself much too thin. We had to move—he was not willing to lose face by taking the boys out of private school, quitting the country club, and selling our house—so we acted like we had some great opportunity in the northern part of Florida. It's been pretty awful, hard on the kids." She looked down at her hands. "I miss my friends, my house, and the only blessing is that we're right down the street from Dad. The boys also seem to like it better in their new school, so that's something."

"I'm sorry," I told her. "That must be hard."

"The hardest part is how it's affected Ken," she said. "The drinking that you saw at dinner that first night is something he's been doing to cope with what's happened. He still pretends like he's a high roller and it's been hard on all of us. This house…" She glanced up at the beach house and back down at her hands. "It's going to save us, but I'm concerned about how it will affect his self-esteem. He'd wrapped his entire identity up in his business—and it went bankrupt. I'm afraid he's going to resent me for stepping in to save the day."

I thought of how kind Ken had been and his efforts to be jovial, in spite of everything going on behind the scenes. He was such a good guy and it made me sad to think that he defined himself by his financial success. It hit me that I had done the same thing. Not at the same level, by any means, because I knew Charlotte was talking an astronomical amount of money, but for months before any of this happened, I had felt like an absolute failure. Well, to be honest, I still did.

"I know what he's going through," I admitted.

"What do you mean?" Charlotte asked.

Keeping my eyes on my plate, I took methodical bites and told her about my company and all the ways it had failed. The ways that I'd failed.

"I came here with nothing," I said, "so it looks like we're in the same boat."

It was ironic to think we had to fight to find that common ground when it had been there the entire time.

"I'm so sorry," Charlotte said. "I can kind of give you Ken's perspective, but I can only guess at how he feels, and the same goes for you. The studio sounds so cute."

"It was," I said. "I didn't like the business side. I wasn't good at that. But I was great at dealing with the kids and coming up with activities. It was so much fun."

"You should try again," she said.

"I don't have the money."

"Do children's art parties," she suggested. "There used to be a woman in town who did that when the boys were younger. People booked her months in advance because she brought the party and the fun."

It wasn't a bad idea. In fact, it was kind of genius. No overhead, other than the supplies, and only one person footing the bill.

"Your advertising costs would be low, too, once you got started," Charlotte said. "Moms book parties based on the parties they went to last. You'd never run out of clients."

"I'll think about it," I said. "No promises."

"That's what this past year taught me." Charlotte looked up at the house. "Even when something seems good, there are no guarantees."

We sat in silence for a moment.

"You know," I said. "I've been thinking a lot about Grandma and why she did all of this. It must have affected her terribly to have us be apart."

Charlotte nodded. "It made her so angry. It's like I said the other night—there were so many times she begged Dad to take me to Ireland, so that I'd have the chance to know you and our mother. He refused, because he didn't think it was fair to put us together only to have us be apart again." She frowned. "I wanted to know who you were. I tried so many times to remember you. I had dreams about you sometimes, but I couldn't remember."

I reached out and held her hand tight. "You know, in the beginning, I worried that Grandma would be disappointed in us."

"I think she'd be proud of us," Charlotte said. "I hope she's looking at us right now."

# CHAPTER TWENTY

I was in my bedroom putting the final touches on some makeup when something that sounded like a raccoon ran across the roof with a loud thumping sound. I hesitated, looking up at the ceiling.

The roofers had done a great job. We didn't need animals up there that could cause additional damage and make it so they had to come back. I also couldn't picture how raccoons would get up there in the first place. There were some big trees but no direct access points. It wasn't like a raccoon could jump like a squirrel.

*Thud.*

I jumped. The sound was right over my head. Maybe it wasn't an animal at all. It sounded like heavy objects were actually falling on the roof.

What on earth was going on?

My heart started to pound as it hit me that the roof might be caving in.

"Charlotte?" I called, rushing out of my room. "Ken?"

I ran down the stairs. They were talking and laughing out on the back deck. Ken waved me over to join them.

"Jayne," he called. "We need a tiebreaker. Charlotte is trying to convince me that most men bring their wives breakfast in bed. What's the verdict?"

"Let me think on that," I said. "In the meantime, something's wrong with the roof."

Charlotte's eyebrows lifted. "It's leaking?"

"No, something's banging on it. I think it's animals or I'm scared that maybe some of the new boards aren't working or…"

There was a loud thump from upstairs that we could all hear.

Charlotte and Ken scrambled to their feet and we all went racing up the stairs and stood in the hallway, staring up at the ceiling. The thumping was relentless.

"It sounds like footsteps," Charlotte said, puzzled. "I heard a crash, though."

"Boys!" Ken shouted. "Where are you?"

The noise came to an abrupt halt. Ken let out some choice curse words and stormed down the hallway. The door leading up to the belvedere was open and he roared, "Why is this unlocked?"

Charlotte froze, her hand on the wall of the hall. "You didn't lock it?"

I swallowed hard. "I didn't know that I was supposed to."

Ken was already taking the steps two at a time and Charlotte was right behind him. I went up more slowly, uncertain as to what I was about to walk into.

Sure enough, one of the windows leading onto the roof was open and the boys were out there. They'd tried to hide behind one of the turrets, probably when they heard Ken shout. In the distance, the ocean stretched for miles. The sight of my nephews so high up made my heart pound.

"Boys, get back in here." Ken's voice was slow and steady. "Get on your hands and knees and crawl."

Josh did what he said. He made it to the window and let himself in, a look of defiance on his face. Evan seemed paralyzed to his spot on the roof.

"Come on, Evan." Charlotte's voice shook. "You're okay."

Evan swallowed hard, his Adam's apple moving up and down with the effort. "No, I think I'm going to fall," he said, his voice starting to crack.

"Come on, man." Josh sounded frustrated. "You're fine. You . were just dancing up there!"

*Dancing?*

Charlotte nearly turned white.

"You can do it, son," Ken called.

"I'm going to fall!"

"You can't fall off the roof," Ken said. "You'll be fine. Imagine a thousand adoring women, cheering you on."

Evan's cheeks turned red. Then he dropped to all fours and did a sudden scramble, making it across the roof and practically falling in through the window.

The second he was in, Ken roared, "What were you two imbeciles thinking? You could have fallen off the roof!"

Evan's mouth dropped open. "You said I couldn't fall off the roof!"

"I was lying," Ken shouted. "Of all the idiotic things I've ever seen in my life, you two thought it would be smart to get out there and try to fly? You're both grounded. No phone for a week."

"Dad!" Josh's face turned to thunder but Evan didn't dare say a word.

Charlotte pulled both of them in for hugs and I stood there in silence. My hands were shaking. The image of Evan crawling across the roof was going to stay with me and the sick feeling in my stomach only served as a reminder that these kids meant something to me.

"There was a crash," Charlotte said. "Were you dropping things off the roof?"

Josh held up his hands. "No, I swear."

"Good. Let's go downstairs and get a snack," Charlotte said. "I think you just aged me ten years."

Ken glanced out the window and shuddered. Once we were all in the hallway, he hung back as the boys and Charlotte headed for the stairs. Then he found the key and locked the door.

"I'm so sorry, Ken," I said. "I didn't know."

"That my kids are maniacs?" He tried to smile, but I could tell he was shaken up. "You coming?"

I rested my hand against the wall, trying to stop my legs from trembling. "Not right now. I have some things to take care of."

Mainly, I wanted to sit in silence and deal with the fact that I'd just made a mistake that could have cost those boys their life. They thought they were invincible but had no idea what could have happened. The idea that they were dancing and stomping around up there? Terrifying.

I was headed in the opposite direction from the stairs, towards my room, when something on the ground near the bathroom caught my eye. It looked like… I took a couple of steps closer and stopped short. There was plaster in the hallway.

Dread settled in my stomach. Letting out a breath, I went to take a look and nearly choked on the cloud of dust in the bathroom.

Charlotte and Ken were back upstairs in a flash at my shout. They stood behind me and stared. The section of ceiling that Charlotte and I had so painstakingly replastered had completely fallen to the ground. Lathe boards, chunks of plaster, and a fine dust covered the vanity and the toilet and practically filled the bathtub.

Ken whistled. "There's your crash." He gingerly took steps into the bathroom, looking up to make sure nothing remained to fall on top of him.

"What happened?" Charlotte whispered.

Reaching up, Ken tugged at a lathe board that half hung from the ceiling and pulled it down. "The boys probably stomped too hard above this."

"It's a roof," Charlotte said. "Ceilings don't cave in because something bumped against the roof."

"We were up in the attic," a small voice said, and I turned to see Evan in the hallway, a hangdog expression on his face. "Before we went up on the roof."

"Honey," Charlotte said, and he held up his hands.

"I'm sorry," he said. "I didn't know that would happen."

"It only happens if your nails aren't long enough to properly connect your lathe boards," Ken said, holding one up as an example. "Or if you don't have enough nails, period. It's supposed to be two for each stud, if I remember right."

Charlotte put her hands to her face and looked at me. We'd run out of the long nails halfway through the process and rather than stopping the project to get more at the hardware store, we'd decided it would be fine to use the shorter nails we had on hand. We hadn't really had enough of those, either.

"Did you do it like this in all the bathrooms?" Ken asked, squinting at the nail.

"No," Charlotte said. "This was our last stop."

Ken ran his hand over his face and I had a feeling it was to hide a smile. "Well, you can thank your sons for saving one of us from a sure and unpleasant ceiling attack. It might not have happened today, tomorrow, or even next week, but it would have happened."

Evan patted his mother on the back. "You're welcome."

Charlotte shook her head at the mess and then looked at me.

I was still baffled by the sequence of events. "Looks like we need to buy more nails."


Once the drywall was back in place with plenty of the appropriate hardware to hold it up, Charlotte and I got to work pulling out the fixtures in the bathrooms. Our last stop was the bathroom in the downstairs hallway in the east wing, the one that was out of the way and barely used. The toilet was firmly attached to the ground and Charlotte and I had to cut and tug to finally loosen it enough to remove it. The water had been off for ages and the toilet was empty, but I still half cringed at that final tug.

"If you would have told me a few months ago that I'd spend my days hugging toilets…" I said, my arms practically wrapped around it.

Charlotte laughed. "I'm tempted to take pictures."

"I've said from the beginning that we should be documenting this. It would be fun to look back over all of this and…" My voice trailed off at her expression. It was clear that she had been joking and the last thing she wanted was a scrapbook of this experience. "Maybe not."

Charlotte unscrewed the toilet. When we lifted it up, we both stopped short. There was a note pasted to the back of it.

"There's another one," she said, her voice dry.

I plucked it off and opened it.

*Present for you inside the sink cupboard.*

"The sink cupboard is already in the dumpster," I said with a groan. "She couldn't have directed us to start with the toilet?"

Charlotte didn't laugh. "Let's take a look when we put this out there."

The dumpster had a ton of space, so the vanity was all the way at the bottom.

"You're the oldest," Charlotte said, scratching the back of her arm. "It's all you."

I sighed. "I'm going to remember that."

The dumpster was too full to open on the side, so I used a stepladder to climb over the top and jump in. There was the vanity, in the mess of boards and rusty nails.

"Be careful," Charlotte called. "There could be rats in there."

"I'm not worried about that," I called, but I did give a quick sweep with my eyes, just to be sure.

I picked my way over to the vanity, already feeling a little short of breath from nerves. What did my grandmother have in store for us this time? It could be anything, and I wasn't sure I was up for it. Charlotte and I had been on such a good path and I didn't want something new to come along that could push us apart.

Bending down, I saw the vanity had a cupboard beneath it that was locked.

"It's locked," I called.

"Break the door," Charlotte shouted back.

I considered the idea. It wouldn't be that hard. I pushed it to the side to see if it might have an additional opening and found a key duct-taped to the back.

"Never mind," I called. "There's a key."

Shaking my head, I detached it and opened the cupboard. There was a stack of old towels thrown about, along with a shoebox taped closed. It was small and black, and for a brief moment, I imagined the effort my grandmother had put into coordinating all of this. It was like the scavenger hunts we did when we were younger, but those days had been a lot more fun.

Now, I passed the box over the edge of the dumpster to Charlotte. "Can you get out?" she called.

I searched for a foothold, but there wasn't enough trash to climb on.

"No," I admitted.

"Do I need to call the fire department?" she called.

I laughed. "Yes, please."

The image of Logan showing up to rescue to me was not unwelcome.

I looked around the metal container, trying to decide the best way out. I could stack some things and hope for the best, but I didn't want to risk getting hurt. Just as I'd decided there was no alternative, the legs of a ladder peeked over the edge.

"Watch out," Charlotte called. "I'm sending you the ladder."

"Wait! How will we get it—" Then I saw she'd attached a blue rope to it that she must have been holding on the other side. "Nice work."

I set it up on a part of the dumpster where there was a flat surface and climbed up to the top. Grabbing the edges, I dropped down and then brushed off my legs. Charlotte had another ladder set up for us to climb up on as we pulled the other out, and I gave her a high five.

"Teamwork," I said.

Mission accomplished, we sat under the shade of the trees and studied the box.

"Ready?" I said.

She hesitated, then opened the lid.

"What is it?" I was sitting on my haunches close to the ground, not quite ready to look.

"There's a letter…"

Charlotte pulled it out and began to read:

*Dear Charlotte and Jayne,*

*I might have mentioned a few times that the summer you came to visit was one of the best summers of my life. It was the type of experience your grandfather and I had always envisioned when we bought this home. Of course, we had only given birth to your father, so we did not have the full and bustling home that we had hoped for. I finally had the opportunity to experience it that summer when you girls were here.*

*Perhaps you do not remember, but the two of you made friends with a group of kids on the beach. That summer, there were times that the entire crowd traipsed through my kitchen to raid the freezer of its Popsicles, Fudgesicles, and ice cream. They left sand on the floor, dirty fingerprints on my walls—and, girls, I loved every blessed second of it.*

Charlotte blinked. "I haven't thought of that in years."

"I talked about it with my friend Lauren," I said. "She remembers coming up here."

"Who?" Charlotte said, looking confused.

"Lauren. She owns a coffee shop on Main. She's also Logan's sister."

Charlotte smiled. "Well, that's convenient," she said. "I don't remember anyone from that summer. The only thing I remember is spending time with you."

The words touched my heart. I stood up and peered over her shoulder at the rest of the letter.

*My hope is that these pictures will spark a positive memory and a measure of delight. I always hope it will remind you girls of what this house could be, and the fun times that can be had. Enjoy your time here—goodness, I hope you chose to do this during the summer. Otherwise, brrr…*

*With love,*
*Your grandmother*

Together, we sifted through the box. Our grandmother had supplied us with endless images of that time. Pictures of us on bike rides, taking dips in the ocean, and collecting seashells along the sand. Lying on the beach, building forts, eating ice cream… The pictures were like memories floating by me like clouds that finally stood still long enough to be seen clearly.

In the pictures, Charlotte and I seemed so close. So happy. Like two girls who would be friends forever.

Charlotte paused at one where we were walking up the staircase from the beach, our hands entwined and heads close together as we whispered a secret.

"We were so naïve." She threw the picture back into the box. "It makes me so mad."

"I know," I said, touching her arm.

"It wasn't right." Her face was red. "I mean, I appreciate what Grandma tried to do, bringing us both here, but it set up false expectations. The idea that we suddenly had this long-lost bond is ridiculous. Do you remember Grandma showed us *The Parent Trap* one of our first nights there? The old one?"

I nodded. "Yes, I loved that."

"Of course you did. We both did. But as an adult, I can look at the situation objectively," Charlotte said. "I look at that picture and I see two girls who have no idea about the reality of their life situation. It wasn't right to try and force a friendship that was going to end with land mines like the ones we've dealt with. It's not right that she's trying to do that again from beyond the grave. I think this whole thing is cruel. Why put us back together to separate us again?"

"You mean, now?" I said, confused. "Or then?"

"Both."

Something cold settled in my stomach. "Both?"

She smoothed her ponytail. "We have our own lives; we don't live in the same town. You don't even want to talk to Dad..."

"There's more to it than that—"

"Yes, but it's going to complicate things." Charlotte let out a breath and stared at the dumpster. "What's that expression? Dumpster fire? That's what this feels like. All of it."

My throat went tight. "Charlotte, I know that this is a lot. I feel the same. Let's not make the mistake of turning on each other. I am here for you and we will talk about all of this, okay?"

I squeezed her hands tight and she nodded. "Listen, I have to get ready for work. If you want to look at the pictures without me, you can. Leave them outside my door when you're done, if that's okay."

Before she could respond, I headed for my room. There, I buried my face in the soft starch of the pillow and burst into tears.

Yes, I'd been through my own heartache, but it hurt to think of all the heartache she'd been through. I was her older sister. I should have spent my life protecting her. Instead, she'd been on her own.

The idea made my heart break for the two girls I'd seen in that picture who believed that, in spite of it all, they'd finally found their match.

I grabbed my car keys and apron to head out to work. Before I could bring myself to go, I sifted through the pictures and grabbed a picture of me and Charlotte sharing an ice-cream cone. I tucked it into the pocket of my shirt and pressed my hand against it, holding it close.

It was hard to wrap my mind around the fact that Charlotte and I had such a history together, that we had spent so many shared smiles and special moments. It brought to mind the years that I couldn't even remember, when we must have dressed up dolls, made up games, sung songs, and done a thousand other things in our shared world.

Charlotte and I had made such progress in our relationship, but seeing these pictures made all of the old feelings and doubts crop up again. The fact that our parents had chosen to separate us blew my mind. How could they justify that?

My parents had been unspeakably selfish. They should have fought through the pain to keep me and Charlotte together. That's what Logan was doing for his daughters. My parents should not have given up out of fear; they should have fought to keep us together.

*That's what we have to do. Every day.*

Charlotte's reaction to the photographs had scared me. The things that she'd said about setting up false expectations, listing all the reasons it would be difficult to stay in each other's lives… it made me nervous. What if we went through all of this and she walked away again?

I couldn't think that way. For so long, I'd made the choice to give up on Charlotte, and I was not about to make the same mistake again.

Our relationship might not be easy, but it was worth fighting for. I had to keep choosing to move forward regardless of how difficult it might be.

It was a challenge to get out of the car to walk into work. My eyes felt like sandpaper from crying, and my face felt puffy. Still, I pasted on a smile and put one foot in front of the other, the images of me and my sister flooding my mind.

The simple act of getting to work put me in a better place, because I didn't have time to get lost in my thoughts. I needed to bring guests silverware and lemons for their waters and remember the specials. There were moments when a thought would sneak in, like how Charlotte and I were cheated, but I quickly pushed it away.

Even though I was determined to move on, I found it hard to keep up at work. I timed the food wrong, forgot to add substitutions, and when I saw Logan walk in, I was too rattled to even tell him hello. Moments later, someone jostled me as I walked across the deck with a tray and the whole lot fell to the floor with a spectacular crash, shattering two glasses of wine and a dirty martini.

The busboys bustled up to take care of the debris, and my manager told me to take five to try to get the wine off my shirt. I rushed to the side hallway that led to the outdoor bathrooms. There was a flowering tree surrounded by a circular wooden bench, and I sank down on it, putting my head in my hands. Silent, hot tears rolled down my cheeks.

"Hey, are you okay?" Logan had come to find me. He sat alongside me on the bench, concern clouding his face. "I saw what happened out there."

"You and everyone else." One of the purple flowers had fallen and I cradled it in my hand. "I wouldn't be shocked if it's on YouTube," I said, trying to keep a sense of humor about it all. "One million hits by morning."

Logan laughed. "I've already forwarded it to a few people." He rested his arms on his thighs, his forearms strong and tanned. "Really, it was pretty impressive no one clapped. I was tempted to lead the charge but..."

The tug of a smile pulled at the corner of my mouth. Just as quickly, the smile faded. My eyes welled with tears and I had to blink to keep them back.

"I should go get cleaned up." I dried my eyes on my sleeve, embarrassed that I couldn't just keep it light.

"Sure." Logan got to his feet. "I'd like to call you later and check on you, if that's okay?"

"Call me?" I echoed.

"Yeah." His voice was low. "I don't like seeing you like this. Hurting."

Our eyes met for a moment and for the first time in ages, I didn't feel so alone.

"My grandmother left a surprise box of pictures of me and my sister the summer we came to visit." I pulled out the picture from my shirt pocket and handed it to him, grateful that the spilled wine had missed it. "It's the only summer we were together after our parents separated us."

He studied it for a moment. "This reminds me of my daughters, sharing an ice cream. I can't begin to imagine separating them. Not at any point in their lives."

"My parents had no problem doing it to us. Seeing this picture made me think about all we've lost."

One of the waitresses poked her head around the corner. "It's getting busy."

"Be right there," I called.

Logan was close enough that I could smell the faded scent of metal, as if he wore it like cologne. He reached out, his thumb brushing across my cheek. Then he drew back, as if surprised.

"Sorry. You had a little mascara."

"Thank you." I felt as flustered as he looked. "The weepy waitress look probably won't earn me extra tips."

We stood in silence and then I remembered the bustle going on around the corner. It would be hard to jump back into a busy night, but I didn't have a choice.

He pulled out his phone. "I have you in here somewhere." He searched for a minute. "I want to be able to check in, see if you're doing okay. I know what you're going through can't be easy."

"Thanks," I said. "That means a lot."

"Found you." He turned his phone and showed me how he'd typed in my name.

*Sweet Jayne.*

That familiar flush that I felt around him warmed my cheeks.

"You're a fan of Lou Reed," I said.

"No." His eyes held mine. "I'm a fan of Jayne."


Charlotte was already in bed by the time I was done with work, so I decided to take a walk along the beach. It was a beautiful night and hopefully it would bring me back to a place of peace.

The weather was perfect and the stars were out, so several groups of people were out and some had even lit bonfires. I was pretty far from the house when I spotted Josh. He was with a group of boys, passing around a bottle of vodka.

I stood there in shock, watching him. It had been a while since Evan and I had talked about Josh and his drinking. It was one thing to hear the report and another to see it happening. Josh was only sixteen and, even though it was not uncommon to experiment at sixteen, it was too dangerous for him to be doing it by the ocean.

If he went out for a swim, he might not come back. If he passed out and his friends left him on the beach, he could get arrested. Either way it wouldn't end well.

Pulling out my phone, I almost called Charlotte, but it was late and she was asleep. Instead, I let out a breath and walked over to the group of boys. Josh's face fell.

I crouched down next to him. "Time to come home."

"Nah," he said, his eyes glassy in the light from the fire. "You're not my mom."

His friends must have realized what was going on because they moved away from the fire and tried to hide the bottle in the sand. I ignored them, because the only one I needed to worry about was Josh.

"No, I'm not your mom," I said, "but I'll have to tell your mom."

Josh's eyes widened in panic. "Don't. I'll come with you. Don't say anything. Please. I was only trying to make some new friends and I didn't know they'd be drinking. Don't say anything, okay?"

The story was unlikely, given what Evan had told me, but I played along in order to get him safely home.

"Sounds good," I said. "Say good night to your friends."

Josh's face was dark but he followed me with big, stumbling steps. We passed several people and I felt nervous, like every single one knew that he was drunk.

It was a long walk to the beach house and I could feel Josh wilting next to me. Finally, I stopped and turned to him. "Look, I know you're drunk."

His body seemed to freeze for a moment. Then he laughed. "I'm sixteen."

I didn't know if that was supposed to mean that it was impossible because he was sixteen or that I shouldn't be surprised, since it was summer and he was sixteen. His tone could have meant either, but I was not about to let him off the hook.

"Yes," I said. "You're sixteen, which is why this isn't okay. I'm not going to tell your parents—provided you agree to two conditions."

He glared at me with his ice-blue eyes. "Yeah? What's that?"

"First, you cannot leave the house again tonight to try and go anywhere or do anything until you're sober. Two, you cannot drink anything else, other than water or Gatorade. I'll be checking back. Oh, and there's a third—I need you to meet me for breakfast tomorrow morning and talk about this."

"I won't be awake for breakfast."

"Lunch, then. No excuses."

He stared me down, but in the end he shrugged. "Whatever. *Auntie*."

"You can call me Jayne," I said.

He didn't respond, but he didn't say something smart, either. Instead, he gave me some sort of a mock salute and we walked the rest of the way to the house in silence.

Once we reached the stairs, I turned to my nephew. "This can't happen again. Understand?"

He gave a serious nod. "Yeah," he said. "I get it."

We walked up the stairs and he stumbled off to bed. I stood in the living room, wondering if I should wake Charlotte and tell her. Ultimately, I decided the best I could do was keep an eye on the situation and, if anything else happened, I would tell her then.

Josh and I went to lunch in a park nearby that had food trucks around its perimeter. He was sullen and hid behind a pair of sunglasses, but at least he showed up.

"Here." I'd bought BLTs from one of the trucks and he seemed as happy as Evan to start eating.

"So, look," I said. "I wanted to talk to you about what happened yesterday." He didn't answer, so I went on: "I'm not interested in telling you that you shouldn't do this or you shouldn't do that, because I doubt it would do any good. You're a teenager, you want to try things, I get it."

He looked surprised, but kept picking through the French fries and dipping the crispy ones in ketchup. "The real question is, why are you doing this? There has to be a reason."

"Why not?" Josh took a drink of the Coke I'd bought him, and looked at me. "Seriously, that's my answer."

"Look, I've got all day," I said.

It wasn't entirely true. Charlotte and I were slated to get to work, and Logan had called the night before and asked me out to dinner on Friday. I wanted to stop by one of the thrift shops to get the perfect dress for the occasion.

"Because it's boring, you know?" Josh said.

"What is?" I asked.

"School. Life. All of it."

"Josh, you like sports, right?" I asked.

He glared at me. "Did my mom put you up to this?"

"She has no idea that we're talking. I can tell her if you want me to."

"No." He flicked at the lettuce on the sandwich. "I used to play soccer, but my grades dipped so I'm not going to be able to play in the fall. It was the only thing that kept school interesting. I'm not good at it like Evan. I'm just trying to keep myself busy so that I can make it through school and get off to college."

"Why will college be better?"

He looked surprised at the question. "I'll have freedom. Get to do what I want."

"You'll still have to go to class," I said, my voice gentle. "You can still flunk out of college."

"I know, but..."

"Do you like the new school that you're at?" I asked. "Your mom said you and your brother moved, and I know that can make things hard."

"What do you know about it?" he demanded, and I sensed I'd hit on something.

"I had to move from my home to Ireland when I was six," I said. "I didn't know anybody. It wasn't easy."

He kept eating but his bites were much more methodical. Finally, he wadded up the crust. "Yeah. It's sucked. Mom and Dad hate it, too."

I frowned. "Why do you think that?"

"Because I read their text messages," he said, giving me a smug smile. "They had this app set up on my phone to spy on me, so I did the same thing to theirs. They're so clueless."

"They're your parents," I said. "Please show some respect."

He glared at me but didn't respond.

"I didn't bring you here to lecture you," I told him. "I wanted to meet to tell you that I'm concerned. If you need an ear, I'm here, okay?"

Josh didn't answer but we got in the car to head home. When we were almost there, he turned to me, looking young. "Thanks. For trying, you know?"

I smiled at him. "You're welcome."


Now that Charlotte and I had worked our way through the structural repairs, fixing water damage, tile and bathroom fixture removals, we had made it to a fun portion—choosing the tiles, carpet, and fixtures that would serve as replacements.

We sat down and pored over wallpaper and flooring fixtures until they all started to look the same. More than once, she complimented me on my choices.

"You have such an artistic eye," she said with admiration. "I really do think you should consider what I said about doing children's parties. I bet there would even be a market for it here, so you could start working on it now as a practice run."

"I think I have enough on my plate right now," I told her. "Speaking of, I have to get ready for work."

My phone chimed as I headed out of the kitchen and I took a look. My heart skipped to see a message from Logan.

*Are you working tonight?*

I turned right back around and showed it to Charlotte.

"What do you think?" I said.

She grinned. "Put on some mascara."

My nerves were a little on edge to see him again because I'd had it in my mind that I wouldn't get the chance until our date on Friday. It was a relief to focus on the mindless act of taking orders, bringing people their food, and doing my best to make their night pleasant. Towards the end of the night, when I had just brought out a bottle of wine for a table that was celebrating a birthday, Logan walked in.

Spotting me, he winked and indicated he'd be sitting at the bar.

"Happy birthday," I told the woman celebrating, and tried to concentrate on keeping the wine in her glass instead of pouring it all over the table.

Even though it was late, customers kept reordering drinks, requesting dessert menus, and basically making it impossible for me to do anything but my job. At last the evening started to wane and all of my checks were paid. I closed out as the tables finished their wine, and turned in my paperwork.

Logan was busy eating something, so he had his back to me as I approached. He looked up and saw me in the mirror that hung behind the bar. Turning, he smiled. "Listen, I know it's late, but I have a surprise for you. I was hoping you could stop by the shop real quick."

"The shop?" I said. "Oh, is the playhouse done?"

"It's not that." He gave me a shy smile. "Just for a minute." Intrigued, I nodded. "Okay. See you there."

I parked out front and once I saw him pull up and park behind me, I got out. He looked so handsome in his black T-shirt, tan pullover, and jeans that I felt a shiver run through me. I had no idea what the surprise might be.

"I'm so curious about this," I said.

Logan turned his attention from unlocking the shop door and gave me a grin over his shoulder. "I hope you like it."

Once again, I felt that spark pass between us. Dangerous feelings but welcome, considering I was so attracted to him. I had no idea what he planned to show me, but I was perfectly happy to follow him.

He was quiet as he flipped on a small lamp that threw off a dim light. "This way," he said, leading me towards the back.

The smell of metal and woodsmoke was intoxicating, and I tried to think of all the reasons I should not be thinking about being alone in the dark with him. But, if I thought he was about to take me in the back room to push me up against the wall, I was wrong. He flipped on the brightest light in the world, illuminating the space.

"The story of you and your sister has really touched me," he said, as I rubbed my eyes. "It brought up all sorts of thoughts and feelings, and I couldn't get this image out of my mind. So, I made this. It's called *Sisters*. Of course, it's for you."

He pulled a black cloth off a gleaming bronze-and-copper sculpture. Each piece of metal seemed to stretch up towards the sky, the competing colors curving up and then towards one another like a mother holding close her child. It was so precise, so perfect, and somehow, it encapsulated my relationship with Charlotte.

"It's beautiful." Slowly, I ran my hands over the cold metal and my eyes welled with tears. "Logan, this is... I can't stop looking at it."

"I know that feeling." His tone made me turn to look at him. "Maybe I should have called it *Jayne*."

I didn't hesitate. I walked right over and he pulled me in close. I wrapped my arms around him as tight as I could, never wanting the kiss to end.

# CHAPTER TWENTY-ONE

Charlotte was on her computer out on the deck when I returned home the next morning. After grabbing a quick cup of coffee from the kitchen, I went out to join her, a big grin on my face. She was in a meeting but when she saw my expression, she gave me a thumbs-up sign off camera before turning her attention back to the computer.

"This all sounds great," she said. "Let me circle back with you about the numbers. I'll be in touch." She ended the meeting and gave me a knowing look. "*You* did not come home last night."

"No, I did not," I sang.

I had texted Charlotte before leaving the restaurant because I wanted her to know that I was heading to Logan's house and that I was safe. It had been a long time since I'd had anyone to answer to, and it was comforting. It meant so much to have her in my life, which made the sculpture Logan had made matter so much more.

"Tell me everything," she said, reaching for her coffee. It was empty and she made a face. "Can I have a sip of that?"

It felt so good to be back in a good place with one another after the heartache the box of pictures had caused.

I poured half of my coffee into her glass and we cradled our mugs. "So, he's an artist and, as it turns out, he fell into this mad hole of creating something for me. He texted to see if I'd be at work and afterwards, he asked me to come to the shop to see it. Charlotte…"

Hopping up, I ran inside and lugged out the sculpture. Her eyes widened as I set it on the deck with a thump. "Isn't that unbelievable?"

"Goodness." She got to her feet and studied it. "I thought you were going to tell me he made you a mix tape. This is much better."

I laughed, then got serious. "He called it *Sisters*."

Her blue eyes met mine, then looked back down at the sculpture. She immediately rested her hand on top of it. "It's…" Her eyes misted. "Well, he's won me over."

The back door banged and Evan rushed out. "Hi, Mom."

"Morning, sweetie." She stretched to kiss him on the cheek. "How are you?" Her computer pinged and she made a face. "Give me a sec. I'm supposed to jump into this meeting—"

"No worries." Evan squeezed his hands tight. "Jayne, can you make me breakfast?"

"Please," Charlotte corrected.

"Please," he said.

By the look on his face, I could tell this had nothing to do with breakfast, and whatever it was he had to tell me, he did not want to share with his mother.

"I'd love to," I said quickly. "Let's go in." Scooping up the sculpture, I followed him inside, hoping everything was okay with his brother. "What's up?" I asked, once we were safely in the kitchen.

"It's Josh." Evan's words came quickly, a pinched expression on his face. "He took out a boat last night with his friends. They were drinking, out past curfew, all of it."

I shook my head. "Evan, I know you're worried about him, but you need to tell this to your mother. She can help—"

"Wait." Evan grabbed at his hair. "He passed out in the boat, so his friends left him there when they pulled back up to the dock. This morning…" The pinched expression fell away as his face crumbled. "Josh and the boat are gone!"

"Gone?" I echoed. "What does that mean?"

"I don't know." Evan clutched at his hair, pacing the kitchen. "I went in his room this morning and he wasn't there, so I started asking around. No one remembers what time they left him there. They tried to get him out of the boat, but he said he wanted to sleep under the stars." Evan's breath was coming fast and I gave him a glass of water. "They were drunk, so they don't know if they anchored it or anything."

I swallowed hard. "Okay. Hopefully, he woke up this morning, took the boat out for a joyride, and ran out of gas."

The beach would have been busy first thing in the morning and if there was some passed-out kid lying in the boat, beach patrol would have heard about it. It was more likely that he'd taken the boat out again and it had run out of gas or gotten stalled, or… I shuddered. He could have drifted out to sea in the middle of the night, which was something I did not want to think about.

I didn't know if the Coast Guard would stop a boat that was drifting. Without a distress signal or a report, they might assume it was just out for a late-night ride. I had no idea what the rules were, whether or not he'd have to be at the helm.

"We need to tell your mother," I said. "Right now."

"Please don't." Evan shook his head. "Josh is so weird these days. I'm afraid of what he'll do if you bring Mom into it. He might try to run away or… I don't even know."

"This is serious," I said. "I can't keep something like this a secret. Something could have happened. She needs to know—"

"She'll flip out." Evan grabbed the sides of his head, hopping up and down. It looked like the kid was about to lose it himself. "Please don't tell her. I don't know what Josh would do."

The idea of not telling my sister that her son was missing put my stomach in knots. Charlotte had every right to know that there was something going on. I wanted a relationship with Evan, but I couldn't keep this from his parents.

"I'm sorry, honey," I said. "We can't do this alone."

I ran back outside. Quickly, I briefed Charlotte on what had happened and she shouted for Ken. The terror in her voice was something I never wanted to hear again. The three of us gathered with Evan in the living room so he could tell them the whole story.

"Whose boat was it?" I asked. "Did the kid tell his parents what happened?"

If the boat was already reported missing, there was a good chance that the Coast Guard had started searching for it.

Evan looked down at his feet.

"What?" I said. "Spill it."

"Josh and his friends steal boats."

"What?" Charlotte cried.

"They look for boats where the key's been tucked under a seat, and they take them," he said. "It's usually the people that are gone for the summer. They can tell because the boats are still winterized."

I rested my hand on Charlotte's shoulder. "It will be okay," I murmured, because I had no doubt the idea of her son passed out in the middle of the ocean, drunk on a stolen boat, was not what she wanted to hear.

"I'll call the Coast Guard," Ken said, pulling out his phone.

"We need to get out there and find him," Charlotte cried, gripping Evan's hand tight.

Josh could be out in the ocean right now, treading water or hanging on to a piece of driftwood. Picking up the phone, I called Logan.


"I was about to call you," he said, his voice low and intimate.

In any other situation, I would have felt butterflies, but now, I only felt the crush of time. "I need your help," I said. "Long story short, I've got a drunk teenager missing on a stolen boat. Can you help?"

His voice immediately turned serious. "Tell me what happened."

I ran him through the scenario, and he took in a sharp breath. "Every second counts. We have to report it."

"His father's doing that right now," I said. "Can you take me out in your boat to look for him?"

Logan had mentioned in passing that he had one. I only hoped it wasn't a rowboat.

"Absolutely," he said. "Meet me at the shop."

Ken instructed Evan to stay at home in case Josh came back, then drove me and Charlotte down there, breaking every speeding law in the city. Logan met us at the door, phone in hand, and flipped the sign to *Closed*.

We jumped into his truck and drove in silence to the marina. Logan pulled up behind the deep-sea fishing shop and parked, scrawling a quick note and leaving it in his windshield. Then he rushed us onto the dock and into a black speedboat.

He helped us aboard, and the boat roared to life as I yanked my life jacket on.

"The Coast Guard's started a search," Ken said, scanning the water. "I didn't tell them the boat was stolen. We don't need to address that unless it comes up."

Ken and Logan discussed a plan of which areas to search as Logan cut through the water. Charlotte looked pale and I took her hand, my stomach sick with guilt and worry. I should have told her that I'd seen him drinking on the beach the other night. Evan had told me this was a problem, and I should have said something about it right away instead of trusting it would get better on its own.

"If anything happens to him…" Charlotte broke off, unable to finish, her hands pressed to her eyes.

The mist from the water splashed against my face like tears.

"He'll be fine," I said. "He has to be."

Five minutes later, Evan called. I was still reeling with the pain in my sister's voice, and I watched, hand to my mouth, as she answered.

"He's back," Charlotte cried.

Ken dove forward to hug her and they held each other tight. Charlotte handed me the phone, saying, "Evan wants to talk to you."

"Hello?" I said, gripping the edge of the boat.

"Jayne, I'm scared," Evan said. "He's banging on the bedroom door, saying he's going to beat me up."

"We'll be right there," I said.

Sliding into the seat next to Logan, I said, "He's okay, apparently, but if we don't get back soon, his brother might not be."

"Where are they?" Logan said, his face grim.

"My grandmother's house."

We agreed the best course of action was for Logan to drive us back to get Ken's car, and then we sped to the Row.

"I'll call the Coast Guard," Charlotte said, the relief evident in her voice. "To let them know he's safe."

Logan and I got there first, and the sun was hot on my face as we jumped out and rushed to the front door. I could hear Josh ranting at the top of his lungs as we approached. Logan frowned and tried the door. It was locked.

"Josh," I called, banging on the door. "Let me in."

I half expected him to ignore me, but he threw open the door and glared at me, then Logan.

"Evan," I shouted past him. "Are you okay?"

"I'm still alive," he called back.

"How dare you?" My nephew's pupils were small and pinned me like a laser. "You had no right to get everyone involved."

Logan looked at me. "What do you want me to do here?"

Josh looked drunk and furious, but exhausted. He probably didn't have the energy to get too aggressive, since he'd already used it trying to break down the door to the room where Evan was hiding.

"I'll go in and talk to him," I said.

Logan nodded. "I'll wait out here," he said, after giving Josh a warning look.

Inside the house, I noticed that Josh recked with that wet-dog, sweaty teenage-boy smell, coupled with alcohol. He was sunburned and weaving back and forth.

"Josh, are you okay?" I asked, careful to keep my voice calm. "Everyone's been looking for you."

"You just had to cause trouble, didn't you?" he demanded, lurching forward.

"Josh, that was not my intent." I put my hand up to steady him, but he shook me off. "Let's sit down, okay? Your parents are on the way."

"Do you know what could have happened to my family if anyone found out about this?" He took a step closer to me. "That's exactly why you did it. You want to destroy my mother so that you can keep the house for yourself. You don't have shit, so you think it's okay to take it from other people."

The words stung. They were too close to home but, at the same time, completely unfair. I had worried about whether or not I deserved to have a role in this inheritance since the beginning, so to have Josh speak to my fear hurt, but not as much as he must have wanted. The kid knew what he was doing. He was on the attack to get me to back off.

*Be stronger. Be better. You're the grown-up.*

I wanted to live up to the words but, at the same time, I was not about to let him say things that weren't true. I wasn't out to destroy his mother—I would do anything to protect her, and that meant protecting him, too.

"Excuse me." My voice was sharper than I'd heard it in years. "I got everyone involved *because* I care about your mother, and I was not about to let her suffer through the idea that her son was irresponsible and immature enough to ruin his life and either die or get arrested by driving around drunk in a stolen boat."

His eyes widened. "It wasn't stolen."

"Don't lie to me." I locked eyes with him and when his gaze wavered, I knew the truth. "You might think you're on a sure track to success in your life. A trip to the Ivy Leagues and a high-paying job? That's never going to happen if you keep going down this path. All of your daddy's money wouldn't have been able to do a thing to save you, and now that the money is gone, your parents are counting on you to see your way through. So don't screw it up."

Josh froze. "What are you talking about, the money is gone?"

The bedroom door clicked open.

Evan walked down the stairs, equally stunned. "What do you mean?"

My knees went weak. The stress of the situation, racing to the boat and then the house, had left me tired and my sugar felt low. Charlotte had confided in me about the issue with the money, she'd trusted me, and I blew it. Feeling sick, I fumbled in my pocket for a piece of hard candy and put it in my mouth, trying to feel back to normal.

Thinking fast, I said, "What do I mean? I mean… if you ended up in jail, he'd have been spending all of his money on lawyers and maybe even lawsuits to make up for what you did." The words barely sounded convincing, but Josh was drunk enough that his face showed nothing but relief.

I could tell that Evan, on the other hand, didn't buy it. His parents walked in right at that moment.

"Josh!" Charlotte rushed forward to hug him.

"Excellent, greet the prodigal son," Evan said. "Hey, Dad? I think it's about time you quit bugging me not to invest in cryptocurrency because, unlike you, I haven't lost a dime."

Turning on his heel, he stalked into the bedroom and slammed the door.

"What is he talking about?" Josh put both of his hands on Charlotte's shoulders. "Wait. So it *is* true?"

Charlotte turned to me with a look of utter disbelief. It was the only secret she'd ever told me, and I'd turned around and betrayed her trust.

"I'm so sorry," I said. "I had no idea that you hadn't told the kids. When we were talking about it, you said it had been hard on them."

"I meant the move has been hard on them," Charlotte said.

"I'm so sorry," I repeated. "The moment I saw his face, I realized you hadn't told him."

Ken looked from me to Charlotte. Then he said, "We appreciate your help this morning. Do you mind leaving us for a while?"

"No," I whispered. "I completely understand."

Heart heavy, I met Logan in the front yard. He took one look at me and frowned.

"What happened?" he asked, and I burst into tears.

# CHAPTER TWENTY-TWO

Walking back into my grandmother's house, I listened to see if it was appropriate for me to come in. Logan had asked me if I wanted to come to the shop with him, but I needed to get something to eat. I heard low voices, but it sounded as if they were far off, maybe in the bedrooms.

The statue of the two sisters gleamed from the spot in the kitchen where I'd left it that morning and I studied it, feeling a pang. I couldn't stand the thought that I'd made such a huge mistake by telling Charlotte's boys about their financial issues. It was a major breach of trust, but it hadn't been intentional.

I really hoped Charlotte knew that.

I fixed myself a sandwich and ate it without tasting it. The moment I heard her voice coming down the stairs, I ran into the living room, wringing my hands.

"Charlotte, I—"

"It's fine." She headed for the kitchen. "We'll discuss it later, but for now, I need some water and I'm going to go lie down. I have a headache."

The fact that she'd spoken to me was a good sign, as well as the promise to address the issue later. The afternoon stretched out in front of me and I was too in my head to take a nap, so I decided to get to work on the house, as we'd planned.

I pulled out the wallpaper and flooring samples we'd been looking at, and revisited the colors we'd considered would be right for each room. The process of comparing the colors was soothing to me. It served as a reminder about how much I had enjoyed doing art with the kids at my studio before it all fell apart.

Running my hands over the stiff paper of one of the samples, I thought about what Charlotte had said, about setting up an art-party business. It was a clever idea because it eliminated so much overhead, but also, it would be fun. The idea gave me hope that I might not have to give up my dream of running a children's art studio; I would simply have to reshape it.

There was a creak on the stairs, and I looked over to see Charlotte on her way back down the stairs. For once, she didn't look put together, just tired and more than a little let down.

I stepped out of the kitchen and said, "Hi. Do you want me to make you some coffee?"

When she agreed, some of my nerves faded. It was possible that what had happened wasn't going to put us back at square one but regardless, we needed to talk about it.

"Great," I said. "I'll get some started and bring it out to the back deck."

Charlotte nodded and headed outside, before settling into a chair that overlooked the ocean.

Once the coffee was ready, I brought it out along with a plate of pastries I'd found at a sugar-free bakery. The more time I spent in this town, the more it seemed to have everything I could possibly need. Including Logan. I only hoped this fiasco hadn't scared him away.

"I wanted to tell you I'm sorry." I sat across from Charlotte. "I genuinely thought you'd told the boys but, regardless, I had no business mentioning it."

"That's right, you didn't." Charlotte's voice was light. "How did it come up?"

Letting out a breath, I told her what Josh had said. "Oh, Jayne." Her tone softened. "I'm so sorry. He obviously was not in his right mind. We've had so much trouble with him this past year… It hasn't been good."

"In full disclosure," I said, "Evan has been talking to me about it. He's been worried about Josh's drinking and didn't want to tell you because he didn't want to upset you. He thought you didn't know."

Charlotte drew back. "You knew? Why wouldn't you say something to me?"

"Because Evan asked me not—"

"He's a kid!" She glared at me, her blue eyes fierce. "Don't you understand that Josh could have died today out there on that boat? It's my job to protect him. You want to be the big sister so badly, well, it's your job to protect me! How could you do that?"

"I'm sorry," I whispered. "I should have said something."

"Yes, you should have." Charlotte picked at a blueberry muffin. "We suspected it, but we didn't know for sure. Today was like a slap in the face."

"Where is he now?" I asked.

"In bed." Charlotte sighed. "Ken's going to have a serious conversation with him when he's sober. He needs to understand what could have happened. The good news is that we can all have an honest dialogue about why we had to move and what things will look like in the future. I think he needs a sense of stability that hasn't been there."

"You know, you mentioned that he liked his new school," I said, "but I talked to Josh about it and he said that he doesn't. Evan seems to think that's where he's getting involved in all of this stuff. Do you have additional options?"

Charlotte paused. "Well, that's something I wanted to talk to you about." She squeezed her hands tightly together. "Jayne, this house is such a special place. We've done an outstanding job bringing it back to life. I think that it would mean so much

to our grandmother to see it like this that I'm struggling with a
dilemma of conscience."

I set down my coffee. "A dilemma of conscience?"

"I'm wondering if we should hang on to it."

My stomach dropped. "Keep it?"

Charlotte tucked a loose piece of hair behind her ear. "It's an
heirloom. Yes, we could bring in a high price for it but, Jayne,
this house is priceless. In the future, we could visit it whenever
we wanted, meet up here with our families. And at some point,
if the timing was right, we could sell. For now, I think we should
use it as an opportunity. We could stay here. Keep working on the
house. It's such a nice chance for community, and it would give
the two of us time together, which I've wanted my entire life."

The suggestion floored me. "Wow. That's... I'm surprised.
You don't want to sell?"

"No," she said. "Do you?"

In the beginning, I had worried that Charlotte would do
something like this. That she would want to use the property as
a beach getaway for her family, but I had never once imagined
she would invite me to join them. Besides, how would that work?

Charlotte, Ken, and her boys were a family. I was her sister,
yes, but our relationship was still tentative and I would always be
on the outside. The house would also be expensive to run. Once
the six months were over, I wouldn't have the stipend from my
grandmother and my job waiting tables was seasonal. It wouldn't
be possible for me to survive.

"It's a beautiful idea but, to be perfectly frank, I need the
money. You said you needed the money, too. Did something
change?"

"Well, yes." Her expression was troubled. "That's what made
the conversation you had with my boys easier. On Friday, Ken
signed a deal with an investor here on the coast who is willing
to back him."

"What?" I said.

"I know." She took a drink of coffee. "It's such a small world, and when the guy heard Ken was here for the summer they met up and talked logistics. It's going to save us, but it also means we're going to have to relocate. Here."

The news stunned me. "Hold on," I said, trying to process what she was saying. "You're moving here?"

"Yes." She gave me a cautious smile. "Isn't that wonderful news?"

I was silent. The reality of the situation started to dawn on me and something cold crept into my stomach.

Even though Charlotte had painted a picture of time we'd spend together, I couldn't help but wonder if she and Ken had sought out the opportunity. Maybe they'd hoped for something like this to happen—which was fine, except for the fact that I'd made it clear that I wouldn't be able to keep the house as a vacation home.

Still, I wanted to be careful with my words. I'd just betrayed her trust in a big way, and I didn't want to jump to conclusions.

"When we first started all of this, you said you were willing to sell," I reminded her. "I won't be able to afford to keep the house."

"You could try," Charlotte said. "You don't have a family. You have zero responsibilities… You could live in a setting fit for a princess, rebuild your business, and we could make up for lost time."

"This isn't a fairy tale." Panic set in at the memory of my debt. "We both agreed that the best choice was to sell the house. I wouldn't even be able to afford the taxes on this place."

"Then let us buy you out." Her face was casual, but the offer did not feel that way. "We'll have it appraised and go from there."

"Wait," I said. "You told me that you had lost all your money. That the house was a blessing and you needed to sell."

Charlotte stared out at the water. "This is only about money to you?"

I looked at her in disbelief. "We're not talking about splitting a check at a restaurant. We're talking about a property that is worth millions of dollars."

"We're talking about our grandmother's home." Hurt colored her features. "I asked you to live with me. Why are you acting like this?"

"I'm sorry," I said. "I'm not trying to be ungrateful. I have so much debt, though. I lied to you about why I'm working at the restaurant. I was too embarrassed to admit the truth, but the fact is I have to work there on top of getting a stipend because I'm so deep in the hole. I would love nothing more than to live here with you guys for a few summers but, unfortunately, I don't have the freedom to do that."

I felt a deep sense of shame at the admission. This house was indeed a family heirloom, and I'd barely been a part of the family. I didn't want to take it away from my sister, who had built so many precious memories here. It was so beautiful and unique that it would be hard for me to let it go, and I only had memories from that one summer. I could only imagine how she felt about it.

The disappointment on her face made my heart ache.

"Would you be able to buy me out?" I asked.

Charlotte nodded. "We'd have to work out a payment plan."

My heart sank. "I don't know if that would work," I said quietly.

She took a drink of her coffee and stared out at the ocean. "Well, I'll speak with Ken. He can begin making arrangements to find us a place."

"I'm sorry," I said.

Charlotte gave a stiff nod. "Me, too."

Inside, the sculpture of the two sisters seemed out of place in the living room. I took it upstairs and tried to find a place for it in my room, but nothing seemed quite right. Finally, I put it in the closet.

It was one of the most stunning things I'd ever owned, but at the moment, every time I looked at it, I felt sad.

# CHAPTER TWENTY-THREE

The next afternoon, we got to work on the staircase without discussing the drama of the day before. The tension felt heavy in the house. Ken and Charlotte were both cool with me and Josh refused to speak to any of us. Evan was the only one acting normal, but I could tell he was upset, too.

There were several balusters that were loose and needed to be tightened, while some needed to be replaced altogether. Charlotte and I were working on the project while Ken made business calls. Evan came over to help, and we all worked in silence as thunder rolled outside.

I was in charge of tightening, but it wasn't as easy as it first seemed it would be. The screw in each was hidden from view, often under thick paint. It was frustrating and slow work, so I focused on being patient as the room got darker and the intensity of the thunder increased. Finally, I got up to check on the storm.

It looked bad. The waves on the ocean were crashing against the shore in a frenzy, and dried pieces of seaweed tumbled across the sand in the wind. Lightning streaked across a gray sky in the distance, but it was getting closer by the minute.

I wasn't on the schedule at the restaurant, thank goodness. Most people weren't going to go out in this type of mess, and I didn't want to either. I got back to work, listening as the wind rattled the shingles and howled past the belvedere up above. It started to rain, light at first, then in earnest, and the thunder crashed.

"It's starting to get—" Charlotte started to say, when the lights flickered and then went out.

"Hey," Evan yelped, pulling out his ear pods. "Geez. I'm listening to this podcast about ghosts and it's getting a little scary. To be perfectly honest, I'm freaking out."

Ken's laughter boomed as loud as thunder. "Well, these stairs are scaring me. Great time to make them as unsafe as possible," he said. "When the lights go out."

The battery on my cell had been low because my charger hadn't been working, and when I went to flip on my flashlight, my phone went dead.

"Great," I mumbled.

It was still light enough to see everybody, but a flashlight would have been helpful.

"Charlotte, can I borrow your portable charger?" I said.

"It's in my top drawer." She was attempting to use the electric saw manually, dragging the blade back and forth across the wood. "The left one."

"Ken," I said. "Please make sure she doesn't cut her hand off."

In her bedroom, I opened the top drawer of her dresser and stopped short at the sight of an envelope addressed to me and Charlotte. It was in my grandmother's handwriting.

*Why would Charlotte have this in here?*

We'd agreed to keep the letters, boxes of pictures, and wedding album in the kitchen, because it was a shared space. I pulled the letter out to be sure that I wasn't confused, but no. It was one I'd never seen before.

I took it over to the window to get some light and began to read:

*Dear Jayne,*

*It is not easy to write this letter. I'm sure that the grief that it will cause you will be great, and for that, I apologize. Yet, dear*

*Jayne, you must know the truth about your past if you are to move forward without apology into the future.*

*Your mother was a wonderful woman. When I first met her, I thought to myself, Finally, my son has found the woman he will love for life. I do believe it's true that he loved her for life but was unable to find it in his heart to forgive her. The two hurt each other more than they helped one another to grow, and when they chose to separate, I would be lying if I said I wasn't grateful. I was tired of the hurt and the heartache, but little did I know that the worst was yet to come.*

*Jayne, your mother sent me a letter before she died, one that she asked me to pass along when the time was right. I could never convince myself that it was the right time, and I regret that now. You'll find it enclosed. I hope you will forgive me for the delay and that it will help you move forward.*

*All of my love,*
*Your grandmother*

Baffled that Charlotte hadn't shown me this, I opened the letter from my mother. I read the first words and then stopped.

*Dear Jayne, There is a truth to be told but I am not brave enough to say it…*

It was the letter. The one that I had wondered about for so long. It was on different paper, a formal cardstock as opposed to the notebook paper with lines. Quickly, I read on:

*Jayne, I first arrived in the States so full of plans for adventure. I went to college, where I met Graham. We fell in love in my last year of school, and he asked me to marry him. I wanted so badly to explore the States and live a big, bold life. We broke up, but he stayed in touch, leaving the door open for the future. Well, six months later, I became pregnant with you by another man.*

"What?" I stared at the words in shock.

This couldn't be true. My father was my father. There hadn't been another man. My mother would have told me before this. Wouldn't she?

Feeling sick, I continued reading:

*He was not interested in pursuing a relationship. I imagine you'll have questions about your birth father. He died when you were three, but he never met you, as he had no interest in me or in being a father.*

*However, Graham was still in love with me. I told him what had happened and he promised to raise you as his own. We agreed to keep your parentage a secret, and we got married. Jayne, we were never happy together. It wasn't the life that I wanted. I was ready to return to Ireland, to be with my family. Still, we wanted to try to make things work and we had Charlotte. The years passed and our relationship continued to fall apart. That's when Graham had an affair, and try as we might, we could not recover. I was honest with the courts about your parentage—*

The courts.

I stared at the paper. Could this possibly be true? If my father wasn't really my father, then my grandmother…

Questions swirled in my mind, and I kept reading as the storm raged outside.

*I was granted full custody. However, Graham did raise you for six years of your life, and he considers himself your father to this day. Please think about letting him back into your life, because he never wanted to leave it to begin with.*

*This is a difficult truth. However, it must be said in order to heal the hurts of the past. Please meditate on this, and I hope it will bring you and your sister together with greater understanding and healing.*

*With all of my love,*
*Your mother*

It was the "with all of my love" that made me grab the paper and wad it up with a cry.

"Jayne?" Charlotte called. Footsteps thundered up the stairs, and she rushed into the room, her eyes wild. "Jayne, wait!" I dropped the letter as if it were a gun and backed up, my arms crossed.

"Start talking," I told her.

She looked down at her feet. "I'm so sorry. I really didn't want you to see that."

"You lectured me about telling the truth," I told her. "About trust. The whole time, you were hiding something like this?"

"I didn't want you to get hurt," she said. "I was going to show you when the time was right, but I was as shocked as you are now and I didn't know what to do or what to say. I'm sorry, Jayne. I should have told you right away."

"The house," I whispered. "You held on to this because you want to contest the will. I'm not related to your grandmother at all."

"No!" The surprise in her voice was sincere and I believed her, until I remembered what was at stake. "Jayne, you can't honestly believe that. Grandma considered you her granddaughter. Period."

"When were you actually planning on showing me this?" I asked, grabbing it off the floor. "When did you think it would be the right time?"

Thunder crashed outside as Charlotte took a few tentative steps towards me. "Jayne, I—"

I held up my hand. "Save it. Now is not the time for you to pretend like you're my friend, or even my sister."

"Please, listen," she pleaded, her blue eyes bright. "I know you're upset. But please, know this. I remember everything from that summer, but most of all I remember how hurt I was to lose you. It's been as hard on you as it has been on me to revisit the past, feel those feelings, and learn to let them go. When I saw this..." She shuddered. "I'm so sorry that I tried to hide that letter. I was trying to protect you because I knew how much it would hurt you and I was afraid you would walk away."

The thought made my eyes fill with tears. How could anyone expect me to stand here, listening to a letter tell me that my father wasn't my father? No amount of money was worth it.

"Jayne," she begged, as lightning lit up the room. "Please. Don't let this drive us apart, like it has our entire lives. Let's turn to each other to deal with this."

Without saying a word, I pushed past Charlotte and headed to my room. Blindly, I threw my stuff into my bags. She followed me, her face pale.

"What are you doing?" she cried.

"Exactly what I should have done from the beginning," I said. "I'm leaving."

"Jayne?" Daniel's voice was so familiar, and so far away. It was hard to believe that we had broken up just over three months ago. It felt like a lifetime. "I can't believe you're actually calling me."

The rain pounded on my windshield as my wipers tried desperately to push it away. Gripping my steering wheel, I held on tight as I headed for the nearest exit to the highway home. "Is this a bad time?"

The question sounded ridiculous because on my end, it was a terrible time. My nose was so stuffed up from crying that I could barely speak, the salt from my tears was sticky on my face, and the town that I had fallen in love with had long disappeared in a flash of lightning in the mirror, leading me to long highways and rolling hills.

"No, I'm glad you called." He paused. "How are you?"

"It's not my best day," I said, pulling onto the highway with my hazards flashing.

Driving was dangerous. My phone was attached to my car charger and I had it on speaker, as the rain made it impossible to see anything. It would be smart to pull over and wait out the storm but I couldn't stay here, I couldn't risk making the choice to go back.

"I hear you," Daniel said with a wry chuckle. "I had a lot of those. You broke my heart." I gripped the steering wheel tighter, imagining the kindness in his face, and the way it used to cloud up when something hurt him. "I couldn't eat, breathe, or think for weeks. The thing that I can't understand about the way we left things is that I was in love with you. It's fine if you weren't in love with me, but I thought you were. What happened?"

It wasn't a question that I was expecting.

Yes, I'd cared about Daniel and I'd told him that I loved him, but after even only one night with Logan, I knew the difference. Daniel and I didn't have that intangible connection, that spark that made every moment feel charged and alive. I'd had that with Logan.

For the first time in my life, I'd felt safe enough to let down my walls and give myself permission to fall in love with someone, in spite of the risk that he might not love me back. The pain that I felt at walking away from that feeling left me unable to give anything to Daniel other than complete honesty.

"I did love you," I said, "but not the way that you deserved. You're so kind, and there are so many things I admire about you, but in the end, you deserve so much more than I could give you."

He was silent for a long moment. Then he said, "You did your best. I know that."

We'd talked so many times about the hurts from my past and he'd tried to push me to go further and deeper, but I couldn't do it. Not with him. Daniel was one of the kindest men I'd ever known and someone would be lucky to have him, but it wasn't going to be me.

Letting out a breath, I got to the point. "I called with a favor," I said, "but it sounds like it might be too hard. I was hoping to crash at your place for a while, until I get back on my feet."

"Back on your feet?" he said. "What happened?"

I told him the whole story, which took passing at least two exits, and he whistled. "I'm so sorry, Jayne. That really sucks."

"Yeah," I admitted, watching the trees roll by. "I called the lawyer right before I called you. We're not supposed to leave for more than two days but, given the circumstance, he's agreed to give me time to think about what I want to do. But I never felt I deserved the house, anyway. Now that I've found out I'm not even related to my grandmother, I know I don't deserve it."

"That's not up to you," he said. "Your grandmother gave it to you."

"With conditions," I said. "I don't have it in me to meet them."

"Well, you're more than welcome to stay. I actually left a few days ago to spend a couple of months with my sister, the one out in California? We're going to do some hiking, road trips, all of it. Then the rest of the family's coming out to celebrate my parents' fiftieth anniversary."

The relief that he wouldn't be in town only solidified my resolve that the relationship was long over. The idea of being with anyone other than Logan at this point was impossible to wrap my mind around, but I had to let him go. I hoped it wouldn't hurt him too badly and that he'd only considered me a summer romance, the woman who'd helped him finally move on from his divorce.

Lauren had told me that he'd barely dated until I came along, and I wondered if that would all change now.

"I'll call the landlord and tell him to give you a key," Daniel said. "I'll be gone for the rest of the summer, but then I think it's best if we don't live together. I'm too old to pretend like we're friends, when I'd spend the whole time wanting to be something more."

"Thank you," I said quietly. "You deserve the best."

"Well." He sounded flattered and bummed out, all at the same time. "Thanks. So do you. Talk to you later, Jayne."

We hung up and I stepped on the gas. I just wanted to get there. I had nowhere else to go.

# CHAPTER TWENTY-FOUR

I stared at my laptop and let out a slow breath. "Suck it up and do it. You can do it."

Easy words to say, but no matter how many times I tried, I couldn't bring myself to reach down and hit the button. Letting out a hearty sigh, I got up and shut off the air conditioning. It whirred to a stop with a loud clatter and I opened the window without the unit, letting in the scorched air of the city.

I'd spent the entire week building a website to host art-themed children's parties. I'd done research, set price points, and felt like this was a venture I could actually succeed at. But every time I tried to take the site live, something held me back. Fear, maybe. That I could do everything right and fail in spite of it all.

It was a painful thought, but I needed to get past it. My time was running out. I'd been in Daniel's apartment for six weeks, and I needed to have something in place before he came back to town. There were a few friends willing to give me a couch to crash on, but that wouldn't last long. I needed a career beyond waiting tables, which was how I'd survived once again. The restaurant where I'd worked before had been willing to take me back on a temporary basis, and the entire situation had felt like a gigantic step back.

Walking over to the fridge, I opened it and stared at the contents. One apple, two containers of leftovers from the Thai restaurant down the block, and one container of yogurt. I settled on the apple.

Martin had called me a few times on Charlotte's behalf to see if I was ready to determine my next steps. I wasn't, and he'd told me that I had a year to figure it out, which bought me some time. Save one heartfelt text begging me to reconsider, Charlotte hadn't tried to contact me, and I was not about to contact her.

The one person I had stayed in touch with was Logan. We'd agreed that it made sense to put on the brakes since I was no longer in town, but we'd still managed to call or text each other every day. I had come to rely on that communication, and there were days that I missed talking to him in person more than I would have thought possible.

I had just sliced up the apple and partnered it with some yogurt when the downstairs buzzer sounded. I wasn't expecting anyone, but it was possible one of my friends had been in the area and had stopped by.

"Hello?" I said, pressing the button.

"Jayne, it's Graham Wilmington," a deep voice said. "Do you have a few minutes to come down and talk?"

My hand pressed against the wall so quickly that it saved me from falling down. I rested my other hand on the coffee table by the door, my heart frozen in my chest.

*Breathe.*

I took in a deep breath as his voice came over the speaker once again. "This has to be a shock, and I'm sorry. I would have called, but I figured I'd have a better shot if I made the trip. Please, Jayne. I need to talk to you."

Graham Wilmington. The man who I'd once believed was my father.

I couldn't believe he was here.

"I thought you lived in Florida now," I managed to say.

The steady sound of my voice gave me courage to take another breath.

"I do," he said. "I came to see you. There's a coffee shop on the corner. Would you be willing to meet me there in ten minutes?"

He had traveled all this way to see me? It was such a shock that I had to know why he'd taken those steps now, when he'd never bothered to do it when I was younger. Especially after the whole mess with Charlotte.

"Sure," I said, feeling my anger start to rise. "I think we have plenty to talk about."

If he caught the rage, he didn't acknowledge it. Instead, in a quiet voice, he said, "Yes. I think we do."

When I was younger, I had often fantasized about meeting up with my father. In my fantasy, I met up with him at some place that had ice cream. I'd walk in wearing a pretty dress, and he'd stand up and open his arms. Then I'd run to him and he'd pick me up and swing me around, like in the movies.

Now, I walked into the coffee shop wearing a pair of thick sunglasses, dressed in a dark blue romper, with a scowl on my face. The shop was crowded and I finally spotted him by the window, staring down at his hands. He looked the same as his pictures but with silver hair, and he had the same fit physique as Charlotte.

Spotting me, he got to his feet. "Would you like a coffee?"

In the fantasy that I'd had when I was young, he'd bought me the most expensive banana split on the menu, drizzled in dark chocolate and speckled with gold. They didn't have that here, but I was fine with the idea of having him buy me the most expensive coffee possible. The one with all the bells and whistles.

We walked to the counter in silence and I put in my order, adding sugar-free caramel, whipped topping, and cinnamon sprinkles. I wouldn't be able to drink half of it here, but I could save it for later. Besides, it wasn't about the coffee.

"I'll get a table," I said, once I'd ordered, leaving him to wait.

He returned with a friendly smile and set mine in front of me. The flavored iced latte looked refreshing, especially on such a hot day. He took a seat and got straight to business.

"You probably don't even remember me," he said.

I was not about to reassure him, so I stuck the straw in my coffee and took a long drink. It was sweet and delicious and worked as a salve on the burn that had taken up residence in my heart the moment I'd heard his name over the intercom.

"Jayne, I want to tell you first and foremost how sorry I am for the way that everything has been shared with you. When you were born…" He stopped talking for a moment and I felt surprised to see that he was choked up. "I never would have dreamed that this is how our life together would have turned out."

"What life together?" I said.

"Exactly." He looked helpless, but I didn't feel a bit of sympathy for him. "There's so much to say, but this isn't the place for it. The one thing I can say is that I am sorry that I missed out on the opportunity to raise you. I wanted to be your father more than anything, and the years that we spent apart never stopped weighing on my mind."

"If you were so worried about me, why didn't you and my mother stay together?" I asked. "How dare you show up now, like you're this high-and-mighty problem solver, ready to fix things between me and Charlotte. If you wanted to play the role of the fixer, you should have realized that it was a horrible decision to separate us. I don't care if I was her half sister. I was her sister. You should have…" The words stopped. My father's cheeks were bright red and he had his hand over his mouth, as though he was about to cry.

Well, too bad. He needed to understand the way his actions had impacted my life. If my mother had still been here, I would have said the same, because now that I'd spent time with my sister, I understood how wrong their decision had been.

"What are you doing here?" I demanded. "I didn't ask you to come, and I don't want your help. So, I think you need to go."

"No." His voice was firm. "I'm here because once upon a time, you were my daughter and I loved you with every breath in my body. I spent my whole life hoping we could come back together. Well, I'm done hoping. I'm here."

I snorted. "That's rich. You could have been here my whole life."

"Jayne." His voice was measured. "I tried. Your mother would not let me near you and, because I was not your legal parent, I did not have a claim on you."

My breath caught. "That can't be true."

"I wanted to give you my time," he said. "I asked your mother again and again to work with me to find a way to let us be together. It was impossible. Your mother refused to leave Ireland." He let out a breath. "I think that, deep down, she was scared that you would want to live with us."

I stared down at the wood grain of the table, letting his words wash over me like the tide.

My father's gaze swept the coffee shop and he cleared his throat. "I was there when you were born, Jayne. I spent six years of your life raising you like my own daughter. When your mother told me she was taking you, I…" His eyes filled with tears and he blinked hard, as if remembering that we were in a public place. "The day she left with you was the worst day of my entire life. The worst week, the worst year, the worst decade. I wondered what you were doing, what cute thing you'd said, and what I had done to deserve such an awful outcome.

"I did what I could to make life beautiful for your sister because the truth of the matter is, the two of you were robbed. Your life was not fair. Hers was not fair. If I could have done anything to change the situation, I would have. In the end, I was too weak to do what I should have done all along—I should have let Charlotte go. I should have let the two of you stay with your mother so that you could be together, but I was too selfish. I have to live with that."

My coffee had sat in front of me. Now, I reached for it and took a slow, sweet sip. It was too much, and I pushed it away.

"Charlotte told me about the time the two of you spent together," my father said, when I didn't respond. "We still have time to be a family. My mother left you and Charlotte that house to bring us back together. I am grateful for her, and I am grateful for that. Most of all, I am grateful to be sitting here with you."

The words nearly knocked me down. I wanted to let him in, but I couldn't. I had done that with Charlotte and it had ended with hurt.

"I can't," I said, my voice small. "I wanted you to be a part of my life so badly and you weren't."

"It wasn't my choice," he insisted. "Please, try to understand that."

Emotion had gotten the best of me and my eyes filled with tears. Getting to my feet, I said, "I don't want to see you again."

"Jayne. Please don't do this." Quickly, he handed me his business card. "Here's my number. Take the time you need. When you're ready, I hope you'll call me."

I turned and left the coffee shop.

Halfway down the block, I remembered that I'd left my fancy coffee on the table. Well, forget it. I was not about to go back. It wasn't worth the heartache of seeing him again.


The week passed by in a blur. My friends insisted that I focus on self-care. They took me to karaoke, treated me at some of my favorite restaurants, and took me out for drinks. The activity helped the days pass by, but at night I lay awake in bed and did my best to fight off the memories of the past.

The one thing I kept coming back to was the idea that my mother did not want to marry Graham. She'd gone off to college and had only come back to him once she was pregnant, and he'd made the choice to marry her and raise me as his own. It was startling that he'd made that decision.

Not to mention my grandmother. She had known the truth and yet she'd fought for me and Charlotte to be together because she'd wanted the best for us. This whole time, I'd been worried that I didn't deserve the house, but deep down, I think what I was worried about was that I didn't deserve her love. But both she and my father had given it to me anyway. They had chosen to make me a part of the family, they had chosen to love me, and I had made the choice to push them away.

There was no reason for that. There was room for love, healing, and forgiveness. Before that could happen, though, I had to be brave enough to try again.

The next morning, I contacted my father. He was booked on a flight that afternoon, so we set up a meeting at the same coffee shop. I saw him through the window before I arrived. He sat at the table with the same drinks we'd ordered the first time, his back straight, and eyes alert as he watched the main door.

Tears streamed down my face by the time I made it to the table. "I'm sorry," I said. "It shouldn't have taken me this long."

My father got up and walked over to me, pulling me into his arms. I know that it was impossible—this was a man I hadn't seen in over thirty years—but the very way that he smelled seemed familiar. We held each other for so long that I felt the nearby tables watching us, as if we were sharing some romantic reunion.

"This is my father," I wanted to shout. Patting his lapels, I blew my nose on a napkin and sat down at the table. "We have a lot to talk about," I warned him, and he smiled.

Two hours later, our coffees were empty and we were making future plans to be a part of each other's lives. Fiddling with the straw, I said, "How will Charlotte feel about all of this?"

The last thing I wanted was to give her something new to be angry at me about. Graham was her biological father and if I developed a relationship with him, she might feel like I didn't have that right. The idea made my stomach twist. I wanted a father more than anything in this world, but I had wanted to have a sister, too.

"Who do you think begged me to come talk to you?" he said. "Charlotte was heartbroken when you left. She nearly walked away from the whole thing. That house means so much to our family that she couldn't bring herself to leave it, but she says it will never be the same without you. She wants you to come back."

I thought for a moment, staring down at my hands. Then I nodded. "Good," I said. "Because I want that, too."

# CHAPTER TWENTY-FIVE

The tears I shed with my father were nothing compared to the reunion with Charlotte. She stood out in the driveway as I pulled up and barely waited for the car to stop before she marched over and pulled me into her arms.

"Don't leave me again," she said, holding me so tight that I could barely breathe. "Promise you'll never leave me again."

I pulled back and smiled at her. "That was the last time. I swear."

We grinned at each other. Unloading the car, I took in the front yard. The landscaping had been done. There were new bushes, a flower garden, and a fountain that bubbled with cheer.

"You've been working hard," I said, and she nodded.

"You wouldn't believe the number of videos I had to watch. It wasn't the same without you." She slung a bag over her shoulder and walked with me towards the front steps of the porch. "Oh, and I thought that would look perfect there. I wanted it to welcome you home."

I stopped short at the sight of the sculpture. It was as stunning as I remembered it, and now that it had experienced some wear and weather, it looked even better.

"It's perfect," I said, and she squeezed my hand.

We walked inside and I stared up at the windows. It looked exactly as we had imagined it, and the bright interior that showcased the vast depths of the ocean was so different from the dark, worn house we'd walked into that first day.

"What do you think?" she asked.

"We might be visionaries."

With a grin, she dropped my bag at the bottom of the stairs. "I've got us all set out there." From where we stood, I could see the table on the deck had been arranged with a bouquet of flowers, sparkling water, and what looked like a bowl of fresh strawberries and cut kiwi. "Come on," she said. "We've got a lot of catching up to do."

The moment I stepped onto the back deck and we settled into our old routines, I knew I was exactly where I belonged. We talked about it all, including when the best time would be to invite our father to visit.

The boys returned from the beach and Evan hugged me with the sandy enthusiasm of a golden retriever, while Josh hung back, watching me warily from beneath the protection of his baseball cap. We all played catch-up, then Charlotte got a work call that she had to answer, and the boys decided to go back down to the beach.

I'd headed into the kitchen to replenish our supply of sparkling water, when Josh walked in the kitchen, shutting the door behind him.

The last time I'd spoken to Josh, he'd been drunk and screaming at me. Squeezing the handle of the fridge a little too tight, I steeled myself. He had followed me in here, so he clearly had something to say but I didn't know if I was ready to hear it.

"I'm about to head back out."

Josh held up his hands. "Sure. Cool." He stood at the kitchen table, looking lost. "Is it okay if I talk to you?"

I hesitated, waiting for him to lash out like he had so often before. "Yes, absolutely. It's good to see you, Josh."

He nodded. "Look, Aunt Jayne, I want to say I'm sorry."

Two things stopped me in my tracks. The fact that he'd called me aunt for the first time and the idea that he'd apologized. His face was less confident than usual and his ears, like his brother's and Charlotte's, had turned red because he was nervous.

"Thank you," I said. "It's okay."

He stood there, looking younger by the minute. Then he said, "I screwed up big-time. It's all I've been doing lately. I can't seem to do anything right. It's like…" He blinked rapidly. Then, to my absolute shock, tears came to his eyes. "Do you know how scared I was that day on the boat? I thought I was going to die out there. The fact that you stepped in to try to save me, even though you didn't even know me, it meant a lot."

My throat got tight, but I shook my head. "Don't make me out to be the hero. It was your brother. He made sure that we were looking for you. Your parents would have come to find you, even if I wasn't there."

"No, he wouldn't have told them," Josh said. "He would have been too worried about what they'd do to me. He might have gathered up some friends and… I really thought I was going to die."

"Josh." I took a step towards him. "That had to be so frightening. I'm sorry you went through that."

"It makes me mad, though, because I don't want to be a baby about it."

"You went through something big," I told him. "Give yourself a break. I'm going to tell you something—there are a lot of people who feel like you do, like they can't do anything right. Smart, accomplished boys your age who look like they have everything on the surface. I think you're brave for owning up to your feelings. That's how you get help dealing with things, by talking about them and figuring out what to do next."

He put his face in his hands and rubbed. "Yeah. It's like, half the time, I'm pretending to be okay to make my mother happy."

"Why?" I asked. "Your mother loves you and wants the best for you. She's not going to flip to find out you want to be smart about dealing with the stuff that's worrying you. I think she'd be proud of you."

He stood there for a moment. "I can talk to her for you if you'd like," I suggested. "Or you can do it on your own?"

"Will you talk to her?" he asked.

"Sure," I said, still surprised that he'd come to me. "I'll do it later today."

We stood in silence for a minute. Then I said, "You mean a lot to me, Josh."

He grunted. "Evan means a lot to you, yeah. But me, not so much."

"That's not true," I said. "You're family. I realize that we're still getting to know one another, but I'm going to tell you something. There's no shaking me now. No matter what, I'm always going to be a part of your life."

He nodded. "Good."

We stood there for a moment, considering each other. He kicked at the ground with his loafers, and I smiled.

"Look, as much fun as it is to feel weird and awkward, I also feel hungry," I told him. "Do you want to go back out and get something to eat?"

Relief crossed his face. "Yeah." He looped his arm around me and pulled me towards him for a split second, before letting me go.

"Was that a hug?" I teased. "It was hard to tell, but I think that might have been a hug."

He laughed. "Whatever you say, Auntie."

This time, the term didn't feel like an insult; it felt like a compliment.

I opened the door and we headed out. I was already looking forward to having a conversation with him over dinner. There were a lot of things I'd wondered about the kid, and finally I would have the chance to get to know him.

The next morning, I made the visit I had been looking forward to from the moment I agreed to come back. I rode my bike to Logan's house, which was a cute bungalow just off the water. The front door was open and I walked in, my heart pounding in my throat.

"Hello?" I called.

"Out here," Logan sang.

His voice sounded happier than ever. Rushing out to the backyard, I stopped short at the sight of Logan with his arms around two young girls with brown hair and pigtails. They regarded me with big eyes and even bigger smiles, and they stood in front of a playhouse.

The smaller one stepped forward and I could tell right away she was the brass, the one who ran the show. "Daddy said this was your idea. The house."

I knelt down in front of her on the grass. "Do you like it?"

"We don't like it." She gave a big pout, crossed her arms, and glared at me. Then her eyes widened and her face lit into a huge smile. "We *love it*!" She and her sister broke into peals of laughter and raced inside the pink house with the white trim, slamming the door shut behind them.

Logan shook his head. "I was going to ask them to introduce themselves but…"

"The playhouse is way more fun." I stood up, brushing grass from my knees. "I get it."

Our eyes met and I felt that familiar flush I'd felt from the moment we first met. The birds chattered in the trees and the heady scent of burning leaves perfumed the crisp fall air. Logan peeked in one of the front windows of the playhouse, before taking my hands and leading me to the side.

"They're having a tea party," he whispered. "I think we have a few minutes." Then he gave me that smoldering look that I'd missed with every bit of my heart, and pulled me in for a kiss.

"I'm glad you came back," he said, holding me close.

I rested my head on his shoulder. "Me, too. Because I think I belong right here."

Charlotte, Ken, Evan, Josh, and I settled around the table on the deck outside for a family dinner. Steaks smoked on the grill alongside corn on the cob wrapped in foil, Charlotte had whipped up one of her famous summer salads, and I had made enough rolls to satisfy Evan, who had at least four already stacked on his plate.

"Sorry we're late," Lauren called, walking out onto the deck. "We brought chocolates. Hoping to make a good impression and all that."

Logan's eyes met mine and he grinned, handing me a box.

"Oh, don't worry. You've made an impression," I told him, and gave him a quick kiss.

My nephews groaned and with lots of laughter, our group settled around the table.

The back of the house looked spectacular in the gold light of the evening. There was still plenty of work to do and I couldn't wait to get back into it. The boys were back in school, so it was just me and Charlotte for now. Like she'd once said, it could take a lifetime to remodel and I looked forward to every second of it.

Ken poured glasses of sparkling water and lifted his in a toast.

"Charlotte and Jayne," he said, "thank you for bringing us along on this incredible journey. I have never met two such strong, smart, and resilient women, strengthened by their devotion to family.

As we move forward, I hope that our time together continues to be rich with love and laughter."

"Hear, hear," Charlotte said. Then she lifted her glass. "Also, I would like to make a toast to my sister. The years we spent apart made us stronger and more committed to the time that we could have together. I'm grateful beyond words that you decided to come back."

I smiled at her. "It wasn't that hard. The only thing that I've ever wanted is for us to be together. To be a family. Speaking of that…" I set down a piece of corn on the cob and lifted my glass. "In the spirit of togetherness, I have a proposition." Charlotte and I had spoken about it privately, and she had run it by Ken, who had agreed. "This house has been a tremendous opportunity for growth and change. It's something that allowed us to share a small slice of time, but I would like to increase our time here. I propose we stay on for the year, together. I want to start my business and spend time with all of you. We can talk about selling later if we think it's the right move."

Evan's face lit up. "No kidding? We'd all live together?"

Charlotte reached out and took his hand. "Well, that will be up to you."

"I'm thinking breakfasts every morning, lots of snacks…"

Logan laughed. "I like the way you think, Evan."

He gave a vigorous nod. "I'm in."

"Josh?" Charlotte asked. "How about you?"

Josh tugged his baseball cap low over his eyes. "If I'm going to have another person telling me what to do all the time, it might as well be her."

"High praise," Lauren said, with a serious nod.

"Is that a yes?" I asked him.

The two brothers looked at each other and grinned. "Yes, Auntie," they chorused. "That's a yes!"

Looking from my sister to her family—my family—my heart finally felt full. It had been a journey filled with ups, downs, and misunderstandings but in the end, every moment had been worth it, because we had been together.

Charlotte handed me an envelope. "Grandma left one last letter that she wanted us to read. I saved it, because it didn't seem right to read it without you. Would you do the honors?"

I looked at the house, the ocean, and the faces of the people that I loved. Nodding, I said, "That means a lot to me. Thank you," and began.

*Dear Charlotte and Jayne,*

*This journey has been long but I hope it has been valuable. I have spent countless hours dreaming of the outcome where the two of you have let go of past hurts and regrets, so that you can move forward into the future. Together. Too much of your life together was robbed from you and I want to give it back. It is my wish that you make up for lost time. That you find the relationship that was lost and give it permission to soar.*

*My dear children, life goes so fast. I remember my days as a young girl, the summer that I turned twelve, and the stage of life the two of you are in now. It all feels like yesterday because the days speed by.*

*Please, my girls, make the choice to embrace the opportunity life has given you to be together. To be sisters. To be family. I will go to my grave hoping and praying that this is the outcome but, at the same time, I understand that some hurts cannot be healed. Some wounds refuse to mend.*

*If that's the case between the two of you, then life will go on. You will both live big, glorious lives that sing. Even if it's not a deliberate duet, your voices will still mingle together and dance like drops of sun on the clouds.*

*But if it is together, the angels will sing with you, me the loudest of all.*

*Hugs, kisses, and all my best wishes,*
*Your grandmother*

# A LETTER FROM CYNTHIA

Dear reader,

I want to say a huge thank-you for choosing to read *When We Were Sisters*. If you enjoyed it, and want to keep up to date with all my latest releases, just sign up at the following link. Your email address will never be shared and you can unsubscribe at any time.

*cynthiaellingsen.com*

The story of Charlotte and Jayne began to percolate in my mind during quarantine. I think many of us struggled during that time to maintain connections with the people that we loved and it got me thinking about what it would be like to be separated from someone you wanted to see so very badly. The story grew from there.

I set it against the backdrop of the ocean because the ocean has always served as a source of peace and beauty to me. It's a reminder that life can ebb and flow, which made the ocean the perfect backdrop for a story about reconnecting.

I was glad that Charlotte and Jayne found their resolution. I was also grateful for the reminder that even the best relationships take work and sometimes, courage. But in the end, their reward can be priceless.

If you loved *When We Were Sisters*, I would be grateful if you could write a review. I read every single one of my reviews and

I'd love to hear what you think, and it makes such a difference helping new readers to discover one of my books for the first time.

I also love chatting with my readers—you can get in touch on my Facebook page, through Twitter, Goodreads, or my website. I look forward to hearing from you and thank you again for reading.

All my best,
Cynthia Ellingsen

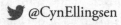 CynthiaEllingsen

🐦 @CynEllingsen

🌐 cynthiaellingsen.com

# ACKNOWLEDGMENTS

Being an author is something I dreamed about as a child and I'm still amazed at the opportunity to do this for a living. Thank you for taking the time to read *When We Were Sisters*. I am beyond grateful for your support.

Bookouture, it is a delight to be one of your authors. A million thanks to Lucy Dauman and Therese Keating, my brilliant editors. You are a joy to work with! Thank you to all of those at Bookouture who have worked tirelessly to make my book shine—cover art, marketing, sales, copy editors, audio, and the entire team—I appreciate you every day.

I am overjoyed to work with Kirsiah Depp at Grand Central Publishing. Thank you so much for including *When We Were Sisters* in the Forever imprint. I'll be forever grateful! Lauren Bello, your hard work and keen attention to detail has helped immensely. It takes a team to put a book into the world and working with the team at Grand Central has been a treat.

Brent Taylor, you are a super-agent. It is such a delight to work with you. Many thanks to you and the team at Triada US.

Celine Dunne, thank you for letting me ask you questions about Ireland. It was a treat. Any mistakes are my own.

Another big thank-you goes to Travis and Stan at Mattox Built Homes, Inc., for your input on home remodeling. Much appreciated. Once again, any mistakes are my own.

As always, thank you to my mother for teaching me to believe in my dreams. To my lovely sister, Carolyn, since this is a book about sisters, after all. To Ryan and my family for the endless love and support, you are the greatest.

And to my dad, I knew I'd put a firefighter in one of these days. I love you.